T0196391

The Marriage Ban

YUSUF AHMAD BELLO

ARCHWAY
PUBLISHING

Archway Publishing books may be ordered through booksellers or by contacting:

Archway Publishing
1663 Liberty Drive
Bloomington, IN 47403
www.archwaypublishing.com
1 (888) 242-5904

ISBN: 978-1-4808-5561-8 (sc)
ISBN: 978-1-4808-5559-5 (hc)
ISBN: 978-1-4808-5560-1 (e)

Library of Congress Control Number: 2017918169

Print information available on the last page.

Archway Publishing rev. date: 01/10/2019

To Inna and Baba

Contents

Acknowledgements

To Ruqayya Salihu, Maimuna Ahmad Bello, Musa Ahmad Bello, Khadijah Ahmad Bello, Zainab Ahmad Bello, Nuruddeen Idris, Sulaiman Sani, and Muhammad Nasir. Thank you.

Prologue

It was evening. Falmata stood by the entrance of the mud-walled kitchen in her husband's courtyard, pounding some boiled yams with a pestle and mortar. She was a dark, slender Kanuri woman in her early twenties. She wore a blue blouse and an orange wrapper with a floral design printed in black. Her braids were tiny, and her nose bore a prominent, circular ring. The steam from the yams rose and played over her face. The bangles on her right hand clinked as she raised the pestle and landed it with a thud against the yams.

Tied to her back was her little baby. He was crying. She would pause her pounding intermittently to rock him to silence, but he wouldn't stop crying for long.

She could hear the bleating of goats and sheep from afar. Those bleats announced the homecoming of the shepherds, who had spent the day on the grasslands with their flocks. They always heralded the arrival of her husband. She pounded faster.

An old woman threw open the courtyard door and ran in like a young man. Falmata looked sharply toward her. It was Ramatu, one of her neighbours. Ramatu's eyes exuded fear. Her old looks were overshadowed by an uncanny excitement. Her trembling hands grabbed Falmata's shoulders.

"Tell me, Falmata," Ramatu cried, "is your husband home?"

"He's not home yet. I hope there is no—"

"Everything is wrong, woman! Run from this place now! They are after your life. Do you hear me? Run from here, and come back no more, till it is—"

An explosion of gunshots sounded nearby. Falmata shrieked and threw away her pestle. The shouting of women and children began to rise in the distance. Three more gunshots sounded.

"Do you hear that?" Ramatu barked at her. "Don't stand there like an idiot. Flee from this house at once!" The old woman bolted out of the compound.

Falmata darted out too. In her confusion, she ran in a different direction, along a deserted path. All she could hear were gunshots from several directions. No sound came from the road ahead of her, which gave her hope that she was heading towards safety. She grew even more hopeful when she saw no corpses or wounded people in her path.

She ran hard, her baby crying helplessly on her back. Could he be hurt? When she reached the bush on the town's outskirts, she bent over and panted. She took her baby in her arms and examined his body. He wasn't hurt. She tied him again to her back.

A man came sprinting along the path ahead of her, his shirt bloody. He was one of her husband's friends.

"Tasi'ou! What is going on in the town?" she demanded. He dodged her and ran on. He disappeared around a turn.

A policeman appeared from the same direction from which Tasi'ou had come. He was armed with a rifle and a bloodstained dagger. The dagger was carelessly tucked into his belt and the blood on it stained his brown trousers. He trotted up, eyes darting around.

"Did a man with a wound cross this path just now?" he asked Falmata.

She couldn't utter a word. Her eyes moved from the mouth of the gun to the ruthless looks of the policeman.

"Constable!" a harsh voice cried out. "Get hold of her. She is Chief Ousmane's wife! Quick!" It was another policeman. He approached, pointing at her.

Falmata dashed into the bush. Her legs ran faster than they ever had before.

◄○►

The sergeant looked on as the constable raised his rifle and aimed in the direction Falmata had gone. The constable's finger trembled at the trigger.

"Fire!" the sergeant barked at him.

The constable remained as still as a statue.

"Fire, idiot! Don't let her go. Fire!" The sergeant would have fired his own gun, but he had run out of bullets.

The constable lowered his rifle and returned the sergeant's gaze. "No, sir," he said. "Let this one go, please. She has a baby."

The sergeant's frown eased. He looked thoughtfully at his colleague. The constable was right, but what would their boss say? They had been given strict orders to arrest her. "Okay," he said at last. "But we have to think of how to explain what we've done if our boss asks us questions. Let's go."

They returned to the shaded spot under the tree where they had parked the van they had come in. Their van was one of about fifty that were packed full of policemen and soldiers who had come to attack the town. The van that had brought the sergeant and constable was now packed with bloodstained corpses.

The sergeant and constable jumped into the van, the sergeant slammed the door and they sped off. At the police station, their boss was waiting for them at the entrance, looking like a fierce and bloodthirsty warlord.

The boss marched to the back of their van to look at the corpses. "Good," he said. "I guess that is Chief Ousmane's wife?" he asked, pointing at a woman's corpse.

The sergeant and the constable moved closer.

"Which woman, sir?" the sergeant asked nervously.

"That one with a bullet to her head."

"Um, no, sir, but—"

"No, no! I don't want to hear any stupid stories. Where is Chief Ousmane's wife? She was one of the people I told you to arrest."

"She is not here, sir," the sergeant confessed.

The boss's eyes flashed. His breaths became loud and fast. He looked ready to grab a gun and shoot everyone around him. He threw a slap but the sergeant dodged it. He threw another and it caught the constable on his mouth and nose.

"Are you stupid?" the boss barked. "Are you sure you are policemen? How can you come back without her? I am going to put you both in the guard room. How can you—"

"We are sorry, sir! We couldn't get her because she ran into the bush," the constable explained, rubbing his nose and mouth.

"Idiots! She ran into the bush? Why didn't you chase her?" their boss spat. They were silent.

"Now go to the bush and get her!" the boss ordered. "And don't come back till you have her—dead or alive!"

◄○►

Falmata was deep into the bush. She was sure the policemen had stopped chasing her, yet she kept running. Her baby kept crying. If only she could get to safety to comfort him! As she weaved between the lofty trees, protruding roots, and fallen logs, her pace slowed to a jog and then to a walk.

Why were they after her? What had happened to her husband? Why had Ramatu asked about him? Could he have been killed for spearheading the burning of the town's brewery the day before? Tears streamed down her cheeks at these thoughts.

Nightfall caught up with her in the depths of the bush. Birds ceased to sing, and crickets began to chirp. The darkness became so heavy that she could hardly see what was in front of her. Her heart palpitated against her chest out of fear of evil spirits, bandits and the unknown.

She suddenly recognised the path she was treading. It led to a hut where a woman called Kande sold firewood. Falmata had been her customer for some years now. She trotted to reach Kande's hut but then stopped abruptly and listened. She looked all about her. Could the sounds she was hearing be illusions?

A gunshot rang out in the distance, clearing her doubts. She carried her baby in her arms and moved speedily, like an antelope being chased by a predator. The gun sounded again, and she ran even faster into mud and over huge logs. She tripped on a protruding tree root and landed in a pool of murky water. Her poor baby was protected by the flesh of her arm. In a flash, she was up and moving again.

She began to see the piles of wood that Kande had stacked up for sale. The woman's little hut also came into sight. It appeared that she had not retired to her village for the night, as the hut was still lit. Falmata reached it in good time. She threw her weight on its door and it gave way as she fell inside.

"*Kai*! Who is it?" Kande cried, grabbing a stick and springing to her feet.

Falmata stood up.

"Stop there!" Kande barked. "If you come closer, I will hit you. Who are you?"

"Kande, it's me, Falmata," Falmata replied. She fell to her knees, and Kande lowered her stick.

"Falmata! Is that you? What is the problem? Why are you like this?"

"Kande, please protect me – please! The policemen are after my life!"

Kande took the baby from Falmata's arms and ushered her to a warm corner. She began to clean the mud off the baby, who was crying bitterly. She examined his body for any injuries.

"He has a few small bruises," Kande said. "Falmata, there is a hunter not far from here. Let me go and call him. He can protect you better. Breastfeed your baby, so that he keeps quiet."

Kande gave the baby to his mother, and Falmata breastfed him. He sucked noisily.

Kande grabbed a gourd and put out the candle so the policemen would not know there was someone inside. She rushed out of the hut and shut the door. She ran amongst the trees until she reached the hunter's hut. Alas, he wasn't around. He had gone back to his village already.

The hut had a nearby well and she drew water from it with a rubber bucket. She poured the water into the gourd she had with her. Just as the gourd got filled, a loud gunshot startled her. She jumped, dropping the container so that the water poured out. About ten more gunshots sounded. Like the first one, they sounded like they came from the direction of her hut. She began to run back.

She found the door of her hut ajar. The baby's cry rang out. Beside the hut, she saw two men carrying Falmata's lifeless body towards a van, whose headlights were on. One man was holding her legs and the other her arms. It was no use doing anything to stop them. Kande knew that she'd be the next victim if she screamed. She hid behind a tree and watched the men swing the lifeless body into the back of the van. It landed with a thud. They climbed into the van and drove off.

She came out of hiding, ran inside the hut and stared with shock at the bloodstains that coated the hut walls and floor. The baby lay on the floor, wailing.

PART I

THE SUITOR

1

Zaidou was beginning to wonder which was hotter – the heat in his shop or the furnace of Hamisou the blacksmith's workshop a stone's throw away. The sunrays beamed through the window behind him and warmed his neck as he worked on his sewing machine. Sweat trickled down his face and nape and dripped onto the brown fabric he was working on. His white dashiki was soaked. He wiped the sweat from his forehead with his index finger, splashed it onto the floor and resumed his work.

The noise from his sewing machine clashed with the song of a Hausa praise-singer playing on the radio on a table to his left. He felt as if, by the movements he made while sewing, he was dancing to the music. The singer's name was Salisou Mai Ganga, an old man based in a neighbouring town; he always sang to the accompaniment of the *kalangu* drum. His band garnished his sweet voice with a chorus. Zaidou had once heard over the radio that Mai Ganga was the best traditional musician not just in Hasoumiya, but also in West Africa (though Zaidou didn't know much geography). Zaidou had more than ten cassettes of Mai Ganga's songs in a drawer.

Zaidou pulled off his sweat-soaked dashiki so that he had only a singlet on. The singlet was a little bit oversized and revealed much of his slim, fair torso and arms. The town had many other Fulani men like him, with athletic physiques and curly black hair. Unlike many of them, he reared no cattle. When he was a teenager, a cow had knocked him down with its horns. He'd sprained his elbow and ankle and bruised his forehead. Since then, he'd dropped the ambition of having his own flock.

He tossed his dashiki on a table that sat opposite the radio. The table had a pile of unfinished garments on it. Many similar garments filled two baskets under the table to the brim. Masara town had many tailors, even though none of them had as many garments to sew as Zaidou did. He knew it was because he was the best in the town – at least, that was what people said. A customer had once told him that Salisou Mai Ganga had sung his praises. Zaidou had tirelessly searched for a recording of that song, but to no avail. When he challenged the customer to bring him the cassette, the customer had explained that the singer had not recorded the song.

"He sang it during a wedding ceremony, and there was no one to record it," he'd explained.

Zaidou stood at the doorway and perused the street for one of those boys who hawked cold water. Cyclists and pedestrians plied the untarred road, causing its dust to rise and mix with the hot air. Down the road, to his right, was the Marmari market, with stalls of crooked sticks and thatch. It was the biggest market in the town. People hovered around it – customers bargaining fiercely with sellers, people making away with their purchases, and labourers carrying heavy sacks of grains and cereals on their bushy heads or in wheelbarrows. Zaidou's own shop stood in the middle of a block of five provision and grocery shops. Two donkeys, heavily laden with sacks of maize, passed by his shop and headed towards the market. Young boys in tattered farm clothes sat atop the sacks the donkeys carried.

Young hawkers roamed the streets and shouted to others about their wares in sweet, melodious voices. One of them was a boy carrying a bucket of cold water on his head. "*Gaa ruwan sanyi! Gaa ruwan sanyi!*" he cried, his jugular vein bulging.

Zaidou beckoned to him.

The boy came. He uncovered the bucket, fetched water from it with a cup, and gave it to Zaidou.

Zaidou gulped it down. The water gave such a refreshing feeling, and Zaidou wished he could jump into the bucket for the rest of the evening. He paid the boy a one-dirham coin and returned to his sewing machine.

With his thirst slaked, the lyrics from the radio sounded sweeter and clearer. It was as if Salisou Mai Ganga were performing live in his shop, with his band echoing a chorus energetically at the doorway. The singer was singing the praises of the emir of Tarayya city, under whose domain Masara town was placed.

> The whiteness of your turban is more beautiful than
> the clouds;
> Your cloak – more colourful than the peacock's
> feathers –
> Is great and wide. It's wider than the desert of
> Sahara.
> You bring us together as your children.
> Under you, we neither fight nor quarrel.
> Though we are either Hausa, Fulani, or Kanuri,
> At the foot of your throne, we are nothing but a
> people.

As soon as one song ended, another followed. Mai Ganga sang the praises of some rich men and deceased heroes of the country. He sang about the region in which Masara and Tarayya were located – the Hausa-Sahara region. He showed how its different tribes were united by their ability to speak the Hausa language. He portrayed its pre-eminence over the other two regions of the country, the Birni and the Savannah-Fula regions. He sang about its big farms and about how they produced the most plentiful maize in the whole of Africa.

"Good afternoon, my able tailor!" a voice sounded above the radio.

Zaidou looked up and saw a man smiling from ear to ear, carrying some white fabric. He frowned and continued with his work.

"Won't you answer my greeting, Zaidou?" the man asked.

"I heard you," Zaidou replied, his eyes still fixed on his work.

The man sat on a stool opposite Zaidou. "Won't you reply when an elderly man greets you?" The smile on the man's face disappeared.

"I nodded when you greeted me. Didn't you see?"

The man shook his head in disgust. He dropped the material he carried onto the table beside the sewing machine. "I want you to sew a robe for me – a simple one, without embroidery," he said.

All he got for a response was the noise of the sewing machine.

"Do you hear me, Zaidou?" the man said, raising his voice. "I want a robe!"

Zaidou stood up tall, grabbed the fabric and threw it onto the floor. Then he continued working.

"What did you do that for?" the man cried. "Are you mad?"

"I sewed two kaftans for you last year and you've still not paid me! Do you expect me to work for you for free?"

"Did I tell I am not going to pay you?"

"I know you are not going to pay me!" Zaidou said. "I've asked you for my money many times, but you always tell me 'tomorrow'!"

The frown on the man's face eased. "Okay, I will pay you everything when you finish this one. I promise."

"Don't promise me anything. Your promises are meant for the latrine."

"What do you mean by that?" The man's tone became aggressive.

Zaidou picked up his scissors and began to cut some material into shape. "Don't you understand Hausa?" he asked. "I said your promises are meant for the latrine. I won't listen to them."

The man jumped to his feet and pointed a finger at Zaidou. His elderly eyes were strained and red. "Zaidou, you are a rude boy!" he charged.

"I am not a boy."

"You are a stupid boy!"

"No, I am not. I'm over forty years old."

"You are over forty, but you still can't get a wife. And you say you are not a boy? Shame on you! Your mates are grandfathers and you're wasting your time sewing shoddy clothes."

"Even if I'm not married, I'm more handsome than you," Zaidou replied. "I don't move about with a big belly like yours. I have teeth in my mouth, while yours have fallen out. Get out of my shop!"

"Useless boy! I want to see the girl that will marry you! Do you think getting a wife is all about being handsome? Do you think getting married is all about sewing clothes? If it were, you would be married. Idiot! You think you have sense but—"

Zaidou increased the volume of his radio so that it drowned out the man's words. He swayed back and forth to the music, making some stitches.

The man moved closer and raised his voice, pointing a finger in Zaidou's face.

Zaidou increased the volume to the loudest level and began to echo the lyrics.

The man stormed out, leaving his material behind.

Zaidou reduced the volume to a comfortable level and sat still, looking out at the busy street through the doorway.

The man's words attacked him like a lunatic swordsman. It wasn't the first time someone had insulted him because he wasn't married. He grabbed a woven fan and fanned himself.

Why wouldn't people see that his being a bachelor was not his choice, and that he was making efforts to get married? It was a constant frustration to him that he had lacked success with women. Just a few months ago, he'd had to call off his marriage to a girl at the venue of the wedding. He'd been told by a friend that she had sticky fingers and would wipe out all his money in one swoop. He'd rejected many other girls too. Other girls he'd courted had either said no to him or else their parents hadn't liked him.

The weather outside grew dim. A gentle breeze began to blow. Bits of nylon, dust and dried leaves flew about. The hot rays were no longer beaming through the window behind him. He donned his white dashiki again and stood at the entrance, watching people hurrying to reach their destinations before the downpour began. A spark of lightning flashed in the sky, followed by a gentle grumble of thunder. Thick grey clouds swam from the east, gradually eclipsing the sun.

Part of the clouds resembled a woman carrying a bowl. He imagined that the bowl was full of *tuwo* and *shuwaka* soup, and that the woman was Talatou, a woman who owned a restaurant a short distance from the Marmari market. He usually passed by her restaurant on his way back home. He'd been studying the slim, dark-skinned lady for some time. Talatou had found a place in his heart. He loved her smiles and the dedication with which she served her customers. Unlike the case in the other restaurants in town, one would seldom hear a customer complain in her place. She served generously. Her wooden restaurant was always spic and span, with very few flies buzzing around.

After thinking about the idea, he'd decided to talk to her. Every afternoon, he had lunch at her place and they'd chat happily. They had done that for three months. He'd told Larai, his widowed sister who lived in his house with her children, about Talatou. Larai told him that Talatou wasn't really in love with him.

"Why do you say so?" Zaidou asked, almost jumping out of his skin.

"You said you're not the only man she chats with, didn't you?" Larai asked.

"Yes. But she smiles and laughs any time we are together."

"Doesn't she do the same with other men?"

"Well, she does. But I think she laughs louder with me."

"Have you ever told her you loved her?"

"No. Do I need to do that? She can see it already. She can see how happy I am to meet her and to eat her food!"

"No, sir," Larai had said, wagging her head. "Tell her that you love her and that you want to marry her. Then you'll know what she thinks about you."

Just that morning, Zaidou had followed Larai's advice. He'd received the shock of his life when Talatou had told him that she wouldn't marry a man who was as old as forty years old.

The wind began to blow stronger, creating small whirlwinds filled with dust and litter. Zaidou closed his windows and tidied up his shop to go home. As he switched the radio off, Ya'u, his friend from childhood, stormed in and sat on the stool.

"Wait! Don't switch it off," Ya'u cried, grabbing the radio.

"Ya'u! You scared me the way you rushed in. Can't you even greet me first?" Zaidou protested.

"Oh, I'm sorry," Ya'u said, as he tuned the radio. "It's just that I heard a rumour and I want to confirm it from the news."

"It's about to rain now. We have to go home."

"Do you want to go home at 5 p.m., just because of rain? Or is your shop leaking?" Ya'u retorted.

The news had already started. The story being told was about the head of state, Leader Gambo, announcing his appointment of Professor Garba Ya'qouba as the Chairman of the Governors' Commission.

Ya'u laughed and clapped his hands at that news. He shook Zaidou's hand and jumped about the shop, almost knocking down the sewing machine.

Zaidou shrugged his shoulders, walked to the doorway and watched as the first drops of rain fell. They dropped onto the zinc roof, sounding like birds pecking at it. The drops grew into a downpour, and water began to flow on the streets, carrying bits of trash along with it. Droplets from the rain splashed into the shop and touched Zaidou's feet and face. The cool breeze was refreshing.

Zaidou knew what Professor Garba's appointment meant for the people of Masara. In 1947, the federal government had constructed breweries all over Hasoumiya. They were to brew and export beer from crops grown by the local farmers. The brewery workers came with police to collect the people's grain, but they never paid for it. After work, the workers would ride their cars and motorcycles home. They drank and drove, knocking down the townspeople every now and then. Many of the victims died.

The people of Masara grew angry. Chief Ousmane appealed to the government to close down the brewery. He said it was haram. The government refused. Chief Ousmane asked the people of Masara to burn down the brewery, which they did. The next day, government forces attacked the town. Over five hundred people were killed. Hundreds more were arrested, including Chief Ousmane. The chief had been sentenced to five years of solitary confinement.

The appointment of Professor Garba would be the first time that Leader Gambo would appoint a man from Masara to head a government body since the town had been attacked.

"What is wrong with you?" Ya'u asked, joining Zaidou in the doorway. "Aren't you happy about Professor Garba's appointment?"

"I have more serious things to think about, my friend," Zaidou said.

"Everyone in the town has serious things to think about, yet we are happy because of this good news. Why are you different?"

"I don't like politics like you do. Why should I be happy because my kinsman has gotten an appointment? Am I him?" Zaidou switched on the light and picked up some white fabric from the basket. He began to cut the fabric with his scissors.

Ya'u listened to the rest of the news quietly. Zaidou noticed how a smile remained on his friend's face.

"So tell me," Ya'u began, switching off the radio. "What's making you unhappy this evening?"

Zaidou told him about his encounter with the potbellied man. He raised his voice above the noise of the rain. He tossed the fabric and the scissors onto the floor. "He has refused to pay me my money, and now he has insulted me because I don't have a wife. Is it my fault that I'm not married?"

"Don't be angry, my friend," Ya'u said, still smiling. He rubbed Zaidou's chest.

"No, I should be angry," Zaidou insisted. "Why would the idiot withhold my money and then insult me? Does he know the number of girls I have approached? Am I just sitting down doing nothing?"

"It's okay, Zaidou," Ya'u said. "He was only talking out of ignorance. People like me know that you have been doing your best. I know you already have a fiancée – Talatou. Shouldn't that make you happy?"

Zaidou buried his face in his hands and sighed. He looked up at his friend and opened his mouth to speak. No words came out.

"I'm sure Talatou will marry you," Ya'u said. "She's a friendly woman."

"No! Let's not talk about Talatou again, please." Zaidou jumped to his feet as if one of his needles had pricked him.

"Why? Are you quitting on her?"

"I didn't quit. She did," Zaidou said. He told his friend how Talatou had shocked him.

"That's bad news!" Ya'u said. "Anyway, you should be used to being rejected by now. I don't think you should be worried."

"Well, I am worried," Zaidou retorted. "I like Talatou."

Ya'u switched on the radio again and held it to his ear.

Zaidou couldn't clearly hear which programme was airing because of the noise of the rain. Different voices were conversing, and they sounded frivolous.

"Zaidou . . ." Ya'u began, setting down the radio, "I don't want you to let Talatou go. You have courted so many women already. I want you to succeed this time."

"But she said she doesn't want me."

"If you want her, you shouldn't listen to her refusal. I will help you to win her heart. She respects me. I'm sure she'll listen to my advice to marry you."

Zaidou laughed out loud. Not that he found anything funny. It felt as if Ya'u's words had entered his body and squeezed that laughter out of him. "Are you serious?" he asked.

When Ya'u said yes, Zaidou dived at him and gave him a tight hug, patting him on the back. "Thank you! Thank you!" he said.

"Ah! What are friends for?" Ya'u smiled.

The rain stopped. Zaidou carried Ya'u on his bicycle to take him home. Ya'u sat on the frame between the saddle and the handlebar. That arrangement didn't make it easy for Zaidou to manoeuvre between the puddles that dotted the muddy dirt roads, but Ya'u seemed to enjoy every bit of it. He chatted away heartily about Professor Garba's appointment and about how it would cause milk and honey to rain on Masara, the way it had just finished raining.

"Professor Garba has been away from the country for thirty years now," Zaidou said. "Will he come back to take his appointment?"

"Of course he will come back to the country!" Ya'u said. "I am sure he will bring his family with him. He has a house in this town, you know."

"Is that so?"

"Yes, a big house."

"Don't you think he will stay in Birni, since that's where Leader Gambo is?"

"Ah! I think you are right," Ya'u said.

Professor Garba had been Leader Gambo's first foreign affairs minister when the latter had seized power in 1945. After the attack on Masara, he'd been appointed as Hasoumiya's ambassador to Egypt. He'd headed many of the country's foreign missions since then. That was why he and his family had been based in Europe, Africa and the Middle East, in turns, for the past thirty years.

Zaidou didn't reach home until sunset. He met Larai sitting on a mat in the courtyard, cutting spinach leaves. He sat beside her and told her about the potbellied man.

2

Larai told Zaidou that the potbellied man had been her neighbour when she'd lived with her husband before his death. She told him about how the man had become notorious for not settling his debts.

"He collected a sack of corn from my husband's stall in the market. To this day, he has not paid for it," she said.

"Is that so? So, he is a thief!" Zaidou exclaimed. He stood at the doorway of the soot-coated kitchen, watching Larai as she stirred a pot of spinach soup she was cooking over firewood. Larai's three-month-old baby Rabe, strapped to her back, slept as his mother worked. A window in the mud wall opened to the outside and light white smoke from the fire billowed out through it, exchanging with the gentle breeze that was the aftermath of the rain. The coolness of the breeze mixed with the nice aroma of the soup and the smoke of the firewood. Just behind him, in the courtyard, one of Larai's children played with the insects flying about under the yellow light of the bulbs. The older teenage ones pounded yams with pestles and a mortar. The thuds that came from their pounding punctuated Zaidou's conversation with his sister. The thought that those children were the offspring of his younger sister resurrected the feeling that he'd not achieved anything yet in life.

Larai was ten years younger than Zaidou. She was fair like him, but she was plump and reached only up to his shoulder in height. She had some black vertical designs tattooed on her face and her long curly hair was plaited in three braids. Her husband had been killed two months earlier by a drunk driver in Tarayya city. Days after that, the house she lived in had burned down. She was spending her *iddah* in Zaidou's house, which meant that she would spend four months and ten days mourning her late husband.

"If you want to get your money from that potbellied man," she said, "sew the material he brought to you. Then tell him you won't give him the garment until he pays you all your money. Let it look beautiful, so that he won't be able to resist it." Larai put a drop of soup from a ladle onto her right palm and tasted it. She stirred the soup and went out to the courtyard to monitor the yam pounding.

They all sat on mats in the living room for dinner. Larai fed Saminou, her four-year-old son. Her two older boys ate from the same bowl, chewing excitedly and licking the spinach soup off their fingers noisily. Baby Rabe slept on the mat beside Larai, clad neatly in a white shawl. Larai was always wary of him catching a cold because she feared it would suffocate him. Whenever the baby had a cold, Zaidou would watch in amazement as she skilfully sucked out the catarrh from his nose and spat it out.

Zaidou sat opposite his sister and her children, eating his pounded yam and spinach soup. The heat of the food was comforting on such a cold night. The nice taste of the food reminded him of Talatou. That thought sprinkled his pleasant experience with some bitterness. The excitement with which he chewed decreased and his morsels became smaller. He itched to speak to Larai about his pain, but he couldn't say a word because of his nephews.

"Bala, go and fetch me cold water to drink," he instructed one of the bigger boys. As soon as the boy was out, Zaidou opened his mouth to talk, only to realise that another nephew was still present who would understand the conversation.

"Tanko, follow your brother," he said.

The boy reluctantly got up, apparently wondering why he'd have to escort his brother just to get a bowl of water.

Zaidou cleared his throat to speak. Before any sound came out, the boys returned.

The night passed without him sharing his worries with Larai. He spent half of that night awake and the other half dreaming strange dreams of himself flying to paradise with Talatou or eating pounded yam with her from the same plate. In the morning, after he'd returned from the mosque, he met Larai sweeping the dead insects that had littered the courtyard the night before.

"I don't think Talatou understood what I meant," he told her.

Larai stood up tall and looked at him. "What do you mean, sir?"

"She doesn't understand that I want to marry her."

"Didn't you say you told her?"

"I told her, but I am sure she doesn't understand. How can she just say no like that? I am handsome, and I have enough money to take care of her and any children she would bear for me." Zaidou produced a chewing stick from his pocket and pushed it into his mouth.

"My brother, please leave that woman alone," Larai advised. "I tell you, she is not the right one for you. I know it."

Zaidou was amazed at his sister's conviction. He didn't like it. He decided to ignore her pessimism and to listen to Ya'u's advice not to let go. He refused to eat the *tuwo* and *kouka* soup Larai had warmed up for him for breakfast, giving the excuse that he wasn't hungry.

"But it's tuwo and kouka soup – your favourite!" Larai protested.

"I said I am not hungry! Do you want me to make my stomach bigger and put the food inside?" Zaidou walked out of the house.

He rode out into the street on his bicycle. The roads were still muddy with puddles here and there. He rode carefully, to avoid splashing people as they walked to their farms and to the market. Herdsmen were out with their cattle already, goading them along with sticks. Some of the herdsmen were little boys. He was amazed at how they controlled such big cows. Children in their white uniforms walked in tens to school, their bags hung on their shoulders. Traders threw open the doors of their zinc kiosks, while hawkers of bread called out to customers.

Talatou's wooden restaurant was wet from the rain. A big puddle spread across its entrance. A plank had been placed over the puddle to help customers enter. Through the entrance doorway, Zaidou could see that the restaurant was full of men sipping *koko* from their bowls and chatting heartily. He dismounted from his bicycle and went in.

Inside, it was warm and noisy. At the left end, Talatou and her female staff were pouring steaming koko into their customer's bowls. Today's menu also included red balls of *qosai*, as well as the white puffy *masa* served with *taushe* soup. Zaidou decided to go for the masa and the taushe soup, not because he preferred it but because that was what Talatou was serving. His heart beat rapidly and his hands trembled as he wove past the eating men and walked up to her.

"G-g-g-ood morning, beautiful woman!" he stammered.

Talatou smiled. That smile looked like the sun rising and lighting up the dawn. "Good morning, Zaidou," she replied. "You want masa?" Talatou's voice was deep, like a man's. She was slim and had big eyes and thick lips. She wore a brown veil that blended with her brown skin.

"Yes, beautiful woman, I want masa." Zaidou smiled.

Talatou picked up a plate and served him two pieces of masa from a bucket on the table before her. "Is that enough?" she asked.

"No. You know I love your food. I will take six."

"*Six?*"

"Yes. You are special, you know," Zaidou said.

A frown suddenly crossed Talatou's face, turning its brightness to darkness. She looked like a witch.

Zaidou's heart skipped a beat. Then he realised her eyes were not looking at him, but over his shoulder and towards the exit.

"Stop that old man!" she cried, dropping the ladle in her hand. "Thief! Stop him!" She bolted like a deer to the door and grabbed a man by his collar as he tried to exit. She landed three slaps on his cheeks. The man was none other than the potbellied man.

"This is the second time you have eaten here without paying me my money," Talatou cried. She pointed towards the cashier sitting to the left of the serving table. "Didn't you see my cashier? Last night, you didn't pay me when I was leaving your room! Today, I must collect my money."

She tried to dig her hand into his pocket, but he struggled to break free. He begged her to be lenient and not to betray their secret about the night before. Most of the men eating crowded around them to intervene and to hear Talatou's allegations better.

Zaidou was sure he was having a nightmare. "Did she say she slept in his room last night?" he asked a man close to him.

"That was what I heard too! I can't believe this," the man said.

"And to think she would say it when everyone here could hear," another man observed.

"She is a bad woman," a third man added. "I have been in this town for ten years now, but this is the first time I have seen a prostitute – and a shameless one, for that matter."

Zaidou watched till Talatou and her adversary had separated and reconciled. He left for his shop, still feeling he was in a nightmare.

He couldn't eat breakfast. He couldn't do much in his shop. Larai's flair for making correct observations became uncannily glaring to him. His respect for her swelled. How could he have fallen for such a ruthless, dirty and uncouth woman? He resolved to start treating his sister's words like gold bracelets and to forget that she was many years his junior.

He went to the *Dandali* after the *'Isha* prayer at night. Men were chatting and eating snacks at tables. Bulbs fixed to sticks at each end of the Dandali gave off a yellow light. Ya'u and Audou sat at one of the tables. Delicacies of all kinds were for sale. Old women fried and sold qosai at one end. Tuareg men with white turbans sold mint tea at a corner. *Suya* sellers grilled the spiced beef stuck on skewers.

"I hope you have not spoken to Talatou about me yet," Zaidou said to Ya'u, as he sat down beside him.

"No, I didn't visit her place today. I promise I will—"

"Don't do it, please!" Zaidou jumped to his feet, pointing a warning finger at his friend.

"Why?" Ya'u gasped.

Zaidou told him about what had happened at the restaurant.

Audou puffed out smoke from his mouth and nostrils and threw a cigarette butt on the ground. "I am not surprised by your story, Zaidou," he said. "If you had told me about your interest in Talatou, I would have warned you not to approach her. But neither you nor Ya'u told me. Do you know that Talatou has been jailed for armed robbery before?"

"What?" Zaidou yelled.

"She has," Audou said. "She spent three years in prison. It was after she was set free that she opened her restaurant."

Zaidou believed Audou, but he couldn't get Talatou out of his mind.

—◄○►—

Zaidou tried to overcome the love he had for Talatou. It was as hard as fighting a bush fire. Had she cast a love spell on him?

For the next two months, he avoided her restaurant. He changed his route altogether while going to work or returning home. When he wasn't able to have breakfast at home, he ate bread, omelette and tea at the *maishayi*'s table close to his shop, or he would buy qosai from the women frying them across the road.

On his way home from work, he stopped over at Chief Ousmane's mosque to observe the *maghrib* prayer at sunset. It was the biggest mosque in the town. It only got full on Fridays when the chief led the *jum'ah* prayers and people from all over the town attended. On other days, only the people in the chief's neighbourhood prayed in it.

After the prayer, Chief Ousmane began to teach some hadith about marriage. He sat on a tanned ram skin, while the men clustered before him on mats. Under the fluorescent lights, Zaidou could see the streaks of white in Chief Ousmane's thick black beard. He wore a red cap around which was wound a white turban. His white *babban riga* had brown embroidery. His deep voice made his words sound authoritative, making Zaidou feel that marriage was so important and that the efforts he'd made so far to get married weren't enough. When Chief Ousmane talked about the need for men to get married to help them avoid fornication, his eyes looked into Zaidou's several times. Zaidou wondered whether the chief suspected him.

Chief Ousmane called for questions at the end of the lesson. The men asked questions more passionately than they did when the lesson was on a different topic, like ablution, fasting or trade.

"Chief!" a young man cried. "There is this lady who is three years older than me. We love each other. Is it halal for me to marry her?"

"Yes," Chief Ousmane said. "There is nothing wrong with that."

"Chief, I want my daughter to marry my friend, but she doesn't like him. What should I do?" another man asked.

"Let her marry the man she loves!" Chief Ousmane frowned and raised his voice. He wagged his finger at the man and repeated his words two more times. He reminded the men about the hadith that forbade forced marriage.

Zaidou felt encouraged by the questioners' zeal. He took a deep breath. "Chief!" he raised his shaky hand. "There is this woman who sells food. She sleeps around, and she was jailed for armed robbery, but I love her. Should I marry her?"

"I'm sure you are referring to Talatou!" a voice from one end of the mosque cried. "How can you marry that kind of woman?"

"Foolish man!" another barked from the midst of the people.

The congregation began to murmur. Laughs sounded here and there. The noise came from every mouth in the mosque. People turned to look at Zaidou. He wished he could sink into the ground.

Chief Ousmane moved his hands up and down, gesturing at the men to keep quiet. When the men were quiet, he turned to Zaidou with a stern look. Before he opened his mouth to talk, Zaidou shot out of the mosque.

As Zaidou passed through Chief Ousmane's neighbourhood on his way to his shop the following morning, he noticed some youths pointing at him and laughing. Some others marching to their farms greeted him: "Good morning, Zaidou, Talatou's husband!" The mockery caused him to ride in a zigzag fashion, nearly hitting some girls hawking cooked groundnuts.

The men at the maishayi's table discussed the hottest news in the country: Leader Gambo had executed three journalists; a town chief was arrested for refusing to allow a road to be built through his domain; and Professor Garba had suspended the Governor of Birni for embezzling from the region's coffers. Zaidou took his breakfast of bread and tea quietly as he listened.

"Professor Garba is making us proud!" one man said.

"Yes, we have not heard any bad things about him since he became head of the Governors' Commission," another echoed.

"Put your words in a better way, man. We have been hearing good things about the professor!" a third man chided.

"You are right. And he is only two months in office. I remember that he gave a warning to the Governor of Savannah-Fula Region last month. The governor refused to pay Kanuri farmers for their harvest because they are not his tribe. Now we hear that he has suspended the Governor of Birni for stealing."

"Good! He will reduce the wickedness in Leader Gambo's government."

"But he has no power over the leader. If he dares to say anything against Leader Gambo, I swear he will be hanged."

Talatou's smiles came back to Zaidou when he returned to his sewing machine. He imagined the nice smell in her restaurant. Her voice rang in his ears. He recalled her thick eyebrows. But this woman was evil! Why couldn't he get her out of his mind? He sighed.

Whenever he heard the voice of a woman passing by, he'd look out the window to see if it was Talatou. Those voices became a distraction. He played Mai Ganga's songs to take his mind off of them.

He regretted that he hadn't waited to hear Chief Ousmane's reply to his question. The chief would probably have asked him not to marry her; that authoritative reply would have strengthened him to stay away from the wayward woman.

A middle-aged man walked in with his little son. "I want a dashiki with trousers," the man said.

"Do you want pockets for the Talatou?"

"For the Talatou?"

"Sorry, do you want pockets for the trousers?"

"I do. I will need somewhere to keep my money."

"What of the—" Zaidou was hit by the boy who had been jumping all over the shop. "Sit down, boy!" he said.

The boy stopped. He picked up the scissors and tried to cut a new dress lying on the table.

"Drop that! Come and stay with you father!" Zaidou grabbed the scissors.

The boy resumed his jumps. He knocked down the stool. He caused a pile of ready-made clothes to fall off the table.

"Stop that! Stay in one place!" his father instructed.

The boy stood still.

Zaidou looked at the damage the boy had done. "Stupid boy!" Zaidou said. He slapped the boy on his neck.

The boy, on the brink of tears, clung to his father's hand, holding his neck.

"Are you all right, Zaidou?" the man asked, his eyes strained. "I have always known you to be a friendly man. What has come over you this afternoon?"

"I'm sorry," Zaidou said. He pulled the boy close to him and rubbed his head.

3

Zaidou entered his house and met Larai and her sons in the living room. The older ones were doing their assignments, their books spread before them on the mat. The light from the bulb was dull, but they seemed to see well enough under it. Little Saminou was sleeping beside them, while Larai was breastfeeding baby Rabe. The only thing common to them all was their silence.

"Welcome back!" they blurted out.

"Mhmm!" Zaidou hummed, stroking his light beard as a smile spread across his face. Then he wished it were Talatou and the children she'd borne for him that had welcomed him that way. He stopped smiling. He hissed and shook his head, directing his eyes to the floor.

"What is the matter?" Larai asked. "Wasn't business good today?"

"Ah! I was just thinking of the potbellied man. He still has not paid me. I need the money to buy another bag of maize. You know Ramadan begins tomorrow."

"Tomorrow?" Larai and her sons cried.

"Yes, tomorrow. The crescent has been sighted. The imam announced it at the mosque."

"Ah! That's good news." Larai smiled.

"Thank Allah, the fasting is coming in the rainy season," Bala said.

"Yes," Tanko agreed, dropping his pen on his notebook. "The cool weather will help us to endure the hunger."

Larai brought Zaidou his dinner of tuwo and kouka soup. The soup had three pieces of fried ram meat in it. The meat was the first victim of Zaidou's molars. The meat chunks were soft and tasty. If only they had come from Talatou's restaurant! He licked his lips. "Yesterday, you told me that we had no meat left," he said to Larai. "Where did you get this from?"

"I bought it today," Larai replied.

"What? Why didn't you send the boys? You shouldn't be going out during your iddah."

"I finished my iddah yesterday. You have not been counting," Larai said.

Zaidou did a mental calculation of the days that had elapsed since the death of Larai's husband. She was right – she'd completed the four months and ten days of the iddah.

"Time passes quickly these days." Zaidou put a morsel of tuwo into his mouth. "So, you can get married again now, eh?"

"Let's talk about your marriage first!" Larai smiled. "I have tasted marriage already."

In the morning, as Zaidou was going out, Larai told him that he needed to buy beans, which she would use to make qosai for iftar.

"Didn't you buy them when you went to the market yesterday?" Zaidou asked her.

"I am sorry. I forgot."

"Always make a list when going to the market. What else did you forget to buy?" Zaidou sat down on the only wooden chair in the living room.

Larai made a list for him. She wrote in Arabic. Like Zaidou, she'd only been to primary school. She hadn't been to secondary school, where English was taught.

"You didn't include vegetables!" Zaidou observed, looking at the list.

"I got them yesterday. Ya'u gave them to me free."

"Free?"

"Yes. Plenty of them."

"*Kai*! That is nice of him!"

"You have a nice friend in Ya'u!" Larai smiled.

Zaidou decided that he would go to the market in the afternoon. In his shop, he played Salisou Mai Ganga's music, swinging back and forth. He followed his favourite lines of the song, raising his voice over that of the singer.

Ya'u entered the shop, carrying a nylon bag. "Kai!" he cried, switching off the radio. "This is Ramadan. You should be listening to the Qur'an – not vain talk."

Zaidou grinned. "I don't have a recording of it," he explained.

"That is a shame!" Ya'u shook his head. He dropped the nylon bag on the table. "Here are some dates for you for iftar."

"Ah! Thank you, my friend. These will last me the whole month!" Zaidou shook Ya'u's hand. "Larai told me you gave us plenty of vegetables yesterday, too."

"I did. I gave them to her." Ya'u's eyes glittered. "She's such a nice woman! It's sad that she lost her husband at a young age."

"Thank you for the gifts, Ya'u."

"How is the fasting, by the way?"

"We thank Allah for letting us see it. This is just the first day. We have about twenty-nine more to go!"

"I advise you to pray hard this Ramadan to get married!"

"My friend, I am still thinking of Talatou. I love her." Zaidou slapped his forehead.

"Are you crazy?" Ya'u's loud voice gave Zaidou a jolt.

"I am serious, my friend. I have not been to see her for two months now, but I always think about her."

"Then your prayer should be that that witch gets out of your mind! How can you continue to love her after the bad things you have heard about her?" Ya'u frowned. He tuned the radio to listen to the news at 3 p.m. His mood improved as he listened.

Zaidou only noted the newscaster mentioning the names of Leader Gambo, Professor Garba or one of the regional governors. As he sewed, he kept thinking about Ya'u's rebuke and about how hard it would be to stop loving Talatou.

"Professor Garba's family has moved to this town," Ya'u said, reducing the radio's volume.

"Is that so?" Zaidou asked, passing a thread through the eye of a needle.

"It is so. They moved in last week. It took two months to renovate their house."

"You mean the professor himself is in this town?"

"No, just his family. He is in Birni," Ya'u explained.

It began to grow dark, and a breeze began to blow. Ya'u left to go to Chief Ousmane's mosque to listen to the *tafsir*.

Zaidou decided to go to the market before the downpour began. As he locked his shop, he looked up to the sky and saw the clouds gradually covering the sun. When he was small, he used to imagine that the clouds were cotton that the wind had blown off the fields.

Returning his gaze to earth, his eyes met two reddish corneas at the background of black irises. They were smiling eyes. The lips beneath them formed a crescent. The looks, though harmless, gave him a jolt.

"Aren't you happy to see me?" Talatou asked. She had a young girl with her and they both carried big nylon bags. The bags were full, as if they would burst at any moment.

"What are you doing here?" Zaidou's hands were on his chest, as if trying to prevent his heart from flying out.

"I'm here to see you."

"For what?"

"For what?" A frown came over Talatou's face. "Should you ask that of a woman you love?"

"I am sorry. It's just that . . . I didn't think I would see you so suddenly," Zaidou stammered.

Talatou told him that she'd just bought some things for her restaurant from the Marmari market. From her nylon bag, she brought out a pink textile designed with white flowers.

"I bought this too. I want you to sew a dress for me for the Eid al-Fitr." She smiled, revealing her gapped front teeth.

"Okay, I will." Zaidou tossed the material into his shop and locked it again. "I have to rush to the market before the rain comes."

"You have been avoiding my restaurant these past few days," Talatou said, looking gloomy. "I want you to eat iftar at my place today. I will serve you free – only you!"

"Only me?"

"Only you, sir."

"Ah! That's good of you. I will come. Thank you! Thank you!" Zaidou smiled.

At the market, as he bargained for a bowl of beans, he fell into thought. The seller had to tap him so that they could complete the transaction. The paths between the stalls became like a maze. He knocked down a basin full of corn flour from a stall and the contents spilled on the ground. The seller held him by the collar, swearing that he must pay her the cost of the corn flour. It took the intervention of passers-by to pacify her.

Back home, Larai sat in the courtyard to examine the items he'd bought. She hissed as she brought them out of the small basket, one after the other. "It was the white beans I wanted you to buy, not the brown ones, sir," she complained. "And it was maize grains I asked for, not the cobs. The fish are stale! Didn't you look at them?"

"I love Talatou," Zaidou said, looking dreamily at his sister.

"Zaidou!" Larai tapped his shoulder.

He looked into her perplexed eyes. "Yes?"

"Are you okay?"

"Yes!" Zaidou cried. He marched to the living room and sat on the chair, looking out the window.

The clouds cleared and the rain didn't fall. As sunset approached, a nice smell came into the living room from the kitchen. Zaidou's stomach grumbled. He remembered Talatou's invitation and he paced the room, contemplating whether he should honour it. Bala and Tanko laid the iftar on the mat: fried yam steaming in a bowl, red stew, fresh dates, oranges cut into four, and fried chicken.

The sun set, and the muezzin sounded the call to prayer from the neighbourhood mosque. Larai and her children joined Zaidou to break their fasts with dates and water. The food would follow, after the prayer, but Zaidou didn't return from the mosque after the prayer. He rode to Talatou's restaurant.

The restaurant was filled with young men taking koko, qosai, fruits and juices of different kinds. They chatted, laughed, ate and drank. Sweat covered their faces, yet they didn't bother to wipe them off. Most of them were bachelors who didn't have wives to cook for them. The air was stuffy and hot. Talatou and her girls served the men in the queue. They served fast.

Talatou darted to receive Zaidou, wiping the sweat from her face with a cloth. "You are here in good time, my husband!" She ushered him to a mat behind the table where the girls stood serving. No customers were there. She served him a whole grilled chicken, some fries, koko and a soft drink.

From the moment Talatou had addressed him as "my husband", Zaidou had stopped smelling the aroma in the air, hearing the voices of the customers or sensing the taste of his meal. He ate mechanically, as Talatou sat on the mat before him. She told him stories he couldn't hear. The words "my husband" kept running through his head.

"Answer me, my husband, why did you stop coming to see me? Did I offend you?" Talatou plucked at his sleeve. Zaidou swallowed the qosai in his mouth.

"Why do you call me your husband?" he asked.

Talatou giggled. "I want to be your wife," she said. Zaidou coughed several times, gasping for air.

"Sorry, my husband," Talatou patted him on the back. She brought him a cup of water, which he gulped down. "Are you okay now, my husband?"

"I thought you said you won't marry an old man like me," he said.

"No, you are not old. I have gotten proposals from seventy-year-old men. You are only a baby to me – cute and fresh." Talatou rocked an imaginary baby.

"Then why did you tell me no?"

"I was pretending," Talatou explained. "Don't you know we women do that so that we don't look cheap?"

Zaidou pushed his food aside. He held his chin and looked into her eyes. Something nice and comforting radiated from her eyes and caressed his soul. Her lips parted in a smile, revealing her gapped teeth. Could this really be a bad woman? How could such a smile come from a lady who had been an armed robber? She looked away. Ah! Wasn't that the shyness of a chaste woman?

"I was told you have been to prison and that you are a prostitute." Zaidou maintained his posture.

Talatou jolted. "Who told you that?"

"My friend, Audou," Zaidou said. "I also heard you telling a man that he didn't pay you for sleeping with him."

Talatou stared at him, her mouth wide open. Her eyes became teary. "That's a lie!" she whispered, in a quavering voice.

"My friends don't lie," Zaidou said.

Talatou bowed her head.

The noises from the customers had started to reduce. Zaidou could hear the sounds of plates being packed from the mats and set on the table behind him. Talatou's sobs clashed with those sounds. He watched her patiently.

"I didn't rob again since I left prison!" she swore. "I have parted ways with my gang."

"But you sleep in men's rooms."

"It's only one man. I won't do that again. I repent. I repent, my husband – by Allah!" Her sobs grew louder and her shoulders shook.

Was she doing all this because of him? Why on earth should he reject a woman who loved him that much? He reached out to pat her, but he stopped short. She wasn't his wife yet. "It's okay," he said. "It's okay, my bride."

"Have you forgiven me?" Talatou suddenly raised her head, revealing her teary red eyes.

"Yes."

"Will you marry me?"

"Yes, my wife."

◄○►

"You made me cook for you, when you knew you were not going to have iftar at home!" Larai said. She sat on a low stool, washing utensils at the tap in the courtyard. She had two wide bowls before her, one for washing the utensils and the other for rinsing them. The utensils clinked in the water as she washed them.

"I'm sorry," Zaidou said. "I was invited for iftar by a friend, and I was afraid that I would be late. That was why I rushed there without telling you." He was sitting on a mat, wearing a singlet and enjoying the cool night breeze.

"Which of your friends invited you? Ya'u?"

"No."

"Audou?"

"No. It was the woman I will marry," Zaidou said. He pulled a thin stick from a broom, broke it into two and began to pick his teeth with one half. Larai sat up and looked at him.

"The woman you will marry? Who is that?" she asked.

Zaidou looked around and ensured that the boys were in the living room. "Talatou," he whispered.

"Talatou? Which Talatou?"

"The one you know. The beautiful one who cooks good food." Zaidou told her everything that had happened from the time Talatou had visited his shop till the time he had parted from her in her restaurant that night.

"She says she has repented," he said. "You know this is a month of repentance. I believe her repentance is sincere."

"Zaidou!" Larai exclaimed. She stared at him for a while and then continued her work.

Zaidou was glad she didn't say any more. Even if she had, he'd already made up his mind.

◄○►

Zaidou cycled to his shop the following morning, feeling relieved that his dilemma was over. He always had more garments to sew during Ramadan. People asked him to sew for them against the Eid al-Fitr. He stopped sewing all other garments and began to work on Talatou's pink and white textile. It wouldn't match her dark skin, but he'd do a beautiful style that would compensate for that. He wouldn't collect a single dirham from her for the job. He smiled as he worked his machine.

In the afternoon, Talatou entered his shop. The sight of her made him more confident that she was the water that would slake his thirst. She wasn't sweaty like the night before, and she'd rubbed kohl around her eyes and applied a red lipstick. A nice scent came from her, and it filled the shop.

"I am still working on your dress," he told her, smiling.

"I didn't come to ask about my dress. I only came to see you." She sat on the stool, facing him.

"That's kind of you." He laughed. Nothing was funny. The laugh came naturally.

She caressed his sewing machine as if it were the first time she was seeing such a device. There were gold rings on all her fingers except the thumb. Zaidou wondered how those tender fingers could have engaged in robbery. But weren't those rings stolen from somewhere? He looked at her smiling face and remembered her cry of repentance. He took a deep breath.

"This looks new," she said of the sewing machine.

"It's old. I got it ten years ago. It's the second machine I bought since I became a tailor."

"Ah! You keep things well. I am sure you will keep me better when you marry me." She laughed.

Zaidou laughed too, and his laugh was louder.

They talked about their businesses, the forthcoming Eid and their marriage. Zaidou told her that he'd like them to get married shortly after the Eid, and she agreed. He told her that he didn't want a quarrelsome wife, and she promised not to be one.

"Are you sure? You know you've robbed people before." He looked at her through the corner of his eye.

"I fight and quarrel, but I will change when we marry. I will change because of you," she promised.

"That's good of you. I love you!"

"I love you, too," Talatou said.

As she left his shop, she invited him for iftar again. He promised to honour her invitation.

Ya'u stormed the shop like a warrior just as Talatou had left. He was wearing a sleeveless shirt, revealing his dark muscular arms. His breaths were fast and there was sweat on his forehead. His eyes were red. "What was that woman doing in your shop?" he barked.

"Won't you sit down, my friend?" Zaidou pointed at the stool.

"No, I won't!"

"What is the matter? Have I wronged you?"

"Yes! I don't see why I should be friends with a man that befriends a harlot and a killer." Ya'u hit his fist on the table where the unfinished garments lay.

"Ya'u, sit down, please. Talatou has repented, and I love her. Do you know she gave me free iftar yesterday? She doesn't rob now, she gives! She has repented, I tell you."

"Who told you she is not deceiving you? Why do you want to be a fool?" Ya'u hit the table again and stormed out.

Zaidou rested his chin in his palm and looked thoughtfully out the door. He watched Ya'u go towards the market, dodging past donkeys and urchins. Ya'u had been his friend since childhood. What would it be like to lose such a good friend after so many years?

Talatou was looking more gorgeous when he met her in her restaurant. She'd changed her clothes. She wore blue clothing and a white veil draped over her head and around her shoulders. She'd powdered her face, applied kohl and wore a golden necklace. A strong scent came from her. She had left her girls to do the work while she'd waited for him.

"You look like an emir's daughter," Zaidou commented, sipping his koko.

"I am not better looking than you, my husband. Many girls talk about you," Talatou revealed.

"Is that so?" Zaidou smiled, opening his eyes wide.

"Don't tell me you don't know! My friends are jealous that I am your chosen one."

"People are only jealous about good things. My friend, Ya'u, is jealous that I am marrying you. You know he is a widower."

"Don't mind him. If he wanted me, why didn't he talk to me?" Talatou lit a cigarette, pushing it between her lips and puffing out some smoke.

Zaidou stopped chewing and stared at her. The strong smell of the cigarette went up his nose. "What is that?" he asked her.

"This?" Talatou flaunted the cigarette.

"Yes."

"You don't know what it is?"

"It's a cigarette."

"You know what it is. Why, then, do you ask?" Talatou inhaled again.

"I never knew you smoked. I don't want my wife to smoke," Zaidou said.

Talatou laughed. "Many people in this town smoke. Why are you surprised to see me doing the same?" She smiled.

"It's mostly men that smoke. I don't want my wife to smoke." Zaidou dropped his cup on the mat.

"Cigarettes are not bad, my husband. Their smoke is the same as the one women inhale from firewood."

"Is that so?"

"Yes! Even your mother inhaled it when she was alive – three times a day. Cigarettes are made from firewood. They are harmless and nice. You can taste it and see." She lit a cigarette and gave it to him.

Zaidou examined it at arm's length. His eyes moved between it and his fiancée's eyes.

She smiled and nodded. "Inhale. It's as simple as that," she said. She took her cigarette to her mouth, inhaled, and puffed out some smoke.

Zaidou's hand trembled as he took his cigarette to his lips. He inhaled deeply. He coughed and threw the stick out the window.

Talatou laughed. "Sorry," she said. "It's always like that the first time."

After his iftar, Zaidou left for the mosque in his neighbourhood for the *tarawih* prayers. The mosque was full so that there were rows of worshippers even at the mosque grounds. When the worshippers cried *"Amin"* in chorus, he recognised Ya'u's voice beside him. After the prayer, he gave him his hand for a handshake. "*Ina wuni*, Ya'u," he greeted, wearing a smile.

"Mhmm," Ya'u hummed without looking at him. He didn't shake his hand. He rose and marched out of the gate.

4

A car pulled up in front of Zaidou's shop. He stopped cutting the cloth in his hands to look at the car. It was a shiny black Mercedes. The last time a car had passed in front of his shop had been three months ago, when a rich merchant from Tarayya had visited the town. The few vehicles he usually saw were either commercial buses that travelled out of the town or private cars belonging to the rich men in the Arziki Quarter.

The rear door to the driver's right opened and a lady stepped out. Zaidou squeezed his eyes, opened them again and looked more intently at her. She looked foreign, more like the Indian actresses he used to see on posters at the Alheri cinema. The orange veil she wore hung from her head down to her knees. It matched beautifully with her white gown and fair complexion. She was just as tall as he was. With a gentle gait, she walked towards his shop, looking up at the signboard at the top of its doorway. He'd named the shop "Zaidou Tailoring Enterprise". It was written in Arabic.

She looked down from the signboard and through the doorway. Their eyes met. Zaidou swallowed and sat still.

"Good afternoon, sir," the lady greeted him in English, as she entered the shop.

"Good aptanun!" Zaidou sprang to his feet.

"You're a tailor, right?" she asked.

"I don't understand English, madam," he said in Hausa, his heart beating fast.

"Oh, sorry! I'm not fluent in Hausa either. Do you speak Arabic?" she asked him in Arabic. Her Arabic was impeccable – better than that of the newscasters.

"Yes, I speak Arabic!" Zaidou nodded eagerly. "Sit down, please." He pulled a stool from a corner and placed it for her in the middle of the shop.

"I need a tailor. I can see you are one." The lady sat down.

"Yes, madam!"

"Do you sew women's clothes?"

"Yes, madam!" Zaidou dived at the pile of unfinished garments on the table, browsing through them. He produced two unfinished dresses, examined them and quickly returned them. He dashed to another table at the opposite end of the shop, where he'd arranged completed garments.

"Yes, madam. I sew women's clothes. Look at these." He presented a pack of finished garments to her. One of them was Talatou's dress.

The lady looked at them in turn, nodding as she did. "Beautiful! Nice! Hmmm!" she kept saying.

She examined Talatou's dress from all angles. A smile came over her face. She looked at it longer than she did the others. She looked up at Zaidou. Her irises were blue. Her sclera were spotlessly white.

"This is beautiful!" she said, returning her gaze to the dress.

Zaidou was happy that the dress he'd sewn for his wife-to-be evoked so much admiration. "Thank you, madam!" He chuckled.

The lady looked at the dress longer than he expected. "Can you make me something like this?" she asked. Her smiles came with dimples.

"Yes, I can. I can make better ones."

"Great! Do you have a magazine from which I can choose other styles?"

Zaidou scratched his head. "I don't. I have all the styles I do in my head."

"Good. No problem. Make me one exactly like this dress, okay?"

"Okay, madam."

"I'll bring you the material tomorrow. I don't mind what you charge. Just make sure you make it the best you've ever sewn!"

"Okay, madam. I will do my best," Zaidou said.

The lady went out to her car.

Zaidou sat down and sighed. What kind of woman was that? Was she a princess from Tarayya? No, he'd met the emir's daughters before – they were all like the natives of Masara, either Hausa or Fulani. Where did this lady come from? She was certainly not a minister or one of the regional governors. She looked young – about thirty years of age.

"I didn't ask you your name, sir." The lady's voice rang from the doorway.

Zaidou jumped to his feet. "My name?" he asked.

"Yes, sir."

"I am Zaidou."

"I see. You named your shop after yourself, right?"

"Yes, madam."

"My name is Zakiyyah. I'm Professor Garba's daughter," she said.

Zaidou shouted, placing his hands on his head. "Are you serious?" he asked.

Zakiyyah told him that she was serious. She told him that it was her first time in the country and she was finding it strange.

She sat back on the stool. "Hasoumiya is my country, but I feel more at home in the Netherlands," she said. "I heard you have a cruel leader here."

"Yes – a very wicked man!" Zaidou grimaced.

"Oh, really? He kills a lot, doesn't he?"

"A lot!" Zaidou spat. He told Zakiyyah about how Leader Gambo had begun his rule in 1945 with the persecution of the Fulani. Sultan Abdulmoumini and all his emirs had been Fulani. When Leader Gambo overthrew the sultan and made governors take the emirs' powers, he began to torment the Fulani because he feared they'd avenge his coup. They were a minority in Hasoumiya, so they were easy to chase. They were arrested, given show trials and killed en masse. Three million had been killed before Gambo's thirst for their blood had been quenched.

Zaidou paused in his story. He wondered whether Zakiyyah was hurt because he was criticising her father's boss, but she seemed to enjoy every bit of his story. He felt excited about that and finished his narrative.

"He treated the Fulanis the way Pharaoh treated the Israelites!" Zakiyyah observed.

"Many of my people were killed at that time. Thank Allah, my family were not harmed," Zaidou said.

"Good for you. I read in a magazine that Leader Gambo once opened concentration camps for the Tuaregs. Is that true?"

"Concentration camps? What are those?" Zaidou caressed his beard.

"Oh! It was a place to which he packed off the Tuaregs and punished them."

"Ah! He did that. It was just after he'd left the Fulanis alone. I don't know why he did it."

"My father said that the leader has compiled a book called *Kitaabul 'Azaab*. It contains a hundred wicked laws of the ancient kings."

"I have never heard that before!"

"Well, I did. Anytime he wants to punish the people, he consults the book. I wonder what he'll do next. Maybe he'll bring back one of those Pharaoh decrees and stop people from having male children. Or he could ban people from getting married altogether!"

"Ban marriage? No way! Has that ever happened?" Zaidou hit the table with his fist.

"Yes – in Rome during the time of a man called Saint Valentine. I watched a film about him in the Netherlands."

"Where is this Netherlands? Is it in Nigeria?" Zaidou asked.

Zakiyyah laughed. "No. It's in Europe," she said.

Zaidou apologised that he didn't know very many places in the world and so he didn't know what Europe was either.

"Europe is a collection of many countries like Hasoumiya," Zakiyyah explained. "We call such collections continents, and there are seven of them in the world. The one in which we are is called Africa. Hasoumiya is in the western part of Africa."

"Aaaaah!" Zaidou nodded slowly. "Now I understand. You are a good teacher. Many people have explained Africa to me before, but I never understood. It looks as if you have gone to many schools."

Zakiyyah laughed. She told him that she had been to school in Paris and in London. She'd studied law up to the master's level in the Netherlands.

"Is London also in Europe?" Zaidou asked her.

"Of course."

"Is everyone in Europe fair like you? I have never seen a person like you before."

"Really?" Zakiyyah's eyes widened. "The people there are fairer than me."

"Is that so?"

"Yes. I'm like this because my mother is an Arab from Egypt, and my father is from this country."

"Ah! No wonder you speak good Arabic."

"Thank you." Zakiyyah smiled so much so that her front teeth showed. They were white, like that of a baby.

The sky grumbled and Zaidou noticed the clouds forming. Zakiyyah promised to send some material so he could sew for her, and she left.

The rain began to pour just as her car zoomed off. Zaidou watched the rain increase in intensity, blurring the sight of all objects outside. The smell it created by mixing with the soil was fresh and strong. As he watched it creating puddles, streaming down the street, he thought of his encounter with Zakiyyah. He smiled steadily.

The rain decreased gradually. When it stopped, it became clear that nightfall was near.

Zaidou picked up Talatou's dress, locked his shop and climbed onto his bicycle. The dragonflies were everywhere, as if they were holding a durbar to celebrate the cool weather. Street urchins wearing tattered garments moved from house to house, begging for food to break their fasts. They carried hungry bowls.

He reached Talatou's restaurant and leaned his bicycle against a nearby mango tree. As he sat eating, he told his fiancée about how her dress had attracted the admiration of a new customer. Talatou was excited. She admired the dress under the dim light of her restaurant.

"It's really nice!" she said. "I will look like a princess when I wear it on Eid day."

"You are already a princess!" Zaidou said.

Talatou laughed. "But you will sew me a better one for our marriage, won't you?" she asked.

"I will. That one will make you look like a queen." Zaidou sipped his koko noisily.

"I am sure you can sew that! You are the best tailor in town!" Talatou said. She rose to give her girls a helping hand as they served.

Zaidou ate quickly so that he could meet the tarawih prayers.

Talatou returned, smoking. The smoke she exhaled was thicker than that of the previous night. Its smell was stronger and different.

"I feel better when I smoke on a cold night like this," she said.

"This doesn't smell like a cigarette!" Zaidou cried, shifting his head away from her.

"No, it's not." Talatou inhaled and exhaled the smoke from her mouth and nostrils. The smell was nauseating.

"So what do you call this?" Zaidou asked.

"It's *ganye*." She unbundled a piece of paper and showed him some Indian hemp.

"I prefer the smell of the cigarette," Zaidou said. "Is this also from firewood?"

"No. It's from a plant," Talatou explained. She smoked the Indian hemp calmly. Its smell made Zaidou no longer enjoy his food. He took three quick sips of koko and rose to his feet.

"I need to leave to attend the tarawih prayers," he said. He bid her goodnight and marched outside to his bicycle. He rode to Chief Ousmane's mosque.

—◄o►—

Zakiyyah was the first to come to Zaidou's shop in the morning. She'd brought the material for her dress. Zaidou measured it and saw that it was six yards. That was sufficient. It was a black textile designed with prints of orange leaves. He raised the material to the sunlight and admired it.

"This looks expensive, madam!" he cried. "I have never seen its like before. Where did you buy it?"

"Never mind, sir." Zakiyyah smiled.

"Please, tell me. My customers will ask me when they see it."

"It's from the Netherlands. How much will the dress cost me?" Zakiyyah asked.

Zaidou stared at the material. He looked out at Zakiyyah's car, at her gold wristwatch, and at her rings. He scratched his head. "Let's talk about the money later," he sighed.

"Why not now?" A little frown came over Zakiyyah's face.

"I want you to see the dress and be happy with it first."

"No! Tell me now, sir."

"Okay, I won't charge you much, since you are a new customer. Four hundred dirhams," Zaidou said.

Zakiyyah nodded, told him her measurements, and left. He watched the car drive down the road and take a turn. He returned to his seat. He switched on the radio and continued work on a kaftan he had been making. The voices from the radio were distant. They were tainted by a low noise in the background, but he didn't bother to adjust the tuning.

"Sorry, sir!" Zakiyyah said, walking into the shop.

Zaidou jumped to his feet, his mouth dropping open. "Did you forget something, madam?" he asked.

"Yes. I forgot to give you these magazines." Zakiyyah gave him three new glossy magazines.

He browsed through them. They were full of styles for men's and women's clothes. The last time he had seen a fashion magazine had been ten years ago. It had been old and its edges eaten by rats. He'd seen it at another tailor's shop, but the tailor had refused to lend it to him.

"Are these mine?" he asked.

"Yes, sir." Zakiyyah smiled. "They'll give you more ideas." She told him that she'd gotten them at the Tarayya airport when she'd arrived in the country.

Zaidou nodded as he browsed through the different styles. "This is beautiful!" he cried. "Thank you, madam. Thank you."

He wanted to sew two additional dresses for Talatou, including the one she would wear on their wedding day. He took the magazines to her during iftar.

"I got these from a customer," he told her. "Choose the styles you like."

Talatou turned the pages with one hand and smoked with the other. She didn't take her eyes off the magazines until she'd gone through all the pages. She threw the cigarette butt out the window. She pointed out two styles to Zaidou. "These are good," she said. "But I don't have money for them now."

"No! I am doing them for you free!" Zaidou cried. He took two quick sips of koko and put a piece of fried ram meat into his mouth. Talatou had been frying the meat for him since he'd told her that he loved it.

"Free?" Talatou cried.

"Yes, my bride – free! If I don't do it for you, who should I do it for?" Zaidou said.

Talatou grabbed the magazines, browsed through them again and chose two different styles to replace the ones she'd chosen earlier. They had richer embroidery and were more complex.

Zaidou scratched his neck and swallowed his food. "These are expensive," he said. "But I'll do it for my queen."

He chatted with his fiancée until all the customers had left. He missed the tarawih prayers. When he went home, only Larai was awake, waiting for his return in the living room.

"You come home late these days," she complained.

"Are you now my watcher?" Zaidou retorted.

"I am sorry, sir. Would you like something to eat?"

"No. I have eaten. Thank you." Zaidou pulled a thin stick from a broom at a corner of the living room and began to pick his teeth with it. He showed Larai the magazines Zakiyyah had given him.

Larai advised him to show appreciation to Zakiyyah by sewing her garments at no charge.

"I can't be sewing for free for everybody," he lamented. "I am already sewing two expensive pieces of clothing for Talatou for free."

"Why? Is she the only customer you have?" Larai had raised her voice.

"No, she's not. But she's been giving me free iftar for days now. She deserves it more than Zakiyyah," Zaidou said.

Larai shrugged her shoulders, bade him good night and retired to her room.

5

Zaidou watched the smile form on Zakiyyah's face as she raised the dress he'd sewn for her and looked at it front and back. He smiled too. It surprised him the way his work made her ecstatic. She reminded him of his old neighbour who was seeing her first grandson. Zakiyyah's eyes glittered. It was as if she was unaware of every other thing around her. His other customers didn't show so much excitement. Was it because she wasn't used to the native dresses? He looked at the blue abaya she was wearing, clearly foreign and factory made.

"You're a genius, Zaidou!" she cried, still inspecting the nooks and crannies of his latest invention.

"That is what people always say," Zaidou replied.

Zakiyyah folded the dress and put it into a black nylon bag. Her countenance wore a more serious look. "Have you ever exported your work?" she asked him.

"Exported?" Zaidou caressed his beard.

"I mean, have you sold it to customers in foreign countries?"

"Well, the emir of Tarayya used to send material for me to sew for him. I also have customers from neighbouring towns and cities." Zaidou smiled.

Zakiyyah told him about Mark Brown, a tailor in London who'd become an international businessman. He'd grown to own a company that produced designer garments sold across the world.

The name of his brand was Zenith. Zakiyyah told Zaidou that he could be like him.

"How can that be? Is that possible?" Zaidou leaned forward and rested his elbows on the table of his sewing machine.

"It is possible. You are already known locally. You can progress by courting international clients. I can help you do that," Zakiyyah said.

Zaidou swallowed. "Is that so?" he asked.

"I mean it. I know five boutiques in the Netherlands that sell garments they import from Nigeria. They do good business. However, the garments they sell are not as good as the ones you sew. If you can sew many dresses in the styles shown in the magazines I gave you, I can send them to those boutiques. They'll pay you well."

Zakiyyah looked serious, yet Zaidou felt as if she was telling him the folktales of *Gizo* and *qoqi*, which his grandmother used to tell him when he was a boy. He told Zakiyyah that most of the money he made was used to take care of his sister and her children. He didn't have the money to start the kind of business she was talking about.

"Would you mind if I lent you some money?" Zakiyyah wore a frown of concern.

"Are you serious, madam?" Zaidou sat up.

"I want to help you. I want you to grow."

"Why not? I will take it, if you are really serious," Zaidou said.

Zakiyyah told him that she could help him buy all the material he would need. "I know the ones that will sell best," she said. "I'll be travelling to Tarayya city this month. I'll get dozens for you. But I'll give you money to buy other things you need – thread and all."

As she rose to go, her handbag fell. A piece of paper and three wads of new 500-dirham notes fell from it. Zaidou's mouth dropped open. He watched her as she packed them and returned the money into her bag. She unfolded the paper and glanced at it.

"Ah!" she exclaimed. "This was a poem I wrote last month. It's about clothes."

"Clothes?"

"Yes, clothes. You want to hear it?" Zakiyyah asked.

Zaidou scratched his head. "I listen to Mai Ganga's songs but I have never listened to a poem before," he said. "Let me hear it, madam."

Zakiyyah opened her mouth and read out:

> Without you, we are like beasts.
> With you, we are like kings.
> For which king is there without a cloak and a crown?
> Our skins, you protect from the elements.
> And our bodies, you guard from the evil gaze.
> A great companion you are.
> For you're always there for us –
> From the cradle to the grave!

She folded the paper, grinning. "Won't you clap for me?" she asked.

"I don't understand it," Zaidou said.

"Oh, really? Maybe it is because I wrote it in a hurry. But my father said it's a nice poem. Anyway, I must go. Goodbye."

"Goodbye, madam," Zaidou said. He watched her walk to the door, putting her poem into her bag.

"Can you teach me how to sew?" she asked, stopping at the doorway.

"Why not, madam? I can do that," Zaidou cried. Many people had made the same request to him before, but he'd turned them down. His excuse had always been that he had too much work to do. The truth was that he didn't want anyone to learn his sewing tricks.

"Will your wife mind you teaching a strange woman?" Zakiyyah asked, smiling. Her face went red. Her gaze was fixed on her fingers.

"My wife?" Zaidou asked. "I am not married."

"Okay. Goodbye." Zakiyyah went out.

"But . . . but . . . will your husband mind if I teach you?" Zaidou jogged after her.

Zakiyyah smiled and shook her head. "No. My father wouldn't mind," she said.

"What about your husband?"

"I'm not married." Zakiyyah smiled again and left. She left in a hurry.

Zaidou stood at the exit and watched her car driving away. How could such a charming lady be single at such a mature age? The man that would marry her would be the luckiest man in the world!

He returned to his chair and switched on the radio.

◄○►

Ya'u stormed into Zaidou's shop, his face bright with excitement. Zaidou stopped sewing and reduced the volume of his radio. He stared at his friend, memories of how he'd rebuffed him recently flashing through his mind.

"Zaidou!" Ya'u cried. "Who is that lady? What has she been doing in your shop?"

"Which lady?" Zaidou asked.

"The one who just left in a car. The fair lady. This is the second time I have seen you both talking as I passed by."

"She is my customer," Zaidou said, trying to read Ya'u's eyes.

Ya'u told him that Zakiyyah was also his customer. She and her mother had bought vegetables from his stall on two occasions. He said that the two women were gentle and nice. They never bargained the way other customers did. He told him of how urchins had followed them all over the market, singing songs about white people coming to town. The women had given those urchins some money to share.

"They are rich," Zaidou commented, resuming his work. "She is Professor Garba's daughter, you know."

"Ah! I thought as much!" Ya'u punched the air. "But you don't talk as much with your other customers like you do with her."

"Yes, I don't. I think it's because she likes the garments I sew."

"But everyone else likes them."

"No one likes them the way she does." Zaidou increased the volume of the radio. The voice of the newscaster wasn't clear.

Ya'u grabbed the radio and adjusted the tuning until it was clear.

The newscaster was reading a story on how Leader Gambo had ordered the execution of seven judges who had given judgements that were not in agreement with his decrees. In other news, Professor Garba had met with the three regional governors about ensuring food security. Ya'u said that the condemned judges were stupid, likening their actions to those of a man who had thrown himself at a hyena.

Zaidou finished the kaftan he'd been working on. He put it neatly into a crisp transparent nylon bag.

"Let me go home. It's almost sunset," Ya'u said, and left.

Zaidou rushed out so that he could be in Talatou's restaurant in good time for iftar. He found it amazing that he had found a lady who loved him so much, feeding him gratis for many days. He'd never been so lucky. As he cycled, he looked into the faces of the ladies on the road and was sure none of them was as generous as Talatou. He stopped over at a mosque to observe the maghrib prayer. Then he continued his journey.

Talatou did not put on make-up. She shouted at her girls as they served. She didn't smile at any customer. She brought Zaidou his food – roasted chicken, fried yam and koko. She smiled. "Good evening," she said.

Zaidou could see that the smile was forced. And why were the words "my husband" missing?

"Good evening, *my wife*." Zaidou emphasised "my wife". He searched her face for a bigger smile. Her smile didn't get larger. She sat before him, smoking a cigarette and breathing like a warlord. Was she tired of feeding him? Yes, she was. He'd eaten too much and she was angry with him.

"One of my customers promised to help me in my business," he said.

"Mhmm," Talatou hummed, glancing at her girls.

"She is Professor Garba's daughter. She has a lot of money."

"Mhmm," Talatou repeated, craning her neck to see the quantity of qosai one of her girls was serving a customer.

Zaidou continued his story. "She will help me to sell to customers outside Hasoumiya, in the white man's land. I told her I didn't have the money to—"

"*Kai!*" Talatou barked at one of the girls. "Pour only five ladles of koko. Did he tell you that seven men will be drinking with him?"

Zaidou switched his gaze between Talatou and her girl. The girl's hand trembled as she continued to serve. Talatou looked at Zaidou, smiled and then nodded at him to continue. He continued his story, sipping, chewing and swallowing between his words. Talatou's attention kept diverting to the girls. She kept asking him to repeat what he had said.

"You don't look happy tonight," Zaidou observed.

"It is my girls. They are stealing my money and my food. I have been watching them for three days now."

"That is bad of them!"

"*Kai!*" Talatou pointed at her cashier. "What is that you are knotting into your wrapper?" She sprang to her feet and marched to her. "You are tying my money in your wrapper, eh? Thief!"

There was a loud sound, which muted all the voices in the restaurant. Everyone looked in Talatou's direction. The cashier had her hand on her right cheek, her mouth wide open, her eyes staring at her assailant. Talatou raised her hand and slapped her again. The cashier yelped and jumped to her feet.

Zaidou got up to intervene.

Talatou grabbed the cashier and began to punch. The punches were wide, and Zaidou feared he would be hit. He stood back.

The cashier tried to block the blows. She began to retreat towards the serving area, knocking over some containers of food. The food spilled onto the floor and some landed on nearby customers. The affected customers cried from the scalding of the hot food and ran out to safety.

The cashier began to return Talatou's blows. Some customers rushed to intervene, while others ran outside. Screams and curses erupted from the serving girls.

Talatou grabbed a stick and wielded it at the men who intervened. They stepped back and the fight continued. Talatou got on top of the cashier, punching her mercilessly. Some customers tried again to yank Talatou off, but she bit their hands with her yellow teeth.

Five men walked up to Zaidou. "Zaidou, please stop your bride. Maybe she will listen to you," one of them pleaded.

Zaidou's heart pounded hard. Why should he be the one to do that? He heaved himself up and walked slowly, with shaky legs, towards the fighters. He tugged at Talatou's dress. "Talatou, please stop. Don't—"

Her stick hit his head. He yelped and stormed out of the restaurant, rubbing the place where he'd been hit. He looked at his hand under the moonlight. There was no blood. He mounted his bicycle and rode home.

—◄o►—

Larai and her sons were eating when he stormed into the living room. He startled them. They stopped chewing and watched him curiously as he bent over, panting. He sat on the mat, then he lay on his back.

"What is the problem, Zaidou?" Larai asked, standing over him.

He couldn't speak a word in reply. He kept panting.

"Sorry, Uncle," Tanko and Bala said.

Zaidou sat up and asked for water and food. He gulped the water down, took time to calm down again and then started to eat.

"Didn't you eat at Talatou's place tonight?" Larai asked.

"I took a few pieces of fried yam. I vomited them on my way coming back," Zaidou revealed.

"Why? What happened?" Larai asked.

Zaidou told her that Talatou had tried to kill her cashier. He'd tried to save the cashier's life, but his efforts had been in vain.

"Are you sure you tried to save her? Larai asked. "You always run away from fights!"

"I did! Zaidou exclaimed. "I could have died trying to save her!" He showed Larai the mark on his forehead. The place had swollen up.

Larai massaged it for him. He yelped and asked her to stop.

"Sorry, sir," Larai said.

"Sorry, Uncle," his nephews echoed.

"Mhmm," Zaidou hummed, taking a sip from his cup of koko.

Zaidou found it hard to sleep when he went to bed. The moment his eyes closed, scenes of the fight would recur to him. He'd not known that his fiancée was such a good fighter. He'd not known that her temper was that bad. Maybe those qualities would lead her to defend him after their marriage, in case he was attacked. But might he be a victim of her violence? He turned in his bed, sat up, and lay down again. He sat up and prayed. He prayed for a long time.

Larai knocked on his door at 4:45 a.m., telling him that *sahoor* was ready. He joined the others in the living room to eat tuwo and kouka soup. They ate quietly. He could feel the eyes of everyone stealing glances at his swollen forehead. He shielded it with his hand.

At dawn, the muezzin began the call to prayer and they stopped eating to begin the fast. Zaidou went to the mosque to pray. He found it painful to prostrate himself. He managed to do it on the healthy side of his forehead, but even that was painful.

The worshippers began to disperse at the end of the prayer. Zaidou stopped to say hello to some acquaintances at the mosque's grounds. One of them noticed his injury and began to help him massage it.

Zaidou shook his hands vigorously out of pain. Then he began to shout.

"You have to endure this, or else it will take time for the swelling to go," the man advised.

Zaidou tried in vain to yank the man's hands off, yelling louder.

The imam came out of the mosque and intervened, saying that the swelling would disappear even without the massage.

When he returned home, Zaidou got a piece of broken mirror from Larai and examined his injury. It wasn't as big as he'd imagined. It was a vertical swelling, reflecting the thickness and shape of the stick.

He picked up a pen and paper his nephews had left in the living room and began to write. He wrote fast, wearing a frown.

"What are you doing, sir?" Larai asked him. She was holding a broom, ready to sweep the living room.

"I am writing a letter."

"A letter? To whom?"

"I am writing to Talatou. I don't love her anymore." Zaidou didn't look up. The words he wrote flowed like rain.

Talatou,

I told you I loved you and that I wanted to marry you, and you agreed. You gave me free food and I sewed for you without collecting money. I heard many bad things about you, but I still chose to love you. Last night, I learnt my lesson. I am not marrying you.

Zaidou.

6

Zakiyyah brought the fabrics to Zaidou as she had promised. They were packed in three big woven bags. The material was worth three hundred thousand dirhams. Zakiyyah showed him the receipts.

Zaidou screamed and swore that he'd not be able to pay that debt. She reassured him that the money he'd make from exporting the garments would settle the debt. She did the arithmetic for him on paper, and he believed her, even though he didn't understand everything. She unzipped one of the bags, brought out a sample of three fabrics and showed it to him.

"I bought this at Tarayya's Exquisite Shopping Mall today. It's a big place," she said.

Zaidou saw that the fabrics were as good as the one he'd sewed for her. He was surprised that she'd fulfilled her promise so quickly. The journey to Tarayya, there and back, was ten hours. She'd taken that journey and done the shopping all in one day!

"Why didn't you rest before bringing the material to me?" he asked her.

"There's no point, sir. I shouldn't keep you waiting," Zakiyyah said, opening a second bag. The material in the bag was for men's clothes, while the other fabrics were for women's clothes.

Zaidou looked at the bags and wondered how long it would take him to sew all the material they contained. He'd have to stop collecting new orders from people. "I am lucky the fasting will end today if the crescent is sighted. I will have enough energy to sew them all," he said.

"That's true," Zakiyyah said. "So you'll begin work after Eid, right? You won't work on Eid day, will you?"

"No, I will start *today*." Zaidou pointed at the floor to emphasise "today". "I won't rest even on Eid day. This is a serious business for me. Thank you very much, madam. Thank you for your help." Zaidou clasped his hands together.

"It's my pleasure!" Zakiyyah smiled. "Can we start our sewing lessons now?"

Zaidou's mouth dropped open. "Let's start two days after Eid," he suggested.

"We can do something now, no matter how little." Zakiyyah yawned.

Zaidou shrugged his shoulders. He looked around his shop for some material he could spare. He brought out a piece of old material from a basket and began to teach her some basics.

She listened the way a little girl would when listening to a folktale. She grew more excited when he began to tell her his story – how he began tailoring. He told her about how he'd dropped out of school upon the death of his father. He'd learned tailoring from a neighbour, who had taken him on as an apprentice.

"Are you sure tailoring is the right thing for an educated lady like you?" he asked.

"Why not? I can do it as a hobby." She laughed.

"And you are sure your father wouldn't mind you doing a poor man's work?"

"Tailoring is not a poor man's job, sir." Zakiyyah looked serious. "You shouldn't look down at your profession, ever!"

"But it won't make me a big man."

"Mark Brown is a big man, very rich. You can be like him. I could abandon my training as a lawyer to be a tailor. And remember, I don't have a job now. Doing tailoring wouldn't be a bad idea."

"Won't you look for a job?" Zaidou dropped the thread and needle he'd been holding.

"I will. Jobs don't come like magic. You have to make applications here and there and attend interviews," Zakiyyah explained. She told him about interviews she'd attended in the Netherlands and at oil companies in the Middle East. She had gotten a job in Saudi Arabia, but she rejected it because it was too far from her family.

"Why did you apply for that job in the first place?" Zaidou asked.

"The owner of the company wanted to marry me. But things didn't work out," she said. She looked dreamily out the door. She looked hopeless. "I don't have a suitor now," she lamented.

"That is sad, madam," Zaidou said. "You will get one when the time is ripe." He wondered which man in the town would be suitable for such a lady of her status. There were rich men in the Arziki Quarter where she lived. Perhaps one of them would propose.

"Why didn't your father make you stay with him in Birni?" he asked her. "There are many rich men there who could marry you."

"He wants us to taste our hometown," Zakiyyah replied. "He wants us to learn Hausa."

"Learning Hausa is not as important as getting a rich husband!"

"I'm not after riches, sir. I want a kind husband. I want a husband who loves me." Zakiyyah smiled. Her eyes twinkled. They reminded Zaidou of the shiny gold coins he'd seen in a movie – *The Last Don* – in the Alheri cinema some years ago. It was the best movie he'd ever watched.

"What's that on your forehead?" Zakiyyah pointed at his injury.

Zaidou quickly covered it and turned away. "Did you just notice it?" he asked.

"I saw it when I came in. Did something hit you?"

"I got it while trying to save a life yesterday," Zaidou said. He narrated the incident at Talatou's restaurant to her. He gesticulated wildly as he explained how he'd dashed at Talatou and tried to wrestle her off the cashier.

Zakiyyah sympathised with him. She asked whether the police came, and Zaidou said no. How could they come when the station was miles away?

Zakiyyah said she needed to go home and rest. She looked sad and apologised that she was leaving. She bade him farewell and left.

Zaidou wondered why she had apologised for leaving. Was that the custom in the Netherlands? Or did she think she would offend him by leaving?

He brought out the letter he had written to Talatou and read it a dozen times. He locked his shop and rode to her restaurant earlier than usual. He stood before it and stared at it. He recalled the nice moments that he'd spent with Talatou inside it. They still felt nice. However, he was determined to remain brave and leave her.

A new set of girls was working inside, arranging the food containers on the table and sweeping the floor.

Talatou stood akimbo, her back to the door. She barked commands at the girls, pointing here and there. "You! Put that container on the table. Arrange the mats properly. No! Shift it to that corner. Let the mats overlap. Let there be no space between them. You! Bring a rag and clean the table!"

Zaidou stared at her. Was he right to leave her? Wouldn't he come to regret it? He'd come so close to marriage now. Why should he turn back? "Good evening, my wife," he greeted her.

She turned and smiled. The smile looked like a withered leaf. Her lips were swollen, as was her left eye. There was a cut on her forehead.

"Good evening, my husband," she replied. "You are here early today. Kai! What happened to your forehead?" She moved closer to observe his injury.

"You hit me yesterday. Have you forgotten?"

"Me?"

"Yes, you. I tried to stop you from beating up your cashier and you hit me." Zaidou frowned.

Talatou held her head with both hands. "Ah!" she cried. "I didn't do it on purpose. I was so angry I didn't know you were the one. Please forgive me!" She fell to her knees.

"It's okay." Zaidou smiled. He brought out the letter and gave it to her. "Hold this, please."

"What is it?"

"Read it." Zaidou walked to the door with a swagger.

"Are you leaving? Won't you wait to break your fast?"

"No, I won't," Zaidou said. He mounted his bicycle and rode home. After sunset, he ate iftar with Larai and her sons.

◄o►

Ya'u and Audou visited Zaidou in his house early, at 7:30 a.m. They were dressed in white babban rigas. The scent of their perfumes was strong. They ate qosai sandwiched in bread and drank tea. They chatted and laughed. Ya'u joked that Zaidou would soon marry a good and beautiful wife. When Zaidou challenged him to mention her name, he simply said that time would tell.

Larai brought them dates and sliced pineapples in plastic bowls.

"*Barka da sallah!*" she greeted them in Hausa, wishing them happy Eid.

"Barka da sallah!" they wished her the same.

"You didn't bring us vegetables for the Eid!" Larai said to Ya'u, wearing a mischievous smile. "Do you want us to become skeletons?"

"I am saving some for you in my house. You will eat your fill when you finally come," Ya'u said.

They all trooped out for the Eid prayers – Zaidou, his friends, his nephews and Larai. Zaidou carried Saminou, while Larai trailed behind, with baby Rabe strapped to her back. The prayers would be offered at the big field, which was past Zaidou's shop and the Marmari Market. The field was used for many other things: football, political rallies and durbar when a VIP visited the town. Zaidou loved the durbar. He loved to see the horses racing up and down the field, leaving dust in their wake.

Chief Ousmane led the prayers, bowing and prostrating. Everyone looked their best. The farmers, who usually smelled in their tattered clothes, looked clean and nice. The elderly wore babban rigas, but most others wore kaftans. The crowd was huge, and Chief Ousmane looked tiny standing before it as he gave the sermon after the prayer. His apparel wasn't different from his usual garb – a richly embroidered babban riga and a long red cap, around which was wound a white turban – only today he was carrying a staff. It was a staff of authority, which the emir of Tarayya had given him when he'd appointed him as the town head. He spoke through a microphone, and his voice echoed across the field.

With the sermon over, people shook hands, hugged, and began to disperse.

"I will be going to my shop," Zaidou told his companions. "I will see you later."

"What?" Ya'u and Audou cried in unison.

"Yes. I have a lot of work to do."

"Why do you want to work, when the whole town is celebrating?" Audou asked.

Zaidou shrugged his shoulders. He walked to his shop.

The smell of new textiles wafted up his nose as he unzipped one of the bags of material. He pulled off his shirt and babban riga, leaving only his singlet on. He brought out a fabric, switched on

Salisou Mai Ganga's music, and set to work. He was determined that each of the clothing items he made would be better than any he'd made before. He couldn't imagine making shoddy clothes for people who were fairer than Zakiyyah.

By afternoon, he'd sewn ten dresses of different styles. That was enough for the day. He began to beautify them with some elaborate embroidery.

"Zaidou," a woman's voice called from outside. "Don't you know today is Eid? What are you doing in your shop?"

He looked up to see the woman who sold fries opposite his shop. She seemed younger in her purple and white garments. She was holding her grandson by the hand.

"Ah! I have a lot of work to do. There is no time for celebration." Zaidou laughed.

The woman told him that she was out to visit friends and family, and advised him to do the same. Zaidou gave the woman's grandson a gift of a one-dirham note.

The embroidery was delicate. He sweated as he worked his needle and thread. He wished he had a fan in his shop. He'd have bought one, if he'd not had to pay the school fees for his nephews.

The light coming in through the doorway was suddenly blocked.

"Good afternoon, Zaidou," a woman's voice greeted him.

Zaidou looked up and saw an eye swollen like a pebble, and an inflamed upper lip. "Talatou!" he gasped.

"Barka da sallah." Talatou bobbed a curtsey. She was wearing the dress he'd sewn for her. It looked nice on her. Zaidou's heart beat fast. She dropped a bowl of food on his table. "This is your Eid tuwo. One of my customers told me you were here. You didn't come for iftar yesterday."

"Ramadan is over, so don't talk to me about iftar." Zaidou continued his work.

Talatou stared at him, still like a statue. "You will eat my tuwo, won't you, sir?" she asked.

"You can take it back, please. Thank you." Zaidou looked at her and back at his work.

Silence. The silence almost caused him to make mistakes.

"Please forgive me, my husband." Talatou's voice was shaky.

"Forgive you? For what?"

"I read your letter. And you told me yesterday that I hit you. It wasn't on purpose, I swear!"

"I know it wasn't on purpose. I just feel I can't mix cow's milk with lime juice. We can't get married. It won't be good for any of us, I tell you." Zaidou was surprised he had the courage to say all that.

Talatou remained standing. Then she picked up her food and walked out. "Are you sure you want me to leave?" she asked from outside.

Zaidou gestured at her to go away.

"I am sorry," she gasped.

Zaidou ignored her.

"Won't you respond, sir?" Talatou asked.

Again, Zaidou gestured at her to go away.

She disappeared into the distance.

Zaidou sighed. He opened his drawer and browsed his cassettes for a particular one. He found it and pushed it into the cassette player. The voices of Mai Ganga and his band rang out:

> Women, women, women, behave yourselves!
> Women, women, women, behave yourselves! (chorus)
> We men love and marry you.
> We men love and marry you (chorus)
> But you behave as sly as foxes.
> But you behave as sly as foxes (chorus).
> Leading us to miseries and to graves!
> Leading us to miseries and to graves! (chorus)

By nightfall, he'd done much of the embroidery on the first dress. He rode home, feeling tired and dizzy.

7

Within nine months, Zakiyyah had helped Zaidou to export twenty big batches of garments. It was the happiest nine months Zaidou had spent in decades. He didn't bother about girls. He didn't bother about money. Business kept him preoccupied. Zakiyyah cheerfully gave him all the support he needed. He'd never imagined he would get a customer who could be so helpful.

He stood akimbo as he watched the bricklayers doing an extension of his house. He was building an extra bedroom, kitchen and toilet. He would live there with his bride and leave the existing part for Larai and her sons. He watched the bricklayers as they carried concrete blocks, cement and sand on their heads.

All three workers were dusty and untidy and hardly spoke. Their leader was Babawo. He'd worked on most of the beautiful houses in the Arziki Quarter. Rumour had it that he headed the gang of robbers Talatou had once belonged to. He'd been jailed for murder before. Zaidou couldn't verify all the rumours, but Babawo's huge, sturdy, muscular build and unfriendly ways gave the impression that they were true. Babawo's hair was thick and bushy. He had a big nose, and his prominent lips were so thick that the upper lip almost touched his nostrils. The only time he spoke was when he barked orders at the other two bricklayers.

The youngest of the bricklayers was in his late twenties. He always sang Salisou Mai Ganga's songs to himself. He was cheerful and didn't seem to have problems. "This will be a good house, sir," he said to Zaidou. He shovelled cement into a metal container and balanced it on his head.

"I can see that," Zaidou agreed. "My bride will be happy to live in it."

The boy looked at him, the smile disappearing from his face. "You are not married, sir?" he asked. "What are you waiting for?"

"I will marry. Just continue with your work."

"But you should have been married long before now. I married at twenty."

"Mind your business, man, or I will send you away from here!" Zaidou walked away grumpily and entered his house.

In the living room, he picked up Tanko's chemistry textbook and browsed through its pages as if he could understand it. Larai asked him questions about the construction work, but he told her to shut up. He asked her to go out and see the progress for herself. He ate his lunch with a frown, wondering whether it was raw grass he was eating. That night, he went to the Dandali. He rode on his new motorbike, which Zakiyyah had helped him buy from Tarayya out of his profits.

Ya'u was eating masa dipped in pepper. A bottle of cold water stood on the table by his plate. Audou was smoking a cigarette. He had a cup of mint tea before him.

"I didn't see you at your shop today," Ya'u observed.

"I was with the bricklayers working at my house." Zaidou sat between his friends.

"Are you building a new house?" Audou's eyes widened.

"Yes. Since last month." Zaidou beckoned to the man selling tea from a big metal kettle. The tea seller trotted up to him.

"You didn't tell us!" his two friends protested.

"I'm sorry."

"And you didn't tell us you had bought a motorbike either. We just saw it," Audou said.

Zaidou apologised again and watched the tea seller pour steaming tea into a cup for him. The tea smelled of mint. He paid the man and took a sip. It burnt his tongue. He set the cup on the table to let the tea cool.

He started to tell his friends about how comfortable life had become for him. He told them about his plans to buy some farmland and to open a provision shop. "I never knew one could get so much money from selling things to people in other countries," he said. "Better get one of your customers to teach you how to do it!"

"I sell grains and tomatoes," Audou said. "Will the white man buy those from me? Don't they have them in their own countries?"

"And I grow and sell vegetables!" Ya'u said. "When I took them to Kano last month, I didn't make much money. They are everywhere in the world."

"How do you know? Have you gone round the world?" Zaidou sipped his tea.

"No." Ya'u said, "but I don't think the rest of the world will be different from Kano and Yaoundé, which I have visited."

Zaidou pitied his friends for their predicaments. Their inability to export made him more grateful to Zakiyyah. He wondered what he could do to repay her. "Zakiyyah really helped me to get my riches." He sipped his tea.

"Yes, she has been kind to you," Ya'u said, "but you have not met at your shop for two days now."

"Yes, we have not. She has gone to Lagos to talk to a company. She wants a job." Zaidou looked at his friends in turn and sighed. "I love her. I am sure she loves me too. I want to propose to her."

Audou laughed. "You want to propose?" he asked.

"Shouldn't I? She is a kind girl. You can't compare her to Talatou," Zaidou said.

"True, they cannot be compared," Ya'u agreed. "I know you two are in love. She comes to your shop to learn how to sew, but you end up laughing and chatting. I thought you would have proposed long before now."

"It will be good for them to marry," Audou said. "It's just that she will think she should be a big man's wife. She is educated and rich, but Zaidou has not finished school."

"Zaidou is a big man too," Ya'u chided. "How many people in this town have a motorbike like he does? People are building houses with mud, while he is expanding his own with cement. And even before now, he has lived comfortably. He is worthy of her!"

"I'm not saying he shouldn't propose. I'm just saying she might say no. If she says yes, her father might say no. He would want his daughter to marry a governor or an emir." Audou crushed the butt of his cigarette under his slippers.

"Don't discourage our friend!" Ya'u wagged an index finger at Audou.

"I'm not discouraging him. I'm telling him the truth. By the way, you have been troubling Zaidou about marriage, so why not talk about yours? You have lost your wife. When are you remarrying?"

"I have proposed to Larai already," Ya'u said.

"What?" Zaidou yelled. "When did that happen? She never told me."

Men at neighbouring tables turned to look at him.

Ya'u gestured at him not to shout. "I proposed when she came to my stall yesterday," Ya'u whispered.

"Has she accepted?" Zaidou asked.

"Yes." Ya'u smiled. "I am sorry I didn't tell you. I was going to do that before we left here."

Zaidou recalled that Larai had mentioned Ya'u's name several times in his conversations with her. He had never realised that a relationship was on.

"Zaidou," Ya'u began, "don't be discouraged by Audou's words. It is time you got serious about getting married. The right woman has come to you. You should have proposed to her before now. Don't let her go! Propose!" He punched his right fist into his left palm.

Zaidou thought about his friends' conflicting advice as he rode home. They had both looked serious and sincere as they advised him.

Larai was chatting with her sons in the courtyard when he got home. Tanko and Bala told stories of school fights, a strict teacher and their truant classmates. Larai told them about her own short experiences at school, about how she'd enjoyed her mother's folktales and about how she'd met and married their late father.

When Tanko and Bala had gone to bed, Zaidou told Larai about his dilemma. "I have always liked Zakiyyah," he said, "but Audou says she's too big for me."

"Too big?" Larai asked.

"Yes. Too big!"

"How?"

"She is from a rich and powerful family," Zaidou said.

Larai gave a long hiss. "Don't listen to him, sir," she said. "You love her, and she is a nice girl. She has been good to you. She loves you too. You should propose."

Zaidou's heart beat fast. "Are you sure?" he asked.

"Yes. Propose. If you don't, another man will snatch her. And I don't think you can get someone better than her. Propose, sir. Please. Good night." Larai got up and retired to her room.

◄○►

In the morning, Zaidou went out to meet the bricklayers. They'd already resumed work, moving up and down without conversation, like a team of ants. The walls were now up way above his head. The roofing would most likely begin that day.

He went round the building. The room and the kitchen were big enough. The kitchen window looked small. "Why didn't you make it bigger?" he asked the youngest of the bricklayers.

"I don't know, sir," the man replied. "Please ask Babawo. You know he tells us what to do."

Zaidou looked at Babawo's unsmiling face as the man poured cement into a gap between two concrete blocks. Babawo had never spoken to him since the construction work had begun. His silence made Zaidou think that he harboured criminal thoughts, or that Babawo hated him.

"Don't worry. I will talk to him later," Zaidou said to the young bricklayer. He revved his motorbike three times.

"Zaidou!" a loud deep voice called. It sounded like the braying of an ass. Zaidou turned and saw Babawo approaching. His heart skipped one beat.

"Are you going to your shop now?" Babawo asked.

"Yes, yes, yes!" Zaidou nodded several times.

"I want you to sew a babban riga for me. I need it for a party in two weeks' time." Babawo went into the uncompleted kitchen, came back with a black nylon bag and gave it to Zaidou. It contained a plain blue fabric. Babawo explained the style and embroidery he wanted. He smiled as he spoke, and that was the oddest sight Zaidou had seen in years. He zoomed off as soon as Babawo was done, and the relief he felt was immense.

He sat for breakfast at the maishayi's table with men from the Marmari market. His tea was flavoured with cocoa. The bread was getting stale, but it was nicely buttered, which made it tolerable. The crumbs fell on his shirt as he bit off the morsels.

The men were discussing Leader Gambo's eightieth birthday, which had been celebrated the day before in Birni. Ten African heads of state had attended, and Birni had been full of security.

"Let him die and leave us alone!" one man cried.

"True. How long do we have to endure his wickedness?" another wondered.

"Kai!" the maishayi cried, raising his hand at them. "Don't say those things at my table. I don't want to be arrested."

The men laughed, but they stopped wishing the leader dead. They spoke about their businesses, their farms and their families.

Zaidou entered his shop and looked at Babawo's material again. Would Babawo pay him for the job? He looked like the fraudulent type! How would he handle Babawo if he defaulted? He'd certainly not treat Babawo the way he had treated the potbellied man – otherwise, he wouldn't live to marry Zakiyyah.

He measured the material and saw that it was ten yards – just enough. He decided first to finish some embroidery he'd started some days ago on a cloak belonging to the emir of Tarayya. He switched on the radio and set to work.

A car pulled up in front of his shop. His heart began to pound and he felt like jumping out the window behind him. He took a deep breath and rehearsed the words, "Will you marry me?" in his heart. His palms felt sweaty. It all seemed like a dream.

"Good afternoon, sir." The driver of the car entered his shop.

"Where is Zakiyyah?" Zaidou barked.

The driver jolted. "I didn't come with her. She sent me to you," he explained.

"She sent you to me? What did she say?"

"She came back from Lagos yesterday. She wants me to take you with me for a party at their house," the driver said.

Zaidou swallowed. He had never attended a party before, and he always felt intimidated visiting the mansions in the Arziki Quarter. "Right now?" he asked.

"Yes – now. The party has already started."

"What is the party for?"

"I don't know. She will tell you," the driver said.

Zaidou began to think of an excuse not to go. He looked at the quantity of work he had to do. No, that wasn't a good excuse. Did he have any shopping to do for Larai? That wouldn't do either. Should he turn down the invitation at all? No! She'd think he didn't love her.

"Is Professor Garba in the house?" he asked.

"No," the driver said, impatiently. "It is only his family and friends. The professor comes on weekends."

Zaidou felt a bit more confident. He followed the driver to the car and they zoomed off.

It was his second time in a car. He called out to people he knew and waved at them. They waved back excitedly, apparently wondering whether their eyes had deceived them.

Professor Garba's house was the biggest on its street. Through its ornamental gate, Zaidou could see many exotic cars parked in the parking lot. A big, grey, one-storey mansion stood at the breadth of the parking lot, opposite the gate. It had a huge double door at its entrance. A paved path beside the mansion led deeper into the grounds. Flowers of different colours lined the tall fence – green, white, yellow and purple. As soon as he stepped out of the car, an usher led Zaidou down the path beside the mansion.

He was taken to a well-mown lawn, where people were feasting. Though it was afternoon, the lamps were lit. The attendees were the rich and the poor, the young and the old. The young rich ones sat eating on white plastic chairs and tables. The older, poorer ones sat and ate on the lawn. They all ate off of expensive china plates. The place brimmed with laughter, voices and the clinking of cutlery on plates. The air was filled with the nice smell of food from silver-plated containers at one end of the lawn. Zaidou went to have a look. There was rice, grilled fish, masa, roasted and fried chicken, tuwo and three varieties of soup. Everything was arranged on a table lined with a white cloth. People took whatever they wanted.

Zaidou stood in front of the serving area and watched people around it leaving with full plates of food. He was not sure where to begin.

"*Masaa'ul khair*, sir," Zakiyyah's voice greeted him.

He turned to his right and saw her cute, fair, smiling face. His eyes stared into her blue irises. How lovely! How beautiful! How elegant! Was he really worthy of such a lady? He swallowed hard. "*Masaa'un noor*, Zakiyyah," he replied.

"This is my mother." Zakiyyah pointed to a woman beside her. The woman was plump and blue-eyed. She was the same height as Zakiyyah and was dressed in a pink abaya.

"Masaa'ul khair," Zaidou greeted his heartthrob's mother. He was careful to emphasise the syllables as perfectly as a newscaster would.

"Masaa'un noor," Zakiyyah's mother replied.

"Mum," Zakiyyah said, pointing at Zaidou. "This is the Managing Director of Zaidou Tailoring Enterprise."

"I see." Zakiyyah's mother looked at him from head to toe.

He was wearing rubber slippers and a sleeveless dashiki. His cap was pointed at the top and had two flaps at its sides that covered his ears.

Zakiyyah guided Zaidou through the buffet. He took fried rice and turkey. The rice contained lots of vegetables and sliced chicken, and it smelled strongly of curry and lightly of garlic. He sat on the lawn and ate, while Zakiyyah attended to her guests. He licked his fingers clean, crushing all the bones. It was the nicest meal he'd ever had – better than anything Talatou served.

He remained on the lawn, watching the guests leave in ones and twos. The domestic servants went about picking up the bottles, nylon bags and serviettes from the lawn.

Zakiyyah returned and sat by his side. She was wearing the black and orange dress he'd sewn for her.

"You look beautiful," he told her. His voice was shaky.

"Thank you, sir." She smiled.

"What was the party for?"

"I got a job!" Zakiyyah laughed.

"Are you serious?"

"Yes!"

"Ah! That's good news," Zaidou cried.

Zakiyyah told him that the job was at the head office of Pure Platinum Petroleum Company in Lagos. She'd be starting the work in three months' time. She observed that she would be switching between three different societies within a space of one year – The Netherlands, Masara and Lagos. She would also be moving from an idle life to a working life.

"Wouldn't you like to change your house too?" Zaidou smiled.

"Isn't this house good enough? You don't like it?" Zakiyyah ran her hand through the air, pointing at the mansion, the lawn and the surroundings. Her face went red.

"It's good," Zaidou said, looking at the places she was pointing at, as if he were seeing them for the first time. "They are beautiful. I meant to say you should change the house you call your own, since many other things are changing in your life."

"I'm definitely going to get a house in Lagos," Zakiyyah said.

Zaidou took a deep breath and shook his head.

Zakiyyah continued to tell him about her experiences in Lagos. She told him that, even though she'd done an interview, her father's influence was what had given her the job. The chairman of the company was his friend and classmate from when he'd done his master's degree at Oxford University over forty years ago. She had been given her offer letter immediately after she came out from the interview.

She ran upstairs, returned with the offer letter and gave it to Zaidou. It was in English, so he couldn't read it.

"Let me read it for you," she said. She translated the letter as she read, sentence by sentence.

"It's a good job," she said. "They'll pay me many allowances: transportation, feeding, security and many others. That is apart from my basic salary."

"Which type of security are they paying you for?"

"It's to hire a guard for my house."

"Don't you think . . . um . . . you need a better guard than a stranger?" Zaidou stammered.

"A stranger? I'll be careful whom I hire! I won't pick any man I see on the street."

"You don't want a man who loves you to guard you?"

"What do you mean, sir?" Zakiyyah's smile disappeared.

Zaidou scratched his neck. "Marry me!" he said.

His words gave Zakiyyah a jolt and she looked at him as if she were looking at a ghost. "What did you say, sir?" Zakiyyah asked. Her face was red again.

"Will you . . . um . . . marry me, madam?"

"Marry you?"

"Yes, madam – marry me," Zaidou said.

There was silence.

Zakiyyah looked at the ground thoughtfully. Did she really understand what he had said? Or did he need to repeat himself?

"Okay, I'll think about it, sir," she said at last.

─◄○►─

Zaidou did not wave at anybody as the driver returned him to his shop. He felt a lump in his throat. Why had he proposed? Now Zakiyyah would think he was a fool. She'd start saying that he had a greedy motive in their business relationship. She would tell Professor Garba that a tailor had proposed to her because she'd gotten a big job. He fought back his tears.

The driver dropped him off at his shop and left. Zaidou sat behind his sewing machine and picked up his scissors, but remained still, looking thoughtfully at the floor. He remained like that for a long time. He didn't know for how long. He dropped the scissors, mounted his bicycle and rode off.

This was the first time a lady had given him the kind of response that Zakiyyah had given him. All the ladies he'd courted had said either no or yes. For those who had said no, the story had ended there (except for Talatou, who had later said yes). For those who had said yes, either he or they had eventually ended the relationship.

Why was Zakiyyah's response different from those of the others? Maybe that was how Arabs said yes, and she had learnt that culture from her mother?

He entered his house and marched to the courtyard. Larai was sitting on a mat, sifting corn flour into a small bowl. Saminou and Rabe were playing with pebbles close to the tap.

"Welcome back, sir," Larai greeted Zaidou.

"Thank you." Zaidou sat on the mat beside his sister. He buried his chin in his palm and stared at the ground.

"You are back early today. How was work?" Larai asked.

"It wasn't fine." Zaidou exchanged looks with her.

Larai carried the bowl of corn flour and entered the kitchen to set dinner on the fire.

Zaidou loved to make faces at children and see them laugh, but he didn't do that to Saminou and Rabe now, even though they ran up to him and sat by his side. Rabe tugged at his sleeve and sat on his lap. Saminou showed him his collection of pebbles. He ignored them both and continued to stare at the mat.

Larai emerged with a bowl of water and set it before him.

"I met her today," Zaidou said. He took a sip of water.

"Saminou!" Larai called, throwing a rope at her son. "Go to the sitting room and play with your skipping rope, quick!"

Grabbing the rope, Saminou jumped happily and ran to the sitting room. Rabe followed him with quick little steps.

"So you visited her today, eh?" Larai said.

"Yes," Zaidou replied. "She invited me to a party to celebrate her new job."

"She has gotten a job? Where?"

"In Lagos. It's with a petroleum company."

"That's good news. I hope you didn't go to her in those rags."

Zaidou looked down at his clothes, then at his sister. He nodded. Larai slapped her thighs with both hands, wearing a grimace.

Zaidou had never imagined his garments were not good enough. He'd worn them even to visit Chief Ousmane.

"So how did it go?" The concern on Larai's face was glaring. It reminded Zaidou of the looks on their late mother's face, whenever she asked him how he was coping with malaria. She'd touch his neck and forehead as she asked.

"I proposed to her," Zaidou said.

"What did she say?"

Zaidou began to tell her the whole story. She nodded excitedly as she listened. When he asked her what she thought Zakiyyah's response meant, she, in turn, asked him about her mood and expressions.

"She looked scared," Zaidou said.

"Scared? Did you shout the proposal?"

"I think so. I just let the words out of my mouth."

"Ah! That's why. But you shouldn't relent, sir. Push on. *Push!* Did you bring her a gift?"

"No."

"Ah! And then, you went to her in those clothes? No problem, anyway. Just continue pushing. Make sure you dress like a king and give her good gifts from now on," Larai advised.

Zaidou began to plan how he'd go about his next visit. He'd sew five dresses for Zakiyyah as a gift. He'd sew ten expensive robes for himself and wear them whenever he visited Zakiyyah.

He worked day in day out, often dozing off at his sewing machine. One night, he almost dozed off on his motorbike on his way home. He rode over a rock and fell, bruising his elbow. He'd also ridden over a nail at the foot of the rock and his front tyre got punctured. The next night, he had another accident on his bicycle and he punctured its rear tyre.

"Take it easy, Zaidou, please," Larai advised. "It's not a matter of life and death. She loves you, I tell you."

Those words didn't dampen his resolve. He put aside all the jobs for his customers and concentrated on his proposal project. When a customer came for their garments, he made up an excuse.

"I ate spoilt maize yesterday and it gave me runny stomach. I couldn't come to the shop for two days," he told one customer.

"That's a lie! I saw you in the shop yesterday."

"Yes, but that was after I felt a bit of relief. But I couldn't do much, even when I came. Please be patient. Come back next week."

As soon as his angry customers left, Zaidou would resume work on his sweetheart's garments. The only person he was able to satisfy was the potbellied man. He came for his garments and, surprisingly, he settled his debt.

Then Babawo stormed the shop. Zaidou's stomach rumbled. All the skills he had for making up excuses evaporated like a droplet of water in a hot pot. He fell flat on his belly. "Please forgive me, please!" he pleaded, even before Babawo opened his mouth.

"You mean you have not finished my garments?" Babawo barked.

"It wasn't my fault, please."

"It wasn't your fault? It's my fault, eh? Didn't I tell you that I needed my robe today? Which clothes do you want me to wear for the party I am attending? You want my friends to laugh at me, eh? If you knew you couldn't finish my clothes on time, why didn't you tell me?" Babawo's voice seemed to shake everything in the shop.

Zaidou remained lying flat on the thread-strewn floor, asking for forgiveness. Those eyes of his, which could hardly summon the courage to look up at Babawo, received a sudden painful blackout.

Babawo's foot was the culprit. Other kicks and blows followed in quick succession. He screamed for help, as he used his lean limbs to block the blows. His shirt got torn at the neck. He was tossed across the shop like a ball. His head hit several objects and he feared it would break open.

The blows suddenly stopped, and he looked up from the floor. The shop was full of people, some holding Babawo and others spectating. Concerned voices filled the air.

"Stop it!"

"What is the matter?"

"Do you want to kill him?"

Babawo rained curses on Zaidou as he struggled to break free from the men's grip. The men dragged him out of the shop and pacified him. He was escorted away, and the crowd dispersed. A few men remained with Zaidou, helping him to assess his injuries and asking him to narrate what had happened. Zaidou couldn't talk. He remained on the floor, cleaning the blood from his face. There wasn't much blood. Someone remarked that his left eye had swollen up. Zaidou picked up a piece of broken mirror from the floor, looked into it and saw that the man had not lied.

It was evening already, and the Marmari market was closing. As soon as his sympathisers left, Zaidou locked his shop and headed home. It was always rowdy when the market was closing. Out of it emerged energetic men pushing wheelbarrows containing all sorts of items belonging to customers and retailers: sacks of maize, heaps of oranges and bags of rice. Customers with smaller items carried them in nylon bags. Cyclists rang their bells endlessly as they weaved through the rowdiness. Zaidou worked his way through the crowd to a less busy road.

His body ached as he limped along. His injured eye felt heavy. He tried to avoid eye contact with people; he looked either down or sideways, as if he were observing something of interest. Some people called out to him, but he ignored them. The sun had almost set. He wished darkness would set in immediately.

He came to a path, which was a shortcut to his house. It was always quiet and seldom used. He quickly took the right turn onto the path, then he froze. Though one eye was bad, he saw well with the other. It saw two blue, dazzling eyes. He stared for a moment, unable to move. He turned to run.

No! How would she marry him if he ran away from her? He froze again. He turned back and looked at Zakiyyah.

She was still looking at him, standing by her car, her arms folded across her chest. Her driver was trying to change a bad tyre.

Zaidou walked towards her, wearing a smile. If he pretended that he was all right, she might not observe his injuries. "Do you have a bad tyre?" he asked.

Zakiyyah's face had gone red, her mouth wide open. Zaidou wondered whether she was trying to recognise him, or whether she was trying to manage her shock. He continued to smile. "How did it happen?" he asked. "Did the driver drive over a nail? I punctured the tyres of my motorbike and bicycle that way recently." He squatted by the driver and began to examine the punctured tyre.

"*Zaidou!*" Zakiyyah screamed.

He stood up tall and looked at her. "What is the problem, my dear?"

"Zaidou! What happened to you?" she asked.

Zaidou told her what had happened. He didn't mention that he'd caused the calamity by taking other people's garments for granted. He just told her the story of a bully who didn't like him. By the time he was done, the driver had finished fixing the tyre.

"Climb into the car, please," Zakiyyah said. "You need to see a doctor."

Zaidou thought about the bills he'd pay. "No! Don't bother about me, please," he cried. "I am fine."

"No, you're not, sir. Maybe you've got an internal injury!" She said *internal injury* in English, and Zaidou did not understand her.

"I have some herbs at home. They will cure me, I tell you."

Zakiyyah opened the front door of the car. "Climb in, Mr Zaidou," she said.

Zaidou felt he'd be ruining his chances if he declined. He smiled and climbed in. She sat in the rear seat behind him and they zoomed off.

Zaidou thought of where the money for his treatment would come from. It wasn't that he was broke; he just couldn't imagine how much a visit to the doctor would cost. Would it cost as much as the extension he was making to his house? If he mentioned his predicament to Zakiyyah, he'd sound more like a pauper than a prince to her. He hit his fist on his thigh. Hoping that he'd cut some cost by making his bad eye not look so bad, he began to massage it, trying to suppress his shrieks as much as possible.

"Don't do that, sir," Zakiyyah advised. "It will only cause you more pain."

"I was only touching it," Zaidou laughed, quickly taking his hand off the eye. "I dream about you every night, madam. I have never loved a woman like I love you." His heart beat fast. His voice quavered with his next words. "Have you decided on whether you will marry—"

He felt a tap on his shoulder from behind. He looked back and saw Zakiyyah's right index finger standing vertically over her lips. She was shutting him up! That felt more painful than the blows Babawo had inflicted on him.

Had he uttered unpolished love language? Or was she telling him not to talk to her about marriage again? Before he could think of an answer, they arrived at the clinic.

8

Zaidou had heard about the beach at Birni since he was a boy. He'd heard about its waves, cool breeze and plentiful sand from many people who had visited it before. It pained him that he'd never gone beyond the borders of Masara town before, let alone visited the beach.

He didn't know that his fortunes could change this suddenly. He couldn't believe that he was outside Masara town, sitting face-to-face with Zakiyyah on the sands of Birni's beach. The cool breeze from the ocean sang songs of love in his ears, and the shade of the palm trees spoke of the tranquillity of marriage. Zakiyyah's smile was so beautiful, and the lovely emotion that radiated from her eyes was more striking than the sun.

A boy carrying some coconut on a tray came by and gave them one coconut each. There were straws sticking out from holes created in the coconuts. He set his coconut on the sand and took Zakiyyah's own from her. "Let me feed you," he said. "You are now my wife, you know."

She giggled and pushed her head forward as he brought the coconut to her mouth. Then there was an explosion. He threw the coconut away and jumped to his feet. Three more explosions sounded and he quickly sat up, looking about his room in search of Zakiyyah, the beach and the coconuts. Three more knocks sounded, and Larai's voice called from outside, "Zaidou! It's morning already. Are you up?"

Burying his face in his palms, he thought about his dream. When will all these dreams come true? Why was Zakiyyah treating him like this? If she didn't love him, why had she deceived him for so many months? Why was she refusing to say yes to his proposal?

"It's 11 a.m. already, sir!" Larai's voice called again.

He got out of bed lazily. He bent over and grabbed his waist, groaning. He limped to the door, unbolted it and pushed it open. The rays of the morning sun flooded in.

Larai was standing before him, Rabe strapped to her back. Saminou was sitting on a mat sipping at a cup of koko. The thick white drink left a mark around his lips as he took the cup away from his mouth. He licked it off hungrily. He took another sip, not bothering to look at his uncle emerging from his room.

"How are you feeling, sir? Can you make it to the shop today?" Larai asked.

Zaidou groaned and touched his eye. He limped to the mat and sat beside Saminou.

"Are you still feeling pains?" Larai asked, walking up to him.

"Life is terrible, Larai. I am tired."

"Sorry. Should I bring you your breakfast now?"

"What did you cook?"

"Koko and qosai."

"Koko and qosai? No, thank you." Zaidou massaged his eye and some parts of his body. A nurse at the clinic had put a plaster on a cut on his forehead the night before. He touched it to ensure that it was still in place.

"You didn't eat anything last night either! Are you sure you're okay? You have still not told me what happened to you." Larai stood akimbo.

When he'd come home the night before, he had refused to answer the questions she'd asked him about his wounds. He had told her not to disturb him and stormed into his room, bolting the door.

Zaidou produced a chewing stick from his pocket and brushed his teeth with it. He had a cold bath, dressed and limped to the door.

He stopped at the door of the living room and thought. If he worked hard that day, he'd finish sewing all of Zakiyyah's garments. But why should he continue to sew her clothes with passion, when she had shut him up because he'd spoken to her about marriage? Shouldn't he dump them and continue sewing other people's garments? Babawo's babban riga should be his priority.

"Please, Zaidou, tell me, what is the matter?" Larai pleaded. "Please. What is happening to you? You are looking so bruised and worried! Did you have a fight?"

Zaidou looked up and saw his sister coming. "Larai," he grumbled, "I am confused."

"Confused? Why?" Larai asked.

Zaidou told her about Babawo's cruelty, and about how Zakiyyah had taken him to the clinic and paid for his treatment.

"It's not my wounds that worry me now. It's the way Zakiyyah told me to shut up. Why would she do that? I'm confused, Larai."

"Why didn't you ask her what the problem was?" Larai asked.

"I was afraid that she'd shut me up again and embarrass me in front of the driver. I can't continue to push. She has already said no!" Zaidou whimpered. He sniffled and cleared the tears from his eyes.

Larai nodded endlessly. Rabe woke up from sleep and began to cry. She sat down on the mat to breastfeed him. She looked thoughtful as the toddler suckled. "You are looking at things the wrong way," she said.

"What do you mean, my sister?" Zaidou sniffled.

"Did you say this lady took you to the clinic and paid for your treatment?"

"Yes!"

"And you still think she doesn't love you?"

"But she told me to shut up!"

"She did that because you shouldn't be talking to her about love in the presence of her driver," Larai said. "She was shy. I am sure she wasn't frowning when she asked you to keep quiet."

Zaidou remembered the glitter in Zakiyyah's eyes and the smile on her face as she'd placed a finger on her lips. He felt stupid. Why was Larai, a girl ten years younger than he was, able to interpret things better than he did?

"You will be making a big mistake if you stop courting this lady," Larai said. "You must keep pushing. Or do you want to remain single?"

Zaidou bit his lower lip. He must push that "yes" out of Zakiyyah's mouth. It was surely hiding somewhere in her heart. He stormed out of the house and marched to his shop. He finished sewing Babawo's garments. Then he continued his journey to Zakiyyah's heart. He sewed late into the night.

That night, after people had left the streets and silence had enveloped the town, four cars sped past his shop, like arrows fired by a hunter. It was Professor Garba's convoy.

9

It was a cool morning. Professor Garba was sitting on his balcony, staring at his garden of flowers and date palms. He had arrived at Masara from Birni the night before. He was a slim, brown septuagenarian with grey hair and a clean-shaven face.

He'd had a nightmare the night before: his father's ghost had appeared to him while he was having a meeting with Leader Gambo.

"What are you doing with this man?" the ghost had asked him.

"He is my boss. We are trying to move Hasoumiya forward," Professor Garba replied.

The ghost had squeezed his ear and slapped his face three times. "It's a lie!" it cried. "Do you know that he killed me and your three brothers? Yet, you are here supporting his government. Do you recall that you supported him for killing me?"

"I am sorry, Baba."

"Sorry for yourself! Get up! Go home and see the harm you are doing to your daughter by working with this man." The ghost had flown away.

Professor Garba's father and three brothers had been killed when government forces had invaded Masara town in 1947. As the foreign affairs minister, Professor Garba had defended the government's action before the world. Even at that time, he knew that he had not been good to his loved ones.

But what did the ghost mean by saying that he was harming Zakiyyah by working for the leader? Could that be a prophecy that the government would kill her, as it had his father and brothers? He poured coffee into his cup from a flask and took some sips. He set the cup on the table and picked a newspaper, browsing through its pages. He slammed the newspaper on the table, leaned back in his chair and folded his hands across his chest.

"Habibi!" His wife, Kauthar, rushed onto the balcony. "The leader has been attacked and the first lady killed!"

"What?" Professor Garba took off his spectacles.

"You didn't switch on your radio this morning! Soldiers tried to kill Leader Gambo last night. They got his wife instead. She's dead, Habibi! *Dead!*"

"Where did you hear this from?"

"I switched on the television now and saw the news. They said the leader and his wife were alighting from their plane when soldiers attacked them."

"This is serious!" Professor Garba stood up. "Is the leader hurt?"

"No!" Kauthar replied. She held his hand. "Come to your parlour. People are celebrating everywhere."

Professor Garba followed his wife to the parlour. The curtains had not been drawn open yet. The morning sun's rays could not enter. The only light in the room came from the television. It shone on the upholstered couches and glass table at the centre of the room. A news reporter was speaking to the camera with a microphone bearing the inscription HBN, the acronym of the Hasoumiyan Broadcasting Network. The top right corner of the screen indicated that he was reporting from Tarayya city. He had to shout to be heard because, in the background, thousands of people were jumping and shouting in celebration. They carried placards that read, LEADER GAMBO, FOLLOW YOUR WIFE. SOLDIERS, BRING US THE LEADER'S BIG HEAD. LEADER GAMBO, HELLFIRE SALIVATES OVER YOUR FLESH.

Other people were performing stunts with motorbikes and shooting hunting guns and fireworks into the morning air. Street urchins jumped behind the reporter, hoping that their faces would be caught on camera.

"This is crazy! This country is in trouble!" Professor Garba looked at his wife. "Do you think these people will get away with their celebration? Leader Gambo will take none of this!"

The pictures switched between the newsroom, field reports of people celebrating across the country and the scene of the leader's failed assassination. The first lady's blood was shown on the airplane's stairs.

"Kauthar, I must leave for Birni right away," Professor Garba announced. "The Leader would want to hold an emergency meeting."

"You only just came home last night!" Kauthar protested.

"This is an emergency!" Professor Garba stormed off to his room.

◄○►

Zaidou did not join in the celebrations that had followed the first lady's assassination. He had been sewing his garments.

He was sewing his seventh babban riga with a white fabric that he'd bought at the Marmari market. It was the most expensive material he could afford. He'd bought nine other colours of that brand.

The sewing machine created a rhythmic noise as he operated it with both hands and feet. The noise clashed with Mai Ganga's music from the radio, almost drowning it.

> People, people go to school!
> Your lives and success grow with knowledge,
> Just like the plants grow with water.

Knowledge is the sun that lights your ways –
The ways of life, and those of the afterlife!
If you walk in darkness you fall into the ditch,
the river, or the sea. Or you hit a rock,
And you break your neck.
Even the girls won't like you so much—

Zaidou switched off the radio and looked out the door. Could Mai Ganga be right that Zakiyyah didn't like him because he hadn't finished school? Maybe he should resume school to impress her. But it wouldn't feel nice sitting in class with teenagers.

He saw Babawo approaching, holding a club. He grabbed Babawo's babban riga and packaged it into a nylon bag.

"Where are my garments?" Babawo barked, storming into the shop.

Zaidou bowed and gave him the nylon bag.

Babawo removed the babban riga from the bag and inspected it.

Zaidou watched him anxiously, walking backwards slowly towards the exit.

A smile formed on Babawo's face.

Zaidou stopped.

"Hmmm!" Babawo hummed, nodding his head. "This is good."

"Yes, it is!" Zaidou cried, walking back into the shop.

"You are a good tailor!"

"My work is always good."

"But this is better than the ones you have sewn for me before." Babawo folded the garment and returned it to the nylon bag. He counted some money and gave it to Zaidou. "Here are two hundred dirhams," he said.

"I will take only a hundred dirhams," Zaidou said, smiling.

"Why? You told me that the cost was two hundred dirhams."

"I did. But I will take one hundred dirhams from you. I caused you some trouble when I delayed your garments," Zaidou explained.

Babawo jumped up from the chair and hugged Zaidou.

When Babawo released him, Zaidou noticed that the white in Babawo's eyes had turned red. They had always been reddish, anyway, but they had become redder and teary.

"Thank you," Babawo said. "I shouldn't have beaten you the other day. I am sorry, and I thank you again." He disappeared into the boisterous streets, throwing away his club.

Zaidou switched on his radio, danced to some music, and returned to his sewing machine.

The theme music of the 10 a.m. news began to play. Zaidou stopped sewing so that he could hear the headlines. He'd not been following the news since the first lady had been killed.

The newscaster greeted the listeners: "Good morning, and welcome to the news at ten."

"Good morning to you, too," Zaidou replied.

The newscaster read the headlines in a confident, masculine voice, with a pause between each one. The last headline said that Professor Garba would be making some important announcements on behalf of Leader Gambo. Zaidou drew closer to the radio.

Professor Garba's voice came on air. Zaidou felt proud that the man who might be his father in-law was so powerful that he could make announcements on the leader's behalf.

The professor's first announcement was that Alhaji Coulibaly had been nominated as the new governor of the Hausa-Sahara region. His nomination was awaiting confirmation by Leader Gambo.

Professor Garba expressed displeasure over the people's celebration of the first lady's assassination. It showed that the people did not love their leader, and they would do everything to frustrate his government. It also made the whole country guilty of the first lady's assassination. The leader had decided on the appropriate punishments: there would be a one-year pause for welfare packages for the poor, and there would be a five-year ban on new marriages. The ban was to take effect in three weeks' time.

Zaidou yelped. He ran outside and called on people to enter his shop to hear the news he'd just heard. In less than a minute, his shop was crowded with listeners.

◄o►

When Chief Ousmane heard of the marriage ban, he invited all the chiefs of the towns and cities of the Hausa-Sahara region to an emergency meeting in his *zaure*.

By afternoon, all the chiefs had arrived. They were served with roasted ram, tuwo and shuwaka soup. They sat in a circle, with the food at the middle. The youngest was in his late forties while the oldest was in his eighties; he always moved with a walking stick. The chiefs wore babban riga and white turbans. They all had beards: some were as black as charcoal, others had traces of white and others were completely white. One chief had dyed his own orange with henna.

At the centre of the zaure, a big mat was spread, topped by a soft round carpet. Five leather-encased cushions were arranged round the carpet. Chief Ousmane and some of the chiefs were sitting on them. A door at the left end of the zaure led into the harem. Close to that door was a big radio, sitting on a table.

The chiefs didn't touch the food. They frowned as they took turns to speak.

"Leader Gambo is possessed!" the oldest of them said, his jugular veins bulging. "Where in the world have you heard of a ban on marriage? This is rubbish! You can see that I am old, but I have never heard or seen or even dreamt about this kind of—!" He coughed several times, and they asked him to take it easy. He was given some water, which he gulped down.

"The people are scared," another chief in his sixties began. "Even we, the chiefs, are scared. The emirs and the governors are scared. We have been enslaved by the pig we call our leader. My daughter was to get married next month. I have now suspended the marriage. I don't want to go to prison or get hanged!"

"In my city, eight people took their lives!" another chief cried.

Chief Ousmane cleared his throat. "Now," he began, "what do we do? We cannot just condemn the ban and go back to our towns and cities. How can we stop it before it begins? It's just three weeks away." That question reminded Chief Ousmane of how he'd met with the youths of Masara in 1947 to tackle the brewery.

"Let us be sincere with ourselves," a chief in his forties began. "The people caused the problem. Everyone knows how Leader Gambo has been treating disloyal people. We hear it on the news every time! He kills. He *kills*. I suggest that we go to him and ask for forgiveness."

"Who will have the courage to do that?" a chief in his seventies retorted.

"Who else, sir? We have to summon the courage. As leaders of the people, we are the ones to do it," the chief in his forties said.

Some suggested that they all go together to see Leader Gambo. Others said a delegation would be better. Someone said that they needed to carry the chiefs and emirs of the other regions of the country along.

"Listen, my friends!" the chief in his eighties interjected. "Let us not waste our time. Leader Gambo will not listen to apologies. He will not listen! A minister sought forgiveness for Governor Tanimou's stubbornness, but the leader hanged him and the governor. So let us not waste our time. What we should do is to tell our people not to obey the ban! It will die off on its own. Simple."

The chiefs accepted that sage advice without much debate. Chief Ousmane promised to hold rallies across the country to pass the message to the people. It didn't matter if that cost him his life. The chiefs thanked him and promised to support him. They prayed for him and took their leave.

Chief Ousmane got all the imams in Masara to announce the maiden rally in their mosques. The forthcoming event became the story on every man's lips.

On the afternoon of the rally, Chief Ousmane sat in his zaure, reading some talking points from a paper. He always spoke off the cuff whenever he addressed a gathering of farmers and herdsmen or delivered the sermon for the jumu'ah prayer. His impending speech was so important that he couldn't leave anything unsaid.

Flashes of the 1947 incident kept coming to mind. They emboldened him, even though he didn't pray for a bloody confrontation.

Through the zaure's exit, he saw his twenty-year-old son, Mahmoud, approaching.

The boy squatted and panted at the doorway. He had sweat on his face and excitement in his eyes. "Baba," he said, standing up tall, "the crowd has gathered. They are waiting for you."

The paper fell from Chief Ousmane's hand. He picked it up and tucked it into his breast pocket.

"Has the stage been set?" he asked Mahmoud.

"Yes, Baba."

"Good. Call your mother to me," he said.

Mahmoud ran into the harem and returned with his mother. She was wearing a wrapper with faded flowery designs and a scarf. There was red oil on her right fingers.

She sat by her husband. "Are you going out already?" she asked him.

"Yes. The people have gathered." He produced a pink cola nut from his pocket and took a small bite, chewing slowly.

"Won't you have lunch before you go? It will soon be done."

He shook his head. "I will eat when I come back. But I am not sure that I will be back."

"Why won't you be back? Are you travelling to Tarayya to see the emir?"

"No. The police might arrest me. The people, too, can stone me if they think I am saying rubbish."

"You are not going to curse their parents, are you? Why should they harm you?"

"They might fear that my words will incite another attack on the town, like they did thirty-one years ago. I want you to pray that I get their support. I want you to pray that all goes well." Chief Ousmane took another bite of his cola nut.

"It will be fine, my husband," his wife, Amina, assured him.

Chief Ousmane patted her on the shoulder. He bade her farewell and went out with Mahmoud.

"What do you think about the ban?" he asked his son, as they walked through the deserted streets.

"It doesn't make sense, Baba," Mahmoud said.

"No, it doesn't, my son! No one has ever heard of such a stupid ban!"

"I have heard about a similar ban before, Baba," Mahmoud revealed. He told his father about how he'd gone on an excursion to Lagos with his class during his second year at the University of Birni. He'd met young couples partying at the Bar Beach on Valentine's Day. One of the locals at the beach told him about the story behind the celebration: in ancient Rome, the emperor had banned young couples from getting married. A man named Valentine defied the ban and began to tie the knot for some couples. He was caught by the authorities and executed.

"Well, we won't have that kind of ban in Hasoumiya! We won't have it!" Chief Ousmane said.

The stage that had been set for him was at the centre of the big field. Mahmoud and some young men asked people to clear the way for the chief to pass. Greetings were showered on Chief Ousmane as he pressed through the crowd.

He climbed the stage with Mahmoud. Five city chiefs were already on the stage. He shook hands with them. He faced the huge crowd.

The murmurs died down and the people glared at him: the young, the old, the Fulanis, the Hausas – everyone. Women clustered here and there. He could identify them by their hijabs and *gele*. He adjusted the loudspeaker to suit his height and cleared his throat. It echoed in the loudspeaker.

"*Assalaamu 'alaykum!*" he greeted.

"*Wa'alaykumus salaam!*" the crowd thundered back.

He started his speech in a calm voice. He denounced the failed coup, the celebrations that had followed and the marriage ban. He also denounced Alhaji Coulibaly's nomination as governor, asking the people to pray that he shouldn't be confirmed because he wasn't suitable.

His speech became charged. The people listened in silence.

"Does it make sense that we shouldn't get married because Leader Gambo has lost his wife?" he asked. "We don't know rape and fornication in our country, but Leader Gambo has just given us the keys to these dirty things! Our young men will force themselves on our girls. Do you know any bastard children? Well, you will see them in your houses if this ban goes ahead in two weeks' time! Do you want the ban?"

The people did not respond.

"I ask you, my people, do you want the ban?"

"No!" came the response.

He nodded his head. "I say again: do you want rape?"

"No!"

"Do you want bastards in your houses?"

"No!"

"Do you want to get married?"

"Yes! Yes!" the crowd thundered. There were murmurs now.

Chief Ousmane took his mouth to the speaker again. "Should we fight the ban, my people?" he cried.

"Yes!"

"Let me hear you loud and clear!"

"Yes, Chief! Long may you live! Yes! Yes!" the people shouted. They looked like ancient warriors yearning for the battlefield.

Chief Ousmane felt the courage and strength of a warlord. "Then get married. *Wallahi*, get married! Your wives are your lovers. They help you, and you help them. They need you, and you need them! So I say to you again, get married! Marry the girls you want, and do not fear the government! I say again, do not fear the government! They will surely fail! Marry, marry, marry!"

The people responded with a thunderous cheer, throwing their hands in the air.

Chief Ousmane hugged the chiefs, thanking them for coming. They came down from the stage. Chief Ousmane and Mahmoud pressed through the charged, excited crowd and went back home.

Chief Ousmane remained in his room till evening, reciting the Qur'an, musing over the rally and praying for victory. He would be having visitors that evening as usual, but his room felt more comfortable to him at this time. The door was pushed open and it creaked.

"I have taken your food to the zaure," his wife said, popping her head in.

"I will eat it here."

"You have visitors. Wouldn't you like to eat with them?"

"Not tonight. Tell them to come back tomorrow, please." Chief Ousmane turned a page on his Qur'an, which was resting on a wooden holder before his crossed legs. He continued to recite in a low voice.

His wife stood watching him. When he paused to turn another page, she sat before him. "Is everything okay?" she asked. Her eyes seemed as if they were searching for answers from his own eyes.

"I need to rest from the rally," he said.

"You don't look tired. You look worried."

"I will be fine. Just bring my food here and—"

A knock sounded on the door, and Chief Ousmane gave permission to enter. Mahmoud peeped in, holding a big book. He retreated when he saw that his parents were discussing something.

"Come in, Mahmoud," Chief Ousmane said. "Which book are you holding?"

"It is an encyclopaedia, Baba." Mahmoud put the book down, turning some pages. It appeared he'd hurried out of his room, because he wore a singlet. He explained that he'd borrowed the encyclopaedia from the university library to do an assignment, and that he'd just read more about Valentine from it. He read some paragraphs that said that Saint Valentine was killed because he opposed the marriage ban.

"Why are you telling me this story?" Chief Ousmane's voice was calm.

Mahmoud looked up from the book. "I am afraid for you, Baba," he said.

"Afraid? Why?"

"Valentine was killed because of what he did. I am afraid that Leader Gambo will do the same to you."

Chief Ousmane laughed, patting Mahmoud on the shoulder.

His wife didn't laugh. "That is just a story, Mahmoud," she said. "Wish your father well, and don't worry about what you read in a story."

"It's not a story, Mama! It happened in real life."

"Mahmoud." Chief Ousmane became serious. "We shouldn't be afraid of death when we fight for what is right. Do you hear me?"

"Okay, Baba." Mahmoud closed the encyclopaedia with a snap. He still looked worried.

"Now get me my food from the zaure. Tell my visitors to take their share and to come back tomorrow," Chief Ousmane said.

Mahmoud and his mother left the room.

10

Professor Garba thought about Chief Ousmane's rally as he was being driven through the streets of Masara in his black Mercedes. He'd read about it in the newspapers.

He had attended the meeting in which Leader Gambo had decided to punish the people with the marriage ban. The leader had wanted to ban foreign trips also, but Professor Garba and many others at the meeting had prevailed on him not to do so.

The Mercedes stopped in front of Chief Ousmane's house. The other cars in the convoy parked beside the Mercedes. The security detail took positions. Professor Garba emerged from his car's rear seat.

Chief Ousmane's house was a big one made of mud bricks. It was a white one-storey building. On its façade were some elaborate decorations in bas-relief, painted in red, blue, yellow and green. The building had two entrances: the first led into the harem, while the other opened into the zaure.

Professor Garba saw Chief Ousmane attending to two visitors in his zaure. As the chief came out to receive him, Professor Garba faked a smile. "Good evening, Chief Ousmane," he greeted, shaking hands with the chief.

"Assalaamu 'alaykum, Professor!" Chief Ousmane greeted him. "Good to see you. Please come in."

They entered the zaure. Chief Ousmane went into the harem and returned shortly. He whispered to Professor Garba to allow him to finish hearing the case his two visitors had brought before him. The professor agreed.

One of the men was a young Fulani man, while the other was about Chief Ousmane's age. He was cross-eyed and had a potbelly. His white clothes had gone brown and had some stitches at the shoulders. The young man complained that the potbellied man had bought five rams from him the previous year but had refused to pay him.

"He is lying, Chief. I bought those rams on credit!" the older man interjected.

"When is he supposed to pay you?" Chief Ousmane asked the young man.

"Five months ago! I have been going to his house to beg him to pay me, but he keeps sending me away. This morning, he slapped me and told me not to come to him again until he calls me."

Chief Ousmane gave the older man a hard, stern look.

The man coughed and fidgeted. He avoided eye contact with the chief.

"Is this thing I'm hearing about you true?" Chief Ousmane asked him.

"Chief!" The man quickly sat up on his cracked heels, pointing at his adversary. "This boy is rude! Am I his mate? Why should he disturb me just because of dirhams? Did I say I was not going to pay him? I am old enough to give birth to him. Let him respect me." He sat back on his buttocks and looked away.

"Do you have the money to pay him?" Chief Ousmane asked.

The man scratched his neck and looked sideways.

"Answer me!" Chief Ousmane barked.

"I have the money, Chief, but I want to buy a bicycle to ride to my farm. If I pay this boy, I won't have the money to do that and—"

"Keep quiet!" Chief Ousmane's voice rang throughout the hollow zaure. It startled the man. He looked as if he'd just seen a demon.

Chief Ousmane told the potbellied man to pay the Fulani man his money that very day. He asked the Fulani man to come back and confirm to him that he'd been paid in full.

"If you don't pay that money, I'll get the police to arrest you!" Chief Ousmane warned the old debtor.

The men thanked Chief Ousmane and went out.

"Very irresponsible man!" Professor Garba commented.

"We have worse people than him in this town!" Chief Ousmane said, gathering the wide sleeves of his babban riga on his shoulders. He told Professor Garba about some of the cases he'd heard: a man who always extorted money from his wife to get drunk; a father-in-law who habitually robbed his son-in-law; and a fraudster who sold off other people's lands. "How is Birni?" he asked Professor Garba, smiling. "I'm sure the rains are abundant there, because it's beside the ocean. You're enjoying cool weather, I believe."

"Yes, Chief Ousmane," Professor Garba replied, faking a smile once again.

They talked about the floods, the fruits that came with the rainy season, the abundant rains of the year, and the good drainage system in Birni. Chief Ousmane told Professor Garba about his request to the emir of Tarayya to get more boreholes for the town, and of the emir's promise to talk to the regional government about that.

Two young boys entered the zaure from the harem, one carrying two bowls of food and the other carrying two cups and a jug of water. They greeted Professor Garba, set the food between him and Chief Ousmane and walked back into the house.

"Those are my grandchildren," Chief Ousmane revealed with a smile, opening his bowl of food so that the steam billowed out and played over his face.

"That's great!" Professor Garba remarked, pouring water into his cup. "You're a lucky old man! But you still have the strength of a young person."

"Do I?"

"Yes, indeed. If you'd been working in a company, you'd have stopped working by now. At your age, you still handle the affairs of this big town. I read about your rally in the newspaper. I understand it was a big one."

"I wanted it to be big!" I was going to talk about important things – Alhaji Coulibaly's nomination and the marriage ban."

Professor Garba looked at Chief Ousmane thoughtfully as he opened his bowl of food. He cut a morsel of chicken with his fork and put it into his mouth. He fetched a spoon of tuwo, dipping it into the spinach soup. He stopped short of putting it into his mouth. "What do you think about those issues?" he asked. "Do you think Alhaji Coulibaly is a bad nominee?"

Chief Ousmane sipped some water and set down the cup. "There are better candidates," he said.

Professor Garba dropped his fork. "Why do you think he shouldn't be governor?"

"He's my nephew, Professor. He grew up under my care. I know he is not good enough to be governor. He went to France on a government scholarship. Since he came back to the country five years ago, he has not visited me. He's forsaken me for five years, Professor!"

Professor Garba knew that Alhaji Coulibaly had grown up under Chief Ousmane's care. His parents had been killed during the government's attack on the town. However, he didn't know that Alhaji Coulibaly had forsaken Chief Ousmane for so long. "So you don't want him to be governor simply because he's forsaken you?" he asked.

"Anybody who treats his family badly will be a bad leader. I have known him since he was a baby. He has a bad character. I advise you to get us a better governor."

Professor Garba pushed the morsel of tuwo into his mouth, chewed, and swallowed. "Chief Ousmane, let me make this appeal," he began. "I am talking to you as a friend, not as a government official. Stop saying things that will incite the people against Alhaji Coulibaly, please. Do you know that your words can turn this town upside down? Have you forgotten 1947? I have my family in this town, please!"

"Your appeal is not necessary, my friend," Chief Ousmane replied. "I only asked the people to pray we get a better governor than him, which I had every right to do. Are these the kind of words that will cause trouble?"

"Good! What about the ban on marriage? What did you say about it?" Professor Garba asked.

Chief Ousmane stopped chewing. "I learnt that the ban will begin in two days' time," he said.

"That's right."

"Does the ban make sense to you?"

Professor Garba pushed his bowl aside. "It makes perfect sense!" he cried. "Would you like your children to rejoice if your wife were killed? Would you like them to wish you dead? If the leader had not sent soldiers to end the celebrations, there would have been an uprising."

"How does that justify the marriage ban? Why shouldn't we get married for five good years?"

"It's a punishment! Or are you challenging the government's authority to punish people for treason?"

"Is your daughter, Zakiyyah, married?"

"She's not going to get married until the ban is lifted!" Professor Garba said.

Chief Ousmane dropped his spoon and drew closer to him. "Do you really love your daughter, my friend? Do you love your people?" he asked.

"I've had enough!" Professor Garba rose to his feet. "You are nothing but a rebel! You've been one since 1947! But let me warn you: if you rebel against the ban, you are inviting trouble for your people!"

He stormed out of the zaure, climbed into his car and was driven home.

11

Zaidou was lying down on the mat in his living room, staring at the ceiling. He'd been lying there for some hours, turning and thinking. The thoughts he had had been troubling him for three weeks now. They'd made him so sick that he'd had to visit the doctor – for the second time in his life. The doctor had told him that there were no germs in his body. All he needed to do was to stop worrying.

"I can't stop worrying that I won't be allowed to marry the woman I love!" Zaidou protested.

"You have to try, my friend," the doctor said. "We all have to try. My daughter is supposed to get married this week, but she can't. Do you think I'm happy?"

The doctor's words had worsened Zaidou's plight. If a doctor could not cure him, who else could? He'd thought of going to the bush to hang himself. But if he did, how would he marry Zakiyyah?

He turned to lie on his left-hand side, facing the wooden chair. It stood against the white wall. The morning sun shone through the window and created light patterns on the mat. The light reminded him of the image of the sun on the label of the beer the town's brewery produced. He'd heard drinkers saying that drinking beer helped them to forget their worries. One drunkard had told him of how he'd had a fight with his wife and son because they pilfered his money. When he drank beer and got drunk, he forgot about all that had happened.

Zaidou went outside. He walked to the beer parlour that stood close to the brewery. The beer parlour was made of four logs of wood and was roofed by a zinc sheet. A signpost made from a rough plank indicated the name of the enterprise in Hausa – The People's Drinking Place. It was open from 8 a.m. till 11:30 p.m. A dozen men were drinking and chatting at some of the tables. At night, the place was always a beehive.

Zaidou sat at one of the tables. A waiter walked up to him and asked, "Which brand do you want, sir?"

Zaidou swallowed. "Which brand do you have?"

"We have Red Rose, Guitar and Sunshine Stout."

"Do you have that one with the picture of the sun on it?"

"That's Sunshine Stout. It is 10 dirhams. Should I bring some?"

"Yes," Zaidou said.

The man fetched a brown bottle from one of the big drums at one end of the shed. He set a plastic cup on the table before Zaidou, filling it with the dark liquid. He left the half-empty bottle beside the cup and sat down at a nearby table to pick his nose.

Zaidou stared at the stout. Its smell was strange and nauseating. His sweaty hands took the cup to his lips. Chief Ousmane's warnings about imbibing alcohol recurred to him. He shook his head and sipped. "*Pweeeh!*" He jumped as he spat it out. The taste was not the culprit, the guilt of sin was.

Some women were washing cups in big tubs at one end of the shed. He ran to them, fetched some soapy water from their tubs with cupped hands and rinsed his mouth twice with it. Ignoring the women's protest, he fetched cleaner water from a second tub and rinsed his mouth three times with it. He apologised to the women, paid the perplexed waiter and walked away. He repented endlessly as he marched, thanking Allah that he'd been able to fight his temptations.

He reached the maishayi close to his shop and asked him to serve him an omelette sandwiched between a loaf of bread, and a cup of tea.

The maishayi fried the omelette on a stove and it smelled of curry as it was being fried. He poured the tea quickly from one cup to another to cool it. It was amazing how he did it without spillage. "You are my first customer today, so I promise you one free cup of tea, if you need more." The maishayi placed the food on the table in front of Zaidou.

"Thank you," Zaidou said. He ate quietly, not caring to ask the maishayi why other customers had not yet come, even though it was 10 a.m. already.

"You don't look happy," the maishayi observed, as he arranged loaves of bread on his table.

"I am not!" Zaidou's words didn't come out clearly because of the bread he was chewing. "No one is happy in this town. Are you?"

"I am not happy, too! I've always told people that Leader Gambo is a madman!"

Zaidou swallowed and dropped his sandwich on his plate. "Are you married?"

"No. I have a fiancée. We have agreed to marry when the marriage ban is lifted."

Zaidou couldn't imagine waiting five years before he could marry Zakiyyah. Five years? No. They'd been together for almost a year now, and it seemed they'd taken too long already to tie the knot.

Two other customers arrived and sat on the bench beside him. They didn't greet him because they were engrossed in their discussion. They spoke at the top of their voices about the marriage ban.

"Give me koko, noodles and omelette!" one of them ordered.

"Me, I want bread and tea only. Please put three spoons of sugar and plenty of milk in the tea!" the other man said. They resumed their discussion.

"I begged my brother to listen to Chief Ousmane's advice to ignore the marriage ban, but he refused! He has abandoned his fiancée because he didn't want to get arrested," the first man said.

"All my neighbours have vowed to listen to Chief Ousmane," the second man revealed.

"Aren't they afraid that Leader Gambo will send soldiers to arrest them?"

"Who is afraid of soldiers? Look around the town and see. Most people are fixing dates for their children's marriages."

"That's true!" the Maishayi chipped in, emptying a can of milk into a cup.

"That is good!" the first man said. "Let everyone who wants to marry, marry. If they are afraid, let them leave the country and marry elsewhere."

"That is for those who have the money!" the second man said.

Zaidou nodded his head at the thought of exile. Why hadn't he thought about it before? He had enough money to emigrate. The nearest town abroad was Birnin Gero, in Nigeria. It was a journey of twelve hours by road. Those who had visited it said it was more developed than Masara town. He would emigrate there with Zakiyyah if she agreed to marry him.

He walked to his shop and switched on the radio. He danced to Salisou Mai Ganga's music. The singer's voice sounded sweeter than ever, and Zaidou danced till he sweated.

Someone tapped him on his shoulder. He yelped and turned round to look at the intruder. It was an old man holding a bundle of white material.

"Why are you dancing when everyone is weeping?" the man asked.

Zaidou switched off the radio. "I am sorry," he said with a sheepish smile. "I didn't see you come in." He sat behind his sewing machine and invited the man to sit down also.

"You want a babban riga?" he asked, taking the material.

"No. Just a kaftan," the man replied.

Zaidou took the man's measurements, singing in a low tone as he did. Then he measured the material. "This will be sufficient for a kaftan. Do you want any embroidery?" he asked.

"I want something plain."

"Good! I will charge you sixty dirhams." Zaidou flaunted six fingers before the man's eyes.

"When will it be ready?"

"In three days."

The man nodded in satisfaction and stood up to go. He stopped at the door and regarded Zaidou. "You look different today," he said. "I pass by from time to time. For the past few days, I observed that you are either worried or complaining about the marriage ban. Today, you are so joyful. You don't even mind dancing like a small boy! Why is that?"

Zaidou laughed. "It is because I am filled with love for my fiancée. I have found a way to marry her without getting into trouble, and—"

Zaidou stopped and listened. Noise came from the big field, as if something chaotic was happening there. "What's that?" he asked.

The man listened too. Then he nodded. "Yes!" he said. "They have come."

"They have come? Who?"

"Haven't you heard that Alhaji Coulibaly is coming for a rally? He has been going round the region."

Zaidou frowned. "Why does this man want to be governor? Can't he see that no one likes him?" he asked. Looking out through the window behind his chair, he saw people rushing towards the field. The metal doors of the neighbouring shops were being slammed shut and bolted.

"Zaidou!" one of the shop owners called out. "Alhaji Coulibaly is in town. Let's go and see what he's up to."

Zaidou's customer took his leave, as Zaidou locked his shop and joined the crowd.

The crowd was big and included people of both sexes and all ages, all filled with excitement: old men, market women, young boys and girls, and farmers carrying hoes. The adults talked about their dislike for Alhaji Coulibaly, hoping that he would not be confirmed as governor.

A huge crowd had gathered in the field. People craned their necks to see what was happening at the centre. Zaidou craned his neck too.

A stage was set up in the centre of the field, with a big sound system on top of it. Fierce-looking soldiers were stationed all over, preventing the crowd from crossing some improvised boundaries. Each soldier carried a gun and a horsewhip. Five cars formed a motorcade parading slowly round the field; a band played by its side with drums and trumpets. The car in the middle was an open convertible. Professor Garba and Alhaji Coulibaly were in it. The other cars were for some government officials and the security detail.

Alhaji Coulibaly was a dark, plump man of about thirty years of age. He was wearing a blue babban riga and a well-starched cap of the same colour. He smiled as he waved at the crowd. Some people waved back and cheered, though most of them booed. Zaidou saw that the man booing next to him was Babawo. They shook hands and exchanged pleasantries.

"Why are people supporting this man!" Zaidou lamented. "Chief Ousmane has told us that he is not good enough to be our governor."

Babawo smiled. "If you see what's happening at the front, you will know why," he said.

Zaidou climbed up a tree so that he was able to see every corner of the field. Some men were distributing gifts, which they carried in wheelbarrows: waterproof boots, wrappers and biscuits. The people were scrambling to get their share.

Zaidou climbed down. "Some men are sharing gifts!" he cried.

"Alhaji Coulibaly sent them," Babawo replied. "Let me go and get my own share." He began to press through the crowd.

Zaidou followed him. He pressed his way past the smelly, sweaty bodies, enduring the shouts, curses and cheers. He made it to the front at last and began to struggle with the crowd to get some gifts. He got a pair of boots and tucked them under his arm.

As Zaidou turned round to repeat the struggle through the crowd, Alhaji Coulibaly's motorcade came closer. The people went into a frenzy, cheering, booing, waving and cursing more enthusiastically. Zaidou waited to get a close glimpse at Alhaji Coulibaly. The open convertible came closer until it was right before him.

"Stupid boy!" a man close to Zaidou barked at Alhaji Coulibaly. "Go home to your wife. We don't want you!" The man threw his waterproof boots at Alhaji Coulibaly, hitting him in the face. Alhaji Coulibaly buried his face in his hands. Five other men around Zaidou also threw their boots at Alhaji Coulibaly, and he ducked for cover.

Three soldiers pounced on Zaidou and two of the assailants, flogging them and raining curses on them. They began to drag them away. Zaidou bit the hand and ear of the soldier holding him. He bit him hard. The soldier screamed and let go of him. Zaidou ran into the crowd and two soldiers followed him.

The crowd began to panic, and some shouted, "Soldiers! Soldiers!"

"They want to kill us!"

"They are going to shoot! Run! Run for your lives!"

People screamed and ran helter-skelter. Zaidou looked back and saw that the soldiers chasing him were being sandwiched by people. Sirens began to blare out from Alhaji Coulibaly's motorcade, and shots were fired into the air as Alhaji Coulibaly was whisked away to safety. That was how the rally was brought to an abrupt end – with a heavy stampede in its wake.

—◄o►—

Zaidou thought it was miraculous that he'd escaped from the stampede. The soldiers had stopped chasing him, yet he ran like an antelope. He didn't look back. He ducked past cyclists, hawkers, and herdsmen and their cattle. He reached his quiet neighbourhood. His house was locked, so he banged on the door. "Larai! Open the door!" he cried.

As soon as the door was opened, he dived into the living room, bolted the door and turned the key. He panted heavily.

"What's the matter, Zaidou?" Larai asked him.

Zaidou inspected himself – his torn and dusty shirt soaked with sweat, the marks the soldiers' horsewhips had left on his body, and his dusty feet. The feet were bare, as his shoes had come off in the stampede. He had two small cuts on each of his feet, and the blood that oozed from them glided on the dust on his feet.

"What happened, Zaidou?" Larai's eyes looked as if they'd bulge out. Saminou stood with her, gazing at him.

"Give me some water, please!" Zaidou lay flat on his back.

Larai disappeared into the courtyard and returned with a bowl of water and a woven fan. As Zaidou gulped down the water, she fanned him. Saminou began to fan him too, using his hands.

"Sorry! Just calm down, please," Larai said, as Zaidou dropped the bowl and continued to pant, leaning his back against the wall. When he'd calmed down enough, he told her the whole story.

"Are you sure they've stopped chasing you?" Larai asked.

"Yes, but they took some of the men who stoned Alhaji Coulibaly away." Zaidou twisted his arm to examine a cut the horsewhips had made.

"Sorry," Larai said.

"Sorry!" Saminou echoed with his little voice.

"Thank you." Zaidou nodded. "My fear is that they might come back for me. They've seen my face. They saw it very well."

"Don't say that again, please. They won't come after you. You are innocent. They will find that out, if they know how to investigate very well." Larai got up and took warm water to the bathroom for him to bathe.

Despite Larai's reassurance, Zaidou didn't feel safe. He spent the rest of the morning indoors. In the afternoon, when Larai's sons returned home from school, he asked them whether, on their way back, they'd heard anyone talking about his complicity in the stampede or if they had sighted any soldiers in town. They said no, and that eased his anxiety. In the evening, when the sun had set and the muezzin made the call to prayer, he went out to the mosque. He looked apprehensively at the men marching to the mosque, fearing they'd pounce on him; but no one did.

After the prayer, some of the worshippers gathered at the mosque's grounds and began to talk about the rally and the stampede. Zaidou stood at the doorway to listen.

"I tell you," one man cried, "I have never seen such a big stampede in my life!"

"By Allah, neither have I," another echoed.

"It was as if every man in the world were running from a lion!"

"I will go back to the field this night to see how bad the situation is."

"Thirty dead bodies had been counted before I left the field!"

"I counted fifty. I hope there are no more deaths."

Zaidou didn't see any of the things the men described. All he could remember was the way he'd struggled to get himself out of the midst of screaming men and women, and taking to his heels.

One man looked back at him. "I thought I saw you being flogged by the soldiers. Were you the one that stoned Alhaji Coulibaly?" he asked.

"No, no! By Allah, I wasn't the one!" Zaidou removed his slippers and dashed out into the streets.

Darkness had set in. The night was cold and there were only a few bicycles plying the road. The only bright things in sight were the light bulbs of the houses, shops and kiosks situated by the roadside.

He reached the Dandali and saw Audou and Ya'u sipping mint tea at a table. Good. They could make him happy again. He walked up to them, shook hands with them and sat on a chair between them.

"You have arrived early today," Audou observed, looking at his wristwatch.

Zaidou shrugged.

"You are looking sad. Would you like some mint tea?" Ya'u asked him.

Zaidou nodded eagerly.

Ya'u beckoned to a tea seller, who came up quickly, set a small glass cup on the table before Zaidou and poured some steaming liquid into it from a big metal kettle.

Zaidou grabbed the cup and gulped down the brew. He coughed several times, gasping for breath.

"Kai! What's the matter with you tonight?" Audou exclaimed. "Why are you gulping down tea as if you are a thirsty camel?"

"Yes," Ya'u agreed, "you are looking so worried, like a ram about to be killed. And why are you without footwear?"

"Are you sick?" Audou asked him.

Zaidou shook his head.

"Then what's the problem?"

"Don't bother about me," Zaidou pleaded. "Just continue talking and leave me alone."

"Do you want to smoke?" Ya'u asked. "Audou, please give him a cigarette."

"He doesn't smoke!" Audou exclaimed. "What he needs is *Zakiyyah!*" He pronounced Zakiyyah's name in a dramatic whisper. The two men laughed.

Zaidou did not laugh. He smiled.

He bade a quick farewell to his friends and went to one of the suya meat sellers. "Give me three hundred dirhams' worth of suya!" he requested.

The seller warmed some skewers of suya over a grill and wrapped them in a piece of newspaper. Zaidou paid him and hurried out of the Dandali.

He ran to his shop and wore the best babban riga he'd sewn. He wore a cap and shiny black shoes to match. Looking at himself in the big mirror on the wall, he thought he looked like a king. The only problem was that his perfume was at home. He took off, carrying the suya and the garments he'd sewn for Zakiyyah with him.

The Arziki Quarter was quiet and beautiful. Only the rich and famous lived there. Its houses had marvellous architectural designs. They were stars that twinkled in the darkness of the mud houses that dotted the rest of the town.

The gate of Professor Garba's mansion was mighty. The sight of the building alone made Zaidou feel nervous.

A security guard appeared at the other side. "Good evening, sir," the guard greeted him.

"Good evening, my friend. How are you?"

"Do you want to see Professor Garba, sir?"

"No. It's actually . . . um . . . his daughter that I want to see."

"Zakiyyah?"

"Yes."

The security guard observed his attire. "You look rich, sir." He smiled.

"Thank you. Can I come in, please?" Zaidou requested.

The man rubbed his fingers against his thumb.

Zaidou was disappointed. He took some money from his pocket and gave it to the man.

The man thanked him and disappeared into the surroundings.

Zaidou paced about in front of the gate. He practiced a few types of smiles: with his mouth closed, with his teeth showing, and with a little giggle.

Many minutes went by, and they seemed like long hours. The security man did not return. Zaidou wondered what was happening inside the house. Had the guard truly informed Zakiyyah of his arrival? Or had Zakiyyah decided that she didn't want to see him?

"Come inside, sir!" a voice broke into his thoughts. He looked up and saw the security man throwing the gate open for him. He jumped up excitedly.

The guard took him down the paved path that led into the house's grounds. The yard and the lawn were illuminated with beautiful lamps. The scent of the flowers hung in the cool night air. It was all quiet, except for the chirping of crickets.

"Mr Zaidou!" a lady called him. He turned to his left and saw Zakiyyah sitting on a chair in front of a door that led into the house. She was dressed in a white hijab and a long dress of the same colour, which blended beautifully with her fair complexion. She invited him to sit in a chair by her side.

"Masaa'ul khair, Zakiyyah!" Zaidou greeted her, as he sat down.

"Masaa'un noor." Zakiyyah smiled.

"You look pleasant!" Zaidou remarked. The words seemed to have forced their ways out of his lips. He nervously handed her the parcel of suya.

"Is this for me?" she asked, as she received it.

"Yes. It's suya. I bought it at the Dandali. You know you can't get better suya from anywhere else," Zaidou told her.

She opened the parcel slightly and peeped into it. "It has a nice aroma. Thank you. I know my mother will like it – and Moukhtar, too, my little brother. You know, we are only just getting to know the delicacies you have here."

Zaidou gave her the garments he'd sewn for her. They were in a black nylon bag.

She gasped. "Oh! You're such a darling, sir!" she cried. She took the garments out of the bag and unfolded them, one after the other. Her eyes glittered as she admired them, so much so that it looked as if tears would flow out of them. "This must have cost you a fortune!" Zakiyyah unfolded another dress.

Zaidou practiced his smiles again.

"That's a funny smile!" Zakiyyah laughed. "Where did you learn that?"

Zaidou laughed in embarrassment. "I shouldn't be smiling," he said.

"Why not? You're not happy to be with me?" Zakiyyah asked.

Those words resounded a million times in Zaidou's ears. He smiled again. "I am happy to be with you," he said. "I said I shouldn't be smiling because I had a bad day today. A very bad day!"

Zaidou told her the story of what had happened at the big field, and about his fears of arrest. He showed her the marks that the soldiers' whips had created on his skin. "And now, on top of my troubles, there is a nice woman who has refused to say yes to my proposal!" He looked at her face to see her reaction.

Zakiyyah threw down the dress she was holding. "You don't have another fiancée, do you?" She flushed.

"You are the nice lady I am talking about, madam. Are we getting married?"

"Yes." Zakiyyah heaved a sigh.

There was silence. That "yes" hovered in the silence. Zaidou never imagined that the word *yes* could sound so sweet. He'd heard it from other girls before, but this was different. Zakiyyah was looking down.

"I am happy!" Zaidou said. "I am happy, Zakiyyah. But do you think the marriage ban will stop us from marrying?"

"I'll be starting work in Lagos, remember? I'll be leaving in two months. Can we get married there?"

"Lagos?"

"Yes."

"That's good! I have never thought of that! I thought of us running to Birnin Gero!"

"Birnin Gero? Where is that?" Zakiyyah laughed.

"It's in Nigeria, too."

"No, let's go to Lagos, sir."

Zaidou had heard stories about Lagos from Ya'u and Audou, who had been there on business trips before. He had always imagined spectacular images of the city as he'd listened to them talking about its bridges, beaches and tall buildings.

"I suggest that you send your people to see my father so that we can begin serious talk about our marriage," Zakiyyah said. Her face had regained its charm and brightness, and her eyes glittered.

"I will do that, Zakiyyah," Zaidou said. "I will talk to Chief Ousmane."

12

Zaidou rode his bicycle into Chief Ousmane's neighbourhood. He'd taken the bicycle for repairs as soon as the sun had come out; the mechanic had just had to change the front tyre.

It had rained the night before, and the ground was wet. Zaidou weaved around the puddles and mud. There was no one in sight. Some he-goats that didn't seem bothered by the cold roamed the neighbourhood. The weather was dull, and it was clear that there would be another downpour.

Zaidou had left home so early because he wanted to see Chief Ousmane privately in his zaure before it was packed full of visitors.

He alighted from his bicycle and leaned it against a mango tree that stood a little way from the chief's house. He regarded the house. One voice warned him not to enter. Another voice told him to go ahead or he'd lose Zakiyyah. He moved closer to the house and craned his neck to peep into the zaure. Chief Ousmane was reciting the Qur'an. His voice was old but mellifluous. It echoed in the zaure. He didn't falter at all in his recitation.

Zaidou stood still.

Chief Ousmane stopped reciting. "Zaidou!" he called.

Zaidou gasped.

"Zaidou, come in, please," Chief Ousmane invited.

Zaidou moved towards the entrance of the zaure, trembling as he did. As he stepped inside, he tried hard to suppress his trembling lest the chief think he was dancing.

Chief Ousmane was sitting on one of the leather-encased cushions. "Sit down, please," he invited, pointing at the cushion opposite him. The chief looked gloomy and tired. He looked ready to entertain only matters of communal importance.

"Assalaamu 'alaykum, Chief," Zaidou greeted him. He could hear the catch in his own voice.

"Wa'alaykumus salaam, Zaidou," Chief Ousmane replied, closing his Qur'an, which was on a wooden holder. "What makes you come so early?"

"I'm sorry, Chief," Zaidou said.

A smile came over Chief Ousmane's face. "You did nothing wrong," he said. "I was just curious." He turned serious again. He actually looked angry. "I heard that you were one of the men that attacked Coulibaly. Is that true?" he asked.

"No, Chief. It's not true. I would never do that – I swear!"

"So, did the people who informed me tell me lies?"

"I didn't throw anything at Alhaji Coulibaly, Chief. I was only unlucky to be close to the people who attacked him. The soldiers caught me because they thought I was one of the attackers."

Chief Ousmane's frown eased, and he relaxed onto the cushion behind him, resting on his elbow. In a calm, sad tone, he told Zaidou of how the stampede had killed many people and injured many others, including his son, Mahmoud. Mahmoud was in a coma at the clinic.

"I was at the clinic at dawn to see him," Chief Ousmane said. "He is still unconscious. I'll return later in the day to see him again."

"May Allah heal him. I am really sorry about his condition."

"Thank you, Zaidou," Chief Ousmane said.

Zaidou knew he'd only be mixing lemon juice with milk if he went ahead to ask Chief Ousmane to talk to Professor Garba about his desire to marry Zakiyyah. "Goodbye, Chief," he said.

"Are you leaving so soon?" Chief Ousmane asked.

"Yes, Chief."

"Are you sure there is no problem?"

"No, no, no! I am fine. I just came to greet you."

"Thank you. My regards to your people." Chief Ousmane sat up and shook Zaidou's hand.

━◄○►━

As soon as Zaidou left, Chief Ousmane called one of his daughters, Sa'adiya, and asked her to get some food that they could take to the clinic.

Sa'adiya emerged from the harem with a young male servant carrying two bowls of food on a tray. Chief Ousmane led her and the servant to the clinic. He visited all ten wards of the clinic to greet the patients and to sympathise with the victims of the stampede.

Mahmoud was lying on the bed with bandages on his head, left arm and right leg. Nine other victims of the stampede were also in the ward, all with bandages here and there. Chief Ousmane went round and wished them all a quick recovery. His wife, Amina, sat on a chair by Mahmoud's bed, fanning the poor boy with a woven fan. The ceiling fan in the room wasn't working. She switched the woven fan from one hand to the other at intervals, waving it tirelessly.

"He opened his eyes about an hour ago," she revealed. Her eyes were red and sleepy.

"Did he sit up?" Chief Ousmane asked.

"No. His hip is broken. The doctor says it will be some time before he can sit again."

Chief Ousmane looked at his son's body. He could only imagine the pain the boy was suffering. He winced at the thought of death.

A doctor came in, accompanied by a nurse. They greeted the chief with smiles, and the doctor examined Mahmoud's wounds. He checked the drip and gave the nurse some instructions. The nurse changed the dressing on the wounds.

"He is getting better. He won't die," the doctor assured Chief Ousmane.

"I really pray so, doctor. He is my only son," Chief Ousmane replied.

When the doctor and the nurse left, the chief sat at the edge of the bed, talking in low tones with his wife about his upcoming rallies. He glanced at Mahmoud intermittently. Anytime he did, he would touch his son's heart to see if it was still beating.

"I will be leaving for Tarayya city today," the chief announced, rising to his feet.

"For the rally?" his wife asked.

"Yes. It will be the biggest rally. All the town chiefs of the region will attend," Chief Ousmane said. He bade Amina and Sa'adiya goodbye and went out.

The rally was to be held the following day. It would be the fourth that Chief Ousmane would be holding. He was impressed by the people's enthusiasm and that of the media. The whole country was already talking about following his advice to get married. Chiefs from the other regions of the country had started holding rallies on his behalf.

◄o►

The rally in Tarayya was as big as Chief Ousmane had expected. It was the first time all the chiefs of the Hausa-Sahara region had joined him in his rally. It was held at the Sultan Stadium. As he stood on the stage alongside twenty of the chiefs, speaking in a charged tone, he could see human heads everywhere. He couldn't see the grass or any empty seat. The people shouted, cheered and jumped as he spoke. He condemned Alhaji Coulibaly's candidature and attacked the marriage ban.

"Do you want wives?" he asked the crowd.

"Yes!"

"Do want prostitutes?"

"No!"

"Do you want rape?"

"No!"

"Which do you want: children or bastards?"

"By Allah, we want children!"

"The government is telling you to have prostitutes, bastards and rape. But your chiefs here and I are urging you to get married and bear children. Who will you listen to?"

"*You!*" The crowd's response was thunderous.

Before Chief Ousmane could say any more, the MC began to play a new song that had become a hit on radio. It blared out across the stadium. The crowd sang along with enthusiasm:

> We've got a government
> But our leader is Ousmane.
> The government is for evil
> But Ousmane is for good.
> To Ousmane we shall listen
> And the government we ignore!
> Who is my leader?
> Ousmane! (chorus)
> Who is your leader?
> Ousmane! (chorus)
> Who is our leader?
> Ousmane! Ousmane! Ousmaaaane! (chorus)

That song ended the rally. Chief Ousmane came down from the stage with the twenty chiefs. Some young men escorted his taxi up to his hotel, cheering and vowing to protect him from arrest or persecution. Chief Ousmane knew he needed that protection, because security agents were all over the city, watching his every move. A group of policemen in a van spent the night on the grounds of the hotel in which he lodged.

Early the next morning, the chief took a bus back to Masara. He went straight to the clinic and saw Zaidou standing before Mahmoud, examining his wounds. Amina sat on the chair beside the bed, while Sa'adiya sat on a mat. Zaidou greeted the chief and shook his hand. Amina showed the chief a bunch of bananas and some ripe oranges that Zaidou had brought.

Chief Ousmane smiled. "Thank you, Zaidou," he said. He told Zaidou that he'd just returned from a rally in Tarayya.

Zaidou praised his efforts and wished him success.

Mahmoud's eyes were still closed. He was breathing calmly.

Amina told Chief Ousmane that their son was only sleeping and that he'd awakened earlier and had drank some water.

Chief Ousmane nodded with satisfaction. He sat on the bed, placed his hand on the bandage on Mahmoud's forehead and prayed for him.

He then turned to his daughter. "How are you, Sa'adiya?" he asked her. She was an eighteen-year-old girl who had just finished secondary school. "Did any of your sisters not come to replace you since yesterday?"

"Hassana was here, but she left just before you came in."

"Have you said hello to Zaidou?" Chief Ousmane observed Zaidou's expression as he asked the question. He noticed the surprise on it.

Sa'adiya shyly nodded in response to her father's question.

Chief Ousmane got up and asked Zaidou to follow him out of the ward. They went out and walked slowly side-by-side along the corridor.

"How is your business?" Chief Ousmane asked.

"We thank Allah, Chief," Zaidou replied.

"And the rains?"

"We thank Allah, Chief. The farmers are happy. We are all happy," Zaidou replied.

They stopped at the middle of the corridor.

"I hope you have gotten over the soldiers' assault," Chief Ousmane said, facing Zaidou. "I know you did not attack Alhaji Coulibaly, so stop having fears that you'll be arrested. Do you hear me?"

"Okay, Chief."

"Good."

As Chief Ousmane thought about his next words, he felt nervous. It was just one man he was addressing, but it felt more difficult than addressing the crowds he'd been facing at his rallies. He stroked the tail of his turban and gathered the big sleeves of his babban riga on his shoulders. "You like Sa'adiya, don't you?" he asked Zaidou.

Zaidou wore a little frown. He looked like a boy being asked to share his mango with his friend. "I have a fiancée, Chief," he said.

"*Alhamdulillah*! That's good news!" Chief Ousmane shook Zaidou's hand. "I want you to have this marriage as quickly as possible. Don't fear the ban. Do you hear me?"

"I hear you, Chief."

"Who is the girl?"

"It's Professor Garba's daughter, Zakiyyah." Zaidou smiled proudly.

Chief Ousmane frowned. "Professor Garba's daughter?" he exclaimed.

"Yes, Chief." The pride disappeared from Zaidou's face.

"Have you spoken to Professor Garba yet?"

"No. I want you to . . . um . . . do that on my behalf, Chief."
Zaidou scratched his head.

Chief Ousmane remained silent, looking at the floor. He took
a small bite at a yellow cola nut and chewed slowly. "I will not be
able to talk to the professor myself," he said at last. "I will send some
people to talk to him on your behalf."

"Thank you, Chief, thank you!" Zaidou said. He smiled broadly.

13

On one of the shelves of a big cabinet of varnished ebony, *Mickey Mouse* was playing on a television. Zakiyyah and Moukhtar sat on a settee opposite the television. Moukhtar was a boy of about twelve years, and he wore blue jeans and a yellow T-shirt. The warm late-afternoon sunrays beamed through the window opposite the stairway, shining beautifully on the glass table at the centre of the parlour. Beside the stairway, a carpeted walkway led to another part of the house.

Zakiyyah wore a blue dress with white spots. Her long black hair was plaited into a ponytail. She read a magazine on Hausa fashion, while her brother was absorbed in the cartoon. The music from the cartoon was the only sound in the room.

Zakiyyah heard footsteps on the stairs. She looked towards the stairway and saw her mother coming up. She wore a black abaya with a white veil covering her head. She carried a tray with pieces of a strange edible on it. They were white, round, and puffy and had traces of brown on them.

"Mum," Zakiyyah began, speaking in Arabic as usual, "what are those?"

"One of the maids made them," Kauthar replied as she stepped into the living room. "She said they are called masa."

Since the family had moved to Masara, Kauthar had been learning from the aboriginal maids how to make one local dish after another.

"Come and taste them," Kauthar said, placing the tray on the table. She took a piece of masa and sat on one of the settees. Moukhtar and Zakiyyah took a piece each.

"It tastes nice. It's just that there isn't enough sugar," Moukhtar said as he chewed.

"It tastes fine. It's different from a doughnut, so you shouldn't expect as much sweetness," Zakiyyah remarked.

Kauthar looked thoughtfully out the window as she pushed a last morsel into her mouth.

"Mum," Zakiyyah called, "is anything wrong?"

Kauthar smiled and reached for a second piece of masa. "Moukhtar," she said, "take the remaining masa to your father and brothers. They are out on the lawn playing football."

"They are playing football?" Moukhtar cried. "Ah! I shouldn't be left out." He grabbed the tray and dashed downstairs.

"Zakiyyah," Kauthar called in a serious voice.

"Yes, Mum?" Zakiyyah placed her magazine face down on her lap.

"When did you say you are going to start work in Nigeria?"

"In two months' time," Zakiyyah replied. Was her mother eager for her to leave? She tried to read the emotion on her face.

Kauthar walked to the cabinet and switched off the television. She returned to her seat and cleared her throat. "You are about to start working," she began, "and you are lucky that the job is a good one. You will meet rich colleagues. Wouldn't you like to have one of them as a husband?"

"Why are you asking this question, Mum?"

"I just want to know."

"Have you forgotten about Zaidou?"

"Zakiyyah," Kauthar said, her face turning red, "I never knew you were foolish!"

"Mum!"

"I mean it," Kauthar continued, sticking out her index finger. "Some men came to your father yesterday. You never told me what your newfound suitor was like. But those wretched men have told us everything."

"What did those men say about Zaidou?" Zakiyyah demanded. She dropped her magazine on the stool and moved to the edge of her seat.

"They told us the sort of wretched man he is! Couldn't you find anyone other than a miserable tailor who cannot even buy himself a car?"

"Mum!"

"I mean it!"

"Zaidou is not miserable, Mum!" Zakiyyah cried, rising to her feet. "He is good and hard-working. Even if he isn't rich, I love him as he is." She sat down and took up her magazine again. Tears filled her eyes, blurring the pictures.

Kauthar sighed. "I can't say anything more to stop you," she said. "But I tell you: your father is not pleased with your decision."

"Have you been speaking my father's mind?" Zakiyyah asked.

"Yes," Kauthar replied.

Zakiyyah sprang to her feet again and made for the walkway.

"Where are you going?" her mother asked.

"I must see Baba, Mum – I must!" she said. She jogged down the walkway.

◄○►

Professor Garba, dressed in a tracksuit, monitored the dribbles, tackles, shots and passes being displayed by his sons. The players ranged between fourteen and twenty-seven years of age. They were dressed in shorts and T-shirts. The makeshift goalposts reached up to the professor's waist.

Moukhtar kept cheering the side he supported – the younger side. He screamed as they conceded one goal after another. They were twenty-three goals down already. He continued to cheer and lament until Adam scored a goal through a powerful shot.

"Goal! G-o-o-o-oal!" Moukhtar screamed, running onto the lawn to hug the jubilant team members.

Professor Garba saw that the sun was about to set. He blew the whistle to end the game.

Moukhtar fetched the tray of masa from the pavement and passed it round. The boys inspected the masa and asked what it was before taking a bite. Moukhtar told them that it was masa.

As Professor Garba took a piece, he looked up at his balcony and saw Zakiyyah appearing at the balustrade. "Zakiyyah, where have you been?" he asked her with a smile. "You should have come to see your brothers play."

"Yes, Zakiyyah!" Moukhtar added. "Adam played beautiful football today!"

Zakiyyah frowned and turned her back to them, leaning against the balustrade.

Professor Garba pushed the last morsel of masa into his mouth and rushed upstairs. "What's the matter, Zakiyyah?" he asked as he appeared on the balcony. He used a small towel to wipe the sweat from his face.

Zakiyyah had tears in her eyes. Her father asked her to sit down, and he sat on a chair opposite her, with a small table between them.

"Baba," Zakiyyah began, "why don't you want me to marry Zaidou? Just because he is not rich? Mum has told me everything."

Professor Garba rested his elbows on the table, and thought briefly. He had never discussed marriage with his daughter before. Now that he had to do so, he felt like he was learning how to drive. He could hit a pedestrian or crash the car into a river. "Zakiyyah," he began, patting his daughter's shoulder, "listen to me. I don't want you to get arrested. That's why I'm afraid for you to get married. The marriage ban has already begun. So please, wait until the ban is lifted before you get married. It's just five years away."

"Why do we have to listen to such a stupid decree, Baba? No one thinks the ban makes sense! No one does!"

"I don't think it does, either. But I have to do as Leader Gambo says. We all have to be good citizens."

"I shouldn't get married as a good citizen?"

"Yes, sweetheart."

"What then should I do, Baba? Become a prostitute?" Zakiyyah frowned.

Professor Garba buried his face in his hands. He took his hands off his face and looked at his daughter again.

"Zakiyyah," he began, in an imploring tone, "understand me: as your father, I want you to get married. But if you do, I can lose my job! Don't you care for me anymore?"

Zakiyyah gasped. Her eyes grew wide as if she'd seen a ghost. "Baba!" she cried. "Do you care for your job more than you care for me?"

"No, no, no!"

"But you are siding with the leader instead of your daughter just to save your job! You shouldn't do that, Baba."

"Yes, I shouldn't. You're right." Professor Garba scratched his head.

"It's not good to side with anyone against your family. Mum told me that you are regretting that you sided with Leader Gambo against your father. But you are repeating the same mistake with your daughter! Please, Baba, think again! Think!"

Professor Garba removed his eyeglasses. He stared at his daughter with unbelieving eyes. Wasn't she sounding the same warning his father had been sounding in his nightmares?

He stroked his chin and looked out into his garden. Zakiyyah was still talking, but he wasn't listening. The trees swished and birds flew from branch to branch, singing to one another.

"It's okay, Zakiyyah." He patted his daughter's shoulder. "You've made a good case. I will look for a way out for you."

He kissed her forehead and wiped her tears with his hands.

14

Zaidou took a sip of mint tea. It tasted better than any brew he'd ever tasted before. He'd often wondered why things tasted better whenever he was happy. He took another sip, swished it and swallowed.

"Ahhh!" He dropped the cup on the table and turned to Ya'u and Audou, who were discussing loudly.

Ya'u was barking like a dog that had sighted a thief. "We are in trouble in this country!" he cried. "My friend got married two days ago and he was arrested last night. I always knew that the police would trouble us!"

"Chief Ousmane's advice is good, but it is dangerous for anyone to follow it." Audou shook his head, glancing at the people eating and drinking around the Dandali.

Zaidou glanced at the people too. He could see that there were no smiling faces or laughing mouths. Everyone looked bereaved. Many of them were his customers. He brought out a pencil and a rough piece of paper from his pocket and began to scribble down some names of those customers.

"Zaidou!" Ya'u cried.

Zaidou looked up and saw his friend's amazed look.

"It seems you're not concerned that people are being arrested," Ya'u said. "What are you doing?"

"I'm writing."

"Writing?"

"Yes. I'm writing down the names of my customers whose garments I've not finished sewing. I have to finish sewing their garments quickly. I am leaving this town very soon."

"You are leaving this town?" his two friends cried.

"You never told us this, Zaidou!" Ya'u added.

Zaidou gestured at him to lower his voice. "I'm sorry," he whispered. "I wanted to allow you to finish your discussions before I informed you. Do you know that I am going to marry Zakiyyah? She has accepted my proposal!"

The mouths of Ya'u and Audou dropped open.

"Are you mad?" Ya'u cried.

"Are you stupid?" Audou spat.

"Did I say something wrong?" Zaidou protested.

"Have you been listening to our discussions at all? Have you been listening to the news? You want to get arrested, eh?"

Zaidou told them to calm down and give him listening ears. He cleared his throat, and told them that Professor Garba had agreed to allow him to marry Zakiyyah. They would travel to Lagos to live their married lives.

"So you see, we won't be arrested!" he explained, smiling from ear to ear.

"We are happy for you," Ya'u said without smiling. "So when is this marriage of yours?"

"It's next week!"

"Next week?" Audou cried.

"Yes. We will travel to Lagos to do it." Zaidou felt proud.

Ya'u tapped the table with his fingers. "I know you love Zakiyyah," he began, "but if you would listen to my advice – the advice of your friend of over thirty years – I would advise you to delay your marriage till the ban is lifted. I know you'll be travelling out of the country, but the moment the police hear about your plans, you'll be in jail."

"I agree with you, Ya'u," Audou said.

Zaidou frowned and hit the table with his fist. "Thank you for your advice, friends," he said. "Let me go and see Chief Ousmane before it gets late. Good night."

He mounted his bicycle and rode off. He cursed his friends for their bad advice. He wanted to see Chief Ousmane to inform him about Professor Garba's decision, and to thank him for his efforts. What he wasn't sure of was where he'd meet him – at his zaure or at the clinic. He decided to check the clinic first.

He reached the clinic and saw Chief Ousmane coming out with the doctor. Zaidou stopped under a tree and waited. He watched them keenly as they gesticulated gently. They talked for many minutes. Zaidou wondered whether they'd remain there all night. The sky grumbled and a breeze began to blow. Clouds gathered and blocked the moon.

Zaidou alighted from his bicycle and walked slowly towards the two men. They had rounded up a discussion about Mahmoud and started talking about Governor Coulibaly, whose nomination had just been approved by Leader Gambo. Zaidou coughed and hoped that Chief Ousmane would turn to look at him. His cough was followed by the sound of sirens. He looked back and saw a van approaching. Its headlights were shining brightly. Another van followed behind it.

The two vans ground to a halt in front of the clinic. Many policemen, armed with rifles, jumped out of them. The doctor ran into the clinic. Chief Ousmane stood watching. The policemen whisked him into one of the vans and sped off.

Zaidou remained stuck to the spot. He was unable to scream, run or cry. When he finally succeeded in lifting his feet, he jogged to his bicycle and rode homewards. He rode past three houses where he saw some young bridegrooms being dragged out of their houses, handcuffed and whisked away in waiting vans. One of them was his cousin; the other two were his customers.

It started raining. Zaidou got drenched, and riding proved difficult because of poor visibility and the potholes he had to dodge.

When he reached his neighbourhood, he saw a van parked in front of his own house. Its headlights illuminated the raindrops ahead. He turned back to retreat.

He rode faster than he ever had before. He didn't bother to wipe the rain from his face. Neither did he ring his bell, fearing that it would attract the policemen.

He sighted Chief Ousmane's mosque ahead of him, its door left ajar and its lights on. When he reached it, he dismounted his bicycle and took it along with him into the mosque. There was no one inside. He slammed shut all the doors and bolted them. He shut the windows and switched off the light. He sat at a corner panting, listening for the sound of the police vehicle. All he could hear was the rain hitting against the roof. The mosquitoes buzzed too, and bit him mercilessly.

-<o>-

Zaidou was awakened by loud knocks on the metal door of the mosque. He looked about him fearfully. "Please don't shoot! Please!" he pleaded.

It was still dark. When he realised that there were no policemen around, he heaved a sigh.

The knocks sounded again.

"Open the door! Is there anybody in there?" a man called from outside.

Zaidou remained still.

"Open the door. It's time for prayer," the man pleaded again.

Zaidou tiptoed to the window, opened it slightly and peeped out. The lights outside were on and he could see the muezzin at the door. There were no officers in sight, so he opened the door.

"Why did you lock yourself inside? How did you get in, by the way?" the muezzin asked crossly.

"I was hiding from the police."

"The police? Which police?"

"They tried to arrest me last night."

"Arrest you? Why? Did you get married?"

"I don't know why they wanted me," Zaidou said.

The muezzin picked up the microphone and made the call to prayer. His metallic voice pierced through the quietness of the dawn. Men began to trickle into the mosque. They beamed with the leftovers of the night's sleep. By 5:30 a.m., when the prayer was meant to begin, Chief Ousmane did not show up. The muezzin stood before the congregation and led the prayer. After the prayer, people began to look around for Chief Ousmane. Murmurs slipped through the congregation.

"I heard he was one of those arrested last night. Is that true?" one man beside Zaidou asked another.

"I don't know. I haven't heard it."

"Could he be travelling?" another voice asked.

"No. I saw him last night."

Zaidou didn't want to tell anyone about the arrest. The very mention of the word "arrest" scared him. He looked at all the entrances to see if there were officers standing in wait for him.

The muezzin picked up the microphone and blew into it, and the congregation became silent.

"Assalamu 'alaykum!" he greeted.

"Wa'alaykumus salaam!" the men replied.

"As we can all see, Chief Ousmane did not pray with us today. This is unusual, because we know our chief is neither sick nor is he travelling. He was with us last night. Many of us saw him. We all know that many of our brothers and sisters were arrested last night!" The muezzin's voice became laden with emotion. "Sadly for us, our chief was one of those arrested. That is why he couldn't lead us in prayer today. We pray to Allah to bring an end to this trial we are suffering. We pray to Allah to return our chief and our brothers and sisters to us safely."

His last words were followed by a whimper. The congregation began to murmur again, louder than it had done earlier. It broke into small groups of men talking about the development.

When the sun rose, the men went to Chief Ousmane's house to sympathise with his family.

Zaidou sat still.

"Aren't you going with us?" one man asked him.

"I am not going. The policemen are outside. They will arrest me."

"Why will anyone arrest you? You didn't get married, did you?"

"They tried to arrest me last night. I don't know why." Zaidou leaned his back against the wall.

By the time everyone was out, he felt lonely and unsafe. He mounted his bicycle and followed the men.

A crowd had gathered in front of Chief Ousmane's house. People went in and out of the house. Some of the people who crowded outside sat like bereaved men, their chins buried in their palms, their eyes looking blankly at the ground. Others spat angry words about the government. A fat middle-aged man spoke the loudest. He got a lot of attention. His listeners nodded in agreement to his points. He sweated as he spoke, and his shirt got soaked from his sweat. His voice rose and he looked like he would start beating up people. He climbed atop some pavement that protruded from the façade and began to address everybody.

"My people! Listen to me," he cried. "We are going round the town to protest the arrest of our chief. We are not cowards. Leader Gambo is a man like us. We shouldn't be afraid of him."

"Right, we shouldn't! Woe unto him!" the crowd echoed.

"I want us to stage a protest this morning. I will lead the protest. I will lead the struggle to get our chief released. We will go round the town to call for his release. We will storm the police station and warn the police that we want our town head back. Otherwise, there will be consequences."

"Yes! Yes!" the crowd cried.

"If nothing is done – if our chief and our brothers and sisters are not released – I swear we will pick up arms against Leader Gambo. We will fight his government until it is removed. We are going to start a rebellion. We must end—"

Several shots rang in the air.

Zaidou ducked for cover.

Another shot was fired and something flew over him, landing in the crowd. The thing exuded a thick white smoke. Several other canisters flew into the crowd. People began to cough.

Zaidou coughed too, gasping for breath.

The people ran like cockroaches that had been sprayed with insecticide. Policemen appeared from all directions, shooting into the air.

Zaidou mounted his bicycle and rode off. People ran along the road with him, yelling. He hit two men and they fell. He fell to the ground with them. He mounted his bicycle again and moved on. He wouldn't go home because the policemen might still be there. He would run to his shop to hide.

A police van sat waiting in front of his shop. He pulled on the brakes and his bicycle screeched through the muddy ground. Mud splashed passers-by, and they yelled at him. The van's engine was running. As Zaidou turned to retreat, the van began to move. He cycled hard, but the van caught up with him. A policeman inside ordered him to stop. He refused. The van overtook him and blocked his way. He tried to dodge it, but he wobbled and fell. Two police officers jumped out, handcuffed Zaidou and pushed him into their vehicle. The van took off.

PART II

THE CAPTIVE

15

It was dark in the cell, even though Chief Ousmane knew that the sun had not yet set. Whenever the sun set, it got pitch dark, and he could hardly see even the iron bars of his cell's gate. Mosquitoes would sing in his ears and bite him all over his body. He wore only an old singlet and trousers, which made it easier for the bloodsuckers to have a nice dinner.

His imprisonment was like the first time he'd been thrown behind bars after the attack on Masara. It was a solitary confinement. He'd spent five years in jail then. This time, no one had told him how long he'd be in prison because he was never charged in court. The one year he had spent already could be the beginning of fifty years without freedom.

He lay on his back on the cold bare floor. Apart from his frail body, the only other thing on the floor was a bowl. It was a wide bowl, which a man had thrown to him through the cell bars when he'd been brought to the cell.

"That's for your urine and shit!" the man had said.

Every morning, the man came to empty the bowl. Another man would bring him his meals. Those two men were the only people he had seen on a daily basis. Once every two days, he saw five more people – gun-carrying soldiers. The man who emptied his bowl would come with them, and he'd be led to a bathroom along the corridor to bathe with cold water. Those baths had often given him a cold.

Today, the cell got pitch dark for the 547th time. Chief Ousmane got up and performed the Maghrib prayer. He bowed and prostrated, taking a long time in his prostrations to ask Allah for a way out. He fought mosquitoes by slapping all parts of his body. He was surprised that he had not developed malaria all this while, because during his first incarceration, he'd fallen sick more than ten times. Back in Masara, when it rained heavily and puddles formed near his house and attracted mosquitoes, he would get malaria in a matter of days. He had petitioned the regional government many times to make drainages for Masara town, but nothing had been done.

He didn't know in which part of Hasoumiya he was. He'd been blindfolded during his arrest. The policemen who had arrested him had driven him for over twelve hours. The blindfold was removed after he'd been put in jail.

While he supplicated in his prostration, he heard footfalls and a yellow light shone into the cell. It was the food man. He heard the cell gate rattle as the man passed the bowl of food through the cell gate, dropping it onto the floor. The food man always met him in prayer. He would drop the food and leave without saying a word.

The food man's light did not go away this time. Curious though he was, Chief Ousmane prayed for as long as he normally did. He sat up, ended his prayer and praised Allah silently, counting the praises on his fingers. He turned towards the gate. The light from the torch fell on his face. He walked to the gate and picked up his food.

"Assalaamu 'alaykum, Chief," the food man greeted him.

"Wa'alaykumus salaam," Chief Ousmane replied. It had been a while since he'd received such courtesy. He turned to go and eat. The food man still didn't go. Chief Ousmane stopped and looked at him one more time.

"Is everything okay, young man?" he asked him.

"I am sorry there's no salt in the food today."

"You are sorry?"

"Yes."

Chief Ousmane shrugged his shoulders and walked away. He sat at his eating corner, wiped his right hand on his dirty trousers and began to eat. It was rice mixed with raw palm oil. It had stones in it, and he spat them out every now and then. The torch was still shining. It was the first time he would see the morsels he was eating. There was no difference between the rice and the meals he had previously been served. He wondered why the food man was apologetic this time around. He felt uneasy eating under someone's observation.

"*Tanko!* What are you still doing there?" a voice echoed from down the corridor.

The food man withdrew and ran away. Darkness returned to the cell.

That night, Chief Ousmane thought about the food man's compassion. He thought about it side-by-side with thoughts about his family. How was his wife? How were his eleven children? It was the thoughts of Mahmoud that bothered him the most. Was he still in the hospital, back on his feet, or dead? How was Masara town faring in his absence? What had become of the marriage ban? The answers to those questions only came to him in his dreams. At times, he dreamt of weddings and smiling couples and families. At other times, he would dream of fornication and prostitutes. He would wake up frowning, and he'd remain grumpy for the rest of the day. He would not eat for the whole day.

For the next four weeks, no one spoke to him again. His life was full of actions and devoid of words. The food man would drop his food and leave, the bowl evacuator would evacuate the bowl and return it washed, and he'd be taken to bathe in the bathroom, escorted by unfriendly soldiers.

The food man brought him lunch. "I have put meat in your food. It's ram meat." He did not drop the food on the floor. He handed it to Chief Ousmane. It would be the first time that the chief would eat meat in over a year.

For several weeks, the food man didn't say anything again. What could be the reason for his random shows of compassion?

One morning, Chief Ousmane decided to ask him questions. "Young man," he whispered, "do you know anything about my family? Have you heard anything about my son, Mahmoud?"

"I heard in the news that he's dead."

"Dead? When was that?"

The man gestured at Chief Ousmane not to shout.

The chief lowered his head and shook it several times. It was the second time he would lose a son. The first time had been after the attack on Masara. After he'd served five years in prison, he'd returned home and received the news that his baby son and his wife, Falmata, were missing. The police had told him that his wife had been killed, but they had no information about his son's whereabouts. Chief Ousmane had presumed him dead also.

Chief Ousmane looked at the food man through his tears. He tried not to let out the noise of his cry. "How are my people in Masara?" he asked.

The man looked around and ran away. Days later, when he brought lunch, he cast a quick glance around, and began to talk. "The guards are drunk," he whispered.

The man told Chief Ousmane that three of his own sisters had taken up jobs in brothels the government had set up across the country to cushion the effects of the marriage ban. The brothels were called Enjoyment Rooms.

"All my unmarried sisters are pregnant now," he said in a shaky voice. He told Chief Ousmane about some of his female neighbours who had been raped, some to death. Even young boys had become womanisers.

"Are these things also happening in Masara?" Chief Ousmane asked.

"Chief, the whole country has become rotten. I have not ever been to Masara, but from what I hear on the radio and from people, everywhere is rotten. *Rotten!* Many people have strange diseases! I must confess, Chief, I have done it too before!"

"You have fornicated?"

The food man nodded. "Many times. But I am trying to stop. There is an Enjoyment Room opposite my house and I visit it—"

One of the guards came and grabbed the food man by the collar, dragging him away.

—◀o▶—

The next time Chief Ousmane saw the food man, he had bruises on his face. The poor fellow continued to bring food without talking, only nodding by way of greeting. It continued like that for six months.

Chief Ousmane had grown sick seven times within those months. A doctor came to treat him each time. Whenever the doctor was about to give him injection, he would pray that it was not poison. Gladly, it wasn't, because he survived it. But he was lean. His ribs were showing and his limbs were weak.

"I need some fresh air," he begged the doctor.

The doctor advised the prison officials to let him go out.

"He is not meant to go out!" one of the prison officials barked.

"He is not strong. He just needs some fresh air," the doctor said.

"He is meant to be in his cell throughout the day. Do you want him to escape?"

"He won't escape! This is a political prisoner. I'm sure you don't want him to die in your hands, seeing the situation in the country."

"Don't say that, doctor. We know our inmates better than you do," the prison official retorted.

The argument raged on, and Chief Ousmane wished they'd stop. He was ready to sacrifice the fresh air. They agreed that they should seek permission from a higher authority to allow him to go out. They disappeared. Later, three prison officials came in, handcuffed him and chained his legs. They took him out of the cell.

He was led out to the field in the company of two soldiers, three policemen and the three prison officials.

It was evening. Inmates were playing football on the field in the warm sun. Their dark sweaty skins glittered under the rays. The field was green, with patches of sand here and there. The grass was longer at the borders. Some of the players wore blue shirts, while the others wore brown. They shouted instructions at each other as the ball was kicked round the field.

"Pass the ball, pass the ball!"

"You! Mark that man!"

"Hey! Hey! Hey! See me here!"

Other inmates stood at the field's borders, watching. They were of all ages, from teenagers to men who looked older than ninety years. The older ones didn't pay much attention to the match. They sat in groups, chatting. Their green uniforms looked too big for their old, frail bodies. Chief Ousmane was made to sit on a bench some distance away from the rest of the inmates.

The team in brown scored a goal. The prisoners cried, "Goooooal! Goooooaaaal!" One of the scorer's team mates carried him on his shoulder and raced to the middle of the field with him, shouting. The team in blue crowded around their goalkeeper, yelling at him. Wasn't that Zaidou? It was, indeed! He seemed to be apologising to his team for his failure.

Chief Ousmane felt happy to see a familiar face after so many months. He wished he could be allowed to go and shake Zaidou's hand.

The match continued. A striker from the team in brown dribbled two defenders and passed it to another player. The player raced towards Zaidou. Zaidou bounced at the goalpost, staring at him. The player shot, Zaidou dived the wrong way and the ball entered the net. Celebrations followed. The match resumed.

Zaidou's defenders abandoned him and ran to the midfield. As a striker in brown approached, he yelled at the defenders to come back. The striker moved with impressive speed towards Zaidou. The defenders struggled to catch up with him. Zaidou bounced at the goalpost. When the striker was about to shoot, Zaidou dived at him and cleared him off the ground. The striker flew into the air and landed on his shoulder. He gave a loud cry.

The referee blew the whistle, raced to the scene and pointed at the penalty kick spot. The striker rolled in pain on the ground, shouting. Some prison officials came and took him away. Zaidou's team mates crowded around him and yelled at him. One of them smacked him three times on the neck. Zaidou fell to his knees and pleaded for mercy.

A player in brown stood one-on-one with Zaidou to take the penalty kick. The referee blew the whistle. The player raced to the ball and shot. Zaidou dived and punched the ball to a safe distance.

"Beautiful! Ma'sha'Allah!" Chief Ousmane cried, clasping his hands together.

The match continued.

Six more goals were scored against Zaidou. Each time, his team mates would come by and smack him or yell at him.

The match ended. The prison officials ordered the inmates back into their cells. The prisoners trooped in various directions, some passing in front of Chief Ousmane. Many of them greeted him as they passed by.

"Assalaamu 'alaykum, Chief," Zaidou greeted him. There was excitement on his face.

"Wa'alaykumus salaam, Zaidou!" Chief Ousmane jumped to his feet. "I am happy to see you! How are you?"

"I am fine, Chief. I never knew you were here!"

"I have been here for over a year now. Why do you choose to play football? Your team mates don't like you. They will hurt you."

"One woman forced me to do it. She was the one who ordered that we should be grouped into teams. I told her I didn't want to play because I didn't know how to. She said she was a big woman in this place and that if I agree to marry her, she would not make me play again. She would help me escape from prison. She said she would take me abroad to marry me. When I told her no, and that I would marry Zakiyyah, she swore that she would make life difficult for me in this—"

"Kai! That's enough! Leave here!" one of the prison officials guarding Chief Ousmane barked. "Get back to your cell!"

Zaidou waved at Chief Ousmane and walked away.

The following day, the prison officials asked Chief Ousmane whether he still needed fresh air, and he said yes. He was taken to the field. A match was played, but Zaidou didn't play. The chief saw him chatting with a fat female prison official at one end of the field. She looked over forty years of age. They chatted till the match ended and the prisoners were sent back to their cells. Zaidou tried to talk to Chief Ousmane as he walked past him, but he was prevented by prison officers.

On the third day, Chief Ousmane was taken out again. Zaidou didn't play. Chief Ousmane browsed the field for him. He was nowhere to be found. What had happened to him?

On the day Chief Ousmane clocked two years in jail, the food man brought him a letter, which he'd hidden at the bottom of his rice. It was soiled but readable. The food man gave him a torchlight so that he could read the letter. The letter was from an imam in the Savannah-Fula region.

Assalaamu 'alaykum, Chief Ousmane,

It has been two years since you have been taken away from us and silenced. I have come to understand that you are in a bad jail in Birni. If you are still alive, I hope this letter reaches you.

I am in hiding for fear of being arrested and jailed like you. Many of us imams are being arrested and killed by the government because we have been preaching against the ban on marriage and the evils that have followed it – just as you inspired us to do. Our girls are now every man's girls, and our men – young and old – are not responsible any more. On my street alone, every house has either an unmarried girl with a baby or one awaiting one. The government is supporting these evils. They have opened "Enjoyment Rooms", where men and women enter for mutual enjoyment. The whole country has turned upside down. But as I say to everyone—

The sounds of the gate being opened hit Chief Ousmane's ears. A man entered the cell, walked up to him and looked down at him. The letter fell from Chief Ousmane's hand. The man picked it up and read it. He took his time to do that. The longer he read, the faster Chief Ousmane's breaths became.

The man took the letter away from his face and looked hard at Chief Ousmane. "How did you get this?" He held the letter up as if he were displaying it to the whole world.

Chief Ousmane did not say anything.

The man kicked him in the belly and in the face.

Chief Ousmane yelled, held his stomach and lay on his side, groaning.

"Tell me where you got this, or I swear I will kill you!"

That threat was drowned by the pain the chief felt in his stomach. He rolled on the floor.

The officer kicked him on the thighs, pulled him by the singlet and made him sit up. He yelled into the chief's face. "Where did you get this letter from?" His breath smelled of beer and tobacco.

"I saw it in my food," Chief Ousmane groaned.

The man left, locking the cell after him.

Some soldiers came in and thrashed Chief Ousmane with horsewhips, leaving him with cuts all over his body. For the next five days, he could only pray whilst lying down. He could not follow the soldiers to the bathroom to take his bath. He threw up three times in the bowl.

When he'd regained some strength, he was handcuffed, put in a Black Maria and taken to one of the beaches in Birni.

It was afternoon and the sun was shining brightly. The light and the cool air of the beach were refreshing. The waves rose and landed softly on the shore. Chief Ousmane had always visited the beach to relax whenever he came to Birni during his days of freedom.

Stakes had been erected close to the ocean. A crowd milled some distance away, looking towards the stakes. Six other Black Marias arrived. Prisoners were taken out from them. They were all dressed in green prison uniforms. They numbered in the hundreds. From the words of the prison officials handling the prisoners, Chief Ousmane understood that they were activists and imams who had publicly opposed the marriage ban. Others were new husbands. One of the condemned men was brought to him, his hands tied with a rope.

"Do you know this man?" asked the prison officer that had brought him.

Chief Ousmane said yes. The man looked hopeless and weak. Veins bulged on his face and neck. It was the food man. Chief Ousmane grabbed the man and hugged him tight. They cried together.

"Pray for me, Chief!" the man whimpered.

"It shall be well, my son," Chief Ousmane assured him. "May Allah have mercy on you." He looked into his eyes. "Have you said the shahadah?" he asked him.

The food man nodded.

"Good!" Chief Ousmane patted him on his shoulder.

The food man was taken away and tied to a stake, along with the others. The soldiers took up their positions.

Chief Ousmane turned his back to the stakes, facing his minders. He closed his eyes. He quivered like a sneezing man as the shots rang in the air. The executions were done in batches. The lifeless bodies would be taken off the stakes and replaced by other convicts. Chief Ousmane's heart pounded harder than it ever had before. He fell on his knees so that they sank in the sand. Would he be dragged to the stake as well?

He was returned to his cell after the exercise, with the horrors of the executions haunting his mind. They haunted him for many days. He had sleepless nights, nightmares and bouts of tears. The new food man did not even bother to look into his face. Five prison officers stood at his gate throughout the day.

One morning, his cell was cleaned and scented with incense. A light bulb was fixed and switched on. In the afternoon, eight army generals came in. Their leader was a slim brown man in his late fifties. A chair was placed for him at the middle of the cell. He sat on it, placing his right leg over his left leg. His black shoes were well-polished. He was clean-shaven and had a lot of grey hair under his beret. He introduced himself as General Mamman, an ex-Nigerian soldier. He was Hasoumiya's Chief of Defence Staff. The other army generals were unsmiling. They stood behind him in their smart green uniforms.

"You miss your family, don't you?" Mamman asked.

"Yes," Chief Ousmane replied.

"How is your health? Are you sick?"

"No."

"Were you given lunch today?"

"Not yet."

"They feed you regularly, right?"

"Yes."

"Have you ever been tortured?"

"Yes." Chief Ousmane said.

Mamman looked at him with sympathetic eyes. "That's sad," he said. "Would you like to leave this place?"

Chief Ousmane gave him a cold look.

"I mean, do you want to be released and go back to your family?" Mamman paraphrased.

"This is not a place for any man to be, Mamman," Chief Ousmane retorted.

"Good. Do you know what brought you here in the first place?"

"You know the answer as well as I do."

"It was because you were stubborn and mischievous, idiot!" one of the generals barked. "Say it! Don't talk like that to—"

Mamman raised his hand at the general without turning to look at him. The general kept quiet.

Mamman gave Chief Ousmane a typed document. "We are ready to release you," he explained. "But you have to agree to the conditions on this document by signing it."

Chief Ousmane read the conditions, all fifteen of them. Most were trivial, and he could easily keep them. The strictest of them were three: that he would desist from any anti-government activities, including rallies; that he would support the government in all its activities; and that he would hold rallies to calm the people and make them abide by the marriage ban.

"We can give you up to three hours to think about these conditions," Mamman said.

Chief Ousmane gave the document a hard look, and then looked at the officers. "Is my release all I will get for signing this document? Haven't the people suffered long enough for celebrating the First

Lady's assassination? They should be set free too! The ban should be lifted," he demanded.

"All we want you to do is to sign the document, and we'll release you, Chief Ousmane," Mamman said.

Chief Ousmane bowed his head and made a short silent prayer. "What if I ask for the ban to be reduced?" he asked.

Mamman shook his head. "We're not here to negotiate release with you," he said.

Chief Ousmane made another silent prayer and asked for a pen. He signed.

He was led by three prison officers to a waiting car at the field. As he entered the car, he sighted five prison officers leading Zaidou to a Black Maria at one end of the field. He was limping. His hands were handcuffed, his legs chained. His shirt was torn at the back, and his trousers were torn at the side from below his knee down to the hem. As soon as he and the prison officers entered the Black Maria, the vehicle took off.

Chief Ousmane's car took off too. It followed behind the Black Maria. When they were out of the prison gates, the Black Maria went a different way from Chief Ousmane's car. Only Allah knows to where!

16

Chief Ousmane was taken to the hospital straight from prison. The doctors and nurses came regularly to examine him or to take blood or other samples from his body. Unlike the food men and the evacuator, they smiled and chatted with him. They told him how his health was every morning.

The food was better than it had been in the prison. It was splendid. It was always rich in all the classes of food – proteins, carbohydrates, and all other nutrients. The vitamins mostly came from Mamman, who visited him every evening after work. He brought him oranges, apples and mangoes in turn. Chief Ousmane would eat them eagerly as he chatted with the government official, as if they'd been friends for a long time. Something was so nice about Mamman's attitude that the chief did not think ill of him. He regarded him as more of a saviour than a persecutor.

"When will you take me back to Masara? Chief Ousmane asked Mamman one evening, shortly after he'd swallowed some pills a nurse had given him. "Why can't I get all the freedom I deserve right away?"

Mamman was sitting on a chair by the chief's bedside, browsing a newspaper. He took the newspaper away from his face and regarded Chief Ousmane. "We want you to return to Masara a healthy man!" He didn't smile.

"But I am not sick!"

"No one will believe you. You are lean and frail. And the doctors have found that you have some infections for which they are treating you. I'm sure they've told you." Mamman got up from the chair, dropped the newspaper on it and strolled to the window. He looked thoughtfully out of it.

From his bed, Chief Ousmane could glimpse out the window. There was a bridge over a lagoon. It was rush hour, so there was heavy traffic on the bridge.

"There is so much trouble out there," Mamman said. "If we let you go in your frail condition, the trouble you'll witness will finish you!"

Chief Ousmane sat up on his bed. "What kind of trouble?" he asked.

"You've been out of touch with what has been happening in the country for more than two years. The marriage ban has caused a lot of trouble. You wouldn't like to hear it."

"What kind of trouble, Mamman!"

"We'll talk about that," Mamman said. He bid Chief Ousmane good night and left.

Chief Ousmane did not know how long he'd been in the hospital. It wasn't as much as a month, though.

Mamman picked him up after he'd been discharged and took him to his own house. It was a big cream-coloured mansion in a nice quiet part of Birni. It had many flowers and was well-guarded by soldiers.

"You are free now," Mamman reminded Chief Ousmane, as they sat in his opulent living room watching TV. "I only brought you here as my guest. I invite you to spend two days with me. But if you choose, I'll take you to Masara immediately."

Chief Ousmane didn't know why Mamman gave him that invitation, but it sounded like a kind gesture. "I will spend just one day with you, Mamman." Chief Ousmane smiled. "I'm happy at your invitation, but I'm eager to see my family too."

Mamman had a nice gentle family. His wife was Nigerian like him. They had five children. The oldest was twenty and a student at the University of Birni.

The children entered the living room one by one to greet Chief Ousmane. The chief was touched by their smiles and gentleness. They reminded him of his young daughters. Mamman's wife brought some mango juice and water and kept them on a stool that stood between Chief Ousmane and Mamman. "What will you have for lunch?" she asked Chief Ousmane.

The chief thought briefly. "I will eat tuwo and shuwaka soup," he said at last. "I have not eaten that in two years."

"Which type of tuwo? Maize, rice or guinea corn?" she asked.

Chief Ousmane had never heard of tuwo made from rice before. Was that a Nigerian type? He said that he'd like to try it. The wife went to the kitchen.

"Your wife's Hausa accent is different from yours," Chief Ousmane observed.

"I'm from Katsina, while she is from Sokoto," Mamman explained.

"Ahhh! Sokoto! That was the capital of the Sokoto Caliphate, right?"

"Yes. But it is just a state now – one of the biggest we have in Nigeria," Mamman said. He told Chief Ousmane the story of his country: how the Sokoto Caliphate had been merged with other empires by the British to form Nigeria, how the country had struggled for independence and won and how it had survived coups and a civil war. He told him about his experiences during the war: how he'd escaped bomb blasts, launched an offensive and rescued fellow soldiers who had been ambushed. He went to his room and brought out a beret that had two bullet holes in it.

"I almost got killed in the war," he said, showing Chief Ousmane the bullet holes. "I've kept this beret with me so that I can remember how lucky I've been."

Chief Ousmane looked at Mamman's face and was surprised that there was no scar on it. His limbs looked undamaged, too. "We've had one coup in this country," he said. "Leader Gambo came to power through a coup. But we've never had a civil war before."

The maids laid lunch on the dining table. There were fruits, fried chicken, and fried mutton served on expensive china.

Chief Ousmane dipped a spoonful of tuwo into shuwaka soup, chewed it and swallowed. The bitter taste of the soup was perfect. It was well salted and seasoned with thyme. If only Amina would learn how to cook tuwo from rice! He dug his fork into a piece of fried meat and pushed it into his mouth. It was tender as he chewed.

After lunch, they returned to the living room and continued to chat about the marriage ban, life after prison and life as a chief.

"I heard of how you destroyed the brewery in your town over thirty years ago," Mamman said.

"I wish it had not gotten to that extent," Chief Ousmane replied. "My people complained to me about it because it is against our religion. We don't want drunkards in our land. We talked to the government, but they didn't listen."

"You seem to talk to your people often."

"I talk to them every day. They come to my zaure and we discuss their problems. Even the other chiefs of the Hausa-Sahara Region come to me for advice."

"Really?"

"Are you surprised, Mamman? I have been doing that for over thirty years." Chief Ousmane picked a cola nut from the saucer on the stool and took a bite. It was fresh and crunchy.

"I have heard a lot about you, Chief Ousmane," Mamman smiled. "I wish you would stay with me for two days, so that I can hear more from your own mouth."

Later in the afternoon, Mamman took his guest to a room to have siesta.

◄○►

Chief Ousmane looked at the sky and saw that there were no clouds. The morning sun was shining.

The tarmac was busy. Airport officials attended to the aeroplanes that dotted the runway. Vehicles that he would otherwise regard as big looked like shoes as they drove past the airplanes. He watched as a jet raced along the runway with a loud sound. It took off as if it were lighter than a piece of paper. It shrank and soon disappeared into the distance. The last time he had flown had been ten years ago, when he'd gone for hajj.

"The weather is good this morning," he said to Mamman, who was walking by his side.

"Yes, it is good for flight," Mamman replied. "The way it rained last night, I thought it would continue this morning. It rains almost all year round in this city."

"Is that so?"

"Yes," Mamman said. "But it's sad that we have only a few farmers. Everyone wants to move about in suits and work in offices."

They reached a small blue air force jet. The lad carrying Chief Ousmane's luggage climbed in, while the chief stood to exchange parting words with his host.

"Thank you for your kindness, Mamman. Thank you." Chief Ousmane hugged Mamman, patting him several times on the back. He broke the hug, but Mamman held onto his hands, wearing a concerned look.

"You were put in prison because of your struggle, Chief," Mamman said. "I do not wish to see you suffer again. Please take things easy and don't make trouble. Don't listen to any troublemaker, please. I assure you that you will be victorious. I will be meeting you again soon. I promise."

"Thank you, Mamman," Chief Ousmane said, and he entered the plane. There were five air force officers inside. They saluted him as he stepped in. He shook hands with them in turn. "Assalaamu 'alaykum, officers," he greeted.

It felt strange that military officers would salute him. One of them ushered him to a seat in the front and helped him buckle his seat belt. They took off.

Chief Ousmane held fast to his armrests as the plane soared into the sky. It seemed to be struggling to maintain its balance. Through the window, he saw the terminal, vehicles, roads and human beings growing smaller and smaller. Wouldn't the plane fall on them? He looked into the faces of the officers in the plane and saw that they were all calm in their seats, most of them chatting in whispers. He heaved and made a silent prayer.

The plane stabilised and glided noiselessly through the sky. He started thinking about Masara town. Were the people aware that he was on his way? Had another person been appointed chief of the town by the emir of Tarayya? He thought of his wife and children and their lovely faces. He felt sad that he wouldn't see Mahmoud. His grave would be amongst his first ports-of-call. He took out a cola nut and took a bite.

"Would you like some snacks, sir? Or would you prefer jollof rice?" a female officer asked him. She was holding a tray.

"I will have the snacks, my daughter." He smiled. She gave him a parcel, a bottle of juice and another of water. As soon as she left, he set them all on the seat next to him and looked out into the clouds, resuming his thoughts. The pilot announced that they'd be landing in Tarayya city in a few minutes. The plane descended gradually until it touched down and taxied to a stop.

One of the officers carried his luggage for him, and they climbed out. It had been cold on the plane, so the sun felt hot. He was led into a blue air force car. They sped out of the airport. A chase car followed them, blaring its siren as they drove away.

They met a crowd as soon as they were off the airport grounds. People of all ages and genders surrounded his vehicle as if they were flies attacking a ripe mango. They couldn't touch him because the windows were shut.

"Don't open the window, Chief," the bodyguard in the front seat advised him.

Chief Ousmane smiled and waved at the people. The car moved slowly and with difficulty through the crowd. People lined the streets of the city, waving at him.

They got out of the city and began the journey to Masara town. Everything looked the same as it had before his imprisonment. Trailers and lorries travelled with huge bags of maize and other farm produce; Fulani herdsmen drove their cattle under the scorching sun; and the villages they drove through every now and then were as calm as they had always been.

They arrived at a checkpoint. The soldiers manning it stopped them, saluted and peeped into their car. "Assalaamu 'alaykum, Chief Ousmane!" they greeted. They smiled till their teeth showed.

"Wa'alaykumus salaam!" Chief Ousmane raised his hand at them.

The soldiers peeped into the chase car, and then they allowed them to go.

Every few kilometres, the cars arrived at checkpoints and the same procedures were repeated. Why had the checkpoints been put in place? And why would a military convoy be stopped? Would criminals move about in such a convoy?

The driver took a turn that was not familiar to Chief Ousmane.

"Are you not taking me to Masara?" Chief Ousmane asked.

"We are, Chief," the driver replied. "We are just taking a different route. The rebels have taken over the towns along the route you are used to."

Chief Ousmane's mouth dropped open. "Rebels? Which rebels?"

The bodyguard looked back at him. "Are you not aware of the Kwaskwarima?" he asked. "Are you not their patron, Chief?"

"What are you talking about, my friend?"

"You mean you don't know anything about the Kwaskwarima?"

"*Wallahi*, I don't," Chief Ousmane swore. "Who are they?"

"But they've been asking for your release. It was their demands that led to your release! I can't believe you don't know this, Chief. I can't!"

Chief Ousmane relaxed back into his seat. He chewed his cola nut. Its bitterness was sharp. "What are the rebels fighting for?" he asked.

"They don't want the marriage ban. They want Leader Gambo to leave," the driver explained.

"Are there rebels in Masara?"

"There are," the bodyguard replied. "But it is still under government control."

Chief Ousmane took a deep breath.

By afternoon, they'd reached the train station at Masara's outskirts. Soldiers were everywhere. People started chasing Chief Ousmane's car. They grew in number gradually. Chief Ousmane observed them to see if anyone resembled a rebel. They carried no guns, cutlasses or bows and arrows. They jumped and cheered. Some climbed the boot and bonnet of his car.

Tears rolled out of Chief Ousmane's eyes.

"They missed you, Chief," the bodyguard remarked.

"Yes, they did!" Chief Ousmane cried. He sighted some of the elders of the town, and he wound down his window. Tens of hands found their way into the car and struggled to shake his hand. He threw his door open and climbed out, shaking the elders' hands in turn. "Assalaamu 'alaykum! Good to see you again!" he greeted them.

His voice was almost drowned by the people's cheers. "Wa'alaykumus salaam!" the elders responded. "You are welcome back, Chief. You are welcome!"

The crowd scrambled to shake his hands, as if the hands were money being shared. Before he knew it, he was up in the people's hands. They threw him into the air and caught him upon landing. They threw him again and again and he wished they'd stop. When they did, they clamoured to hug him. He hugged as many of them as he could, thanking them for their love and support.

He turned to go back to his car. The soldiers cleared the way for him. Tens of journalists met him at the car. They pushed their microphones and recorders at his mouth. The photographers flashed their cameras a dozen times, while the journalists threw hundreds of questions at him.

"What do you have to say about your release, Chief Ousmane?"

"Will you continue to struggle for the repeal of the marriage ban?"

"Were you tortured in prison?"

"Did you reach any agreement with the government?"

Chief Ousmane waved at them.

The soldiers sent them away.

"We shall see you tomorrow, Chief!" one of the elders said. "We will allow you to rest for today. You are welcome back!"

"Thank you, thank you," Chief Ousmane replied, climbing into the car. A soldier slammed the door shut. Chief Ousmane directed the driver to his house.

His neighbourhood was quiet and empty. Some goats rested at the entrance to his house. It looked as if they had taken over the house. His breathing was rapid as he climbed out of the car. One of the soldiers followed him with his luggage. He marched into his zaure.

There was a girl inside. Her eyes met his.

His mouth dropped open.

She jumped to her feet. "Baba!" she cried. She didn't run towards him. She retreated backwards towards the door that led into the harem. The look on her face was that of horror and disbelief. The baby in her hands wiggled and began to cry.

"Sa'adiya!" he cried. "Whose baby is that?"

She ran into the house.

He followed after her.

17

Babawo took a long gulp from a bottle of Lute Lager Beer. He dropped the bottle onto the table, licking his lips. The People's Drinking Place was filled to capacity. The drinkers came from grasslands, farmlands and markets within the town. One could tell them from their outfits. The farmers wore tattered T-shirts and awkwardly buttoned threadbare shirts. They had stains of wet soil on their feet and clothes. The herdsmen wore sleeveless shirts and had a pile of hair on their heads. Some of them had their wide woven hats hanging from their necks. Others had their goads on the table before them.

The shed was enveloped in yellow light that came from the bulbs hanging from the zinc roof. The music was loud, so the men had to raise their voices as they chatted. The smell of beer hung in the cool night air.

Babawo took another long gulp and dropped his bottle onto the table again.

"You don't like to drink from a cup?" his companion at the table asked him.

The man was a stranger. Babawo always sat with strangers when he drank. He preferred their stories to those of people whose lives he was already familiar with.

"No," Babawo replied. "I prefer to gulp." He took another gulp. "How did you get that cut on your cheek?" Babawo asked the man.

The man smiled, causing the cut to gap wider. He lit a cigarette and began to smoke it. "A woman didn't like the price I offered to pay her," he said. "We had a fight and she used a knife on me."

"Didn't you agree on the price before you did it?"

"No. I always bargain after I'm done."

"That is stupid of you!"

"No, it's not." The man puffed out some smoke.

"It is. If you had bargained at the beginning, you wouldn't have fought."

"I find it easier to bargain at the end. At times, I run away and don't pay anything." The man laughed.

Two men joined them at the table. They greeted them and continued with their discussion. They spoke excitedly in hushed tones. They barked at the waiter to bring them cat flesh pepper soup and Lute Lager beer. The waiter served them and left to attend to others.

The men paid more attention to their discussion than to their food. They'd pause their eating, thrash out a point and then tear big morsels of flesh with their yellow teeth, chewing and talking. Their voices grew louder so that Babawo could hear them.

"The women at the Market Enjoyment Room are better, my friend. They charge less and they are always smiling," one said.

"I don't agree with you. Do you find girls like Asabe over there – Asabe that works at the Enjoyment Room opposite this shed?" the other said.

"Is she not that black one with tiny hands?"

"Her blackness is very nice, my friend. Do you not see the way she shines with that nice-smelling ointment she rubs on?"

"Ah! You can see many better girls than her in the Market Enjoyment Room – many! The ones opposite this shed are mostly short and thin. In the Market Enjoyment Room, you can find all sorts – black, fair, fat, thin – any type, my friend. Many of them come from Kwakwa village. You know they are beautiful."

"I think I will follow you there tonight. You said they are cheap, right?"

"Yes, they are. I'll take you there. I'll pay for you, since it's your first time. You'll never go anywhere else after that – I tell you."

They licked their fingers clean and stormed out of the shed.

Babawo paid attention to the music, tossing his head to and fro. Though the song was in English and he could not understand it, he loved it. Its beats were fast and they filled him with energy. He preferred it to the ones that were slow and made him feel sleepy.

"Were you among those that received Chief Ousmane today?" Babawo's companion asked him.

"Is he back?"

"You didn't hear? He came back in the afternoon. They said two fine military cars brought him. A crowd received him. I'm surprised you missed such a big crowd."

"I was at the bush, training with the Kwaskwarima throughout today."

"Ah! So you are one of us!" The man saluted and shook hands with Babawo. He told him how he'd missed the day's training because he'd had to attend to some domestic issues. He told him about how the whole town had been converted into a partying ground upon Chief Ousmane's return.

"It's good the government is listening to us," Babawo said.

"It is better for them."

"Two years in jail is a long time!"

"It is. It's sad that, after those years, he is returning home to see that his son is dead and his daughter raped." The man emptied his bottle of Sunshine Stout into his plastic cup. He sipped.

"Rape is the thing that is helping us these days. I was the one who cornered that his daughter. I couldn't help it," Babawo said.

The stout in the man's mouth spurted out, splashing on Babawo's face. The man did not apologise. His eyes were fixed on Babawo as if he were looking at a jinn.

Babawo cleaned off the mess from his face with the hem of his shirt. "Don't be shocked because I did it, my friend," he said. "I miss my wife. She died during the stampede Governor Coulibaly's rally caused two years ago – she and my only son. I'm not happy with Governor Coulibaly at all! He killed my wife, and now he and the leader don't want me to take another wife."

The man found his voice. "You raped Chief Ousmane's daughter?"

"Tell me the truth, my brother: in these two years since the ban began, haven't you raped?" Babawo asked.

The man rested his elbows on the table and buried his forehead in his hands.

"Confess to me, my friend," Babawo insisted.

"Why would you rape innocent girls, and Chief Ousmane's daughter for that matter?" the man asked. "Do you know that she's given birth? You've given Chief Ousmane a bastard grandchild, and you're happy!"

"Listen, I had no choice. The Enjoyment Rooms are expensive. I can only go there if I have money. Like this night, I'm in the mood, but the only money I have is for my breakfast tomorrow. What do you want me to do?"

The man shrugged his shoulders and took three sips. "Rape is a wicked thing." The man dropped his cup on the table. "All three of my daughters got raped. One of them died during childbirth. So I know how bad rape is."

"If you are so concerned, better go and tell the government to allow us to get married!"

"Well, that's what the two of us are trying to do, by joining the Kwaskwarima," the man said.

Babawo raised his bottle to see how much beer remained. He drank it up in five gulps. Throwing the bottle onto the ground, he walked out of the shed without bidding his companion goodnight.

The Enjoyment Room across the road was a three-storey building with four big rooms on each floor. Babawo stood in front of it. Music blared from all its rooms. Some of the rooms had their lights on, while others were dark. Women in skimpy clothes posed around the building. Some were chatting with men. He counted the money in his pocket, shook his head and walked away.

The music receded as he walked further away. Soon, he was walking on the cold quiet streets. Only a few pedestrians and cyclists were in sight. The only source of light was the moon.

He reached a deserted dirt road. The chirping of crickets was perhaps the only sound in the air. He sat on a small rock, brought out some Indian hemp rolled in a piece of paper, lit it and began to smoke.

A boy and a girl appeared from around a corner. They were each carrying a tub on their heads. They were barely teenagers. He threw the roll of hemp onto the ground and crushed it under his foot. He pushed his leg in front of the boy and made him trip. The boy yelled as he fell. The maize grains in the tub he was carrying spilled onto the ground.

"Why did you do that?" he cried. "Why?"

"Sorry, poor boy! It was a mistake." Babawo stood up and looked down at the grains. "You'll have to pack them back into the tub. You're going to the mill, *ko*?"

"Yes," the boy replied, squatting to pack the grains.

The girl squatted to assist him.

"Oh, girl!" Babawo cried. "The mill will soon close. You need to keep going. Your brother will meet you on the way."

"My father said we should walk together. There are bad men on the way," the girl said.

"I will escort you," Babawo said. "I will show you a shortcut to the mill. I won't allow any man to trouble you."

The girl hesitated. She looked at her brother. He was busy with his task.

Babawo helped her put her tub back on her head. "Let's go, girl. You have nothing to fear," he assured her.

He made the girl walk in front of him. He gave her directions: "Turn left. Now go straight. We are going right, now."

They came to a bush with tall trees.

"This is not the road I know," the girl complained.

"I know it is not. This is the shortcut I told you about," Babawo replied. He took the tub from her to relieve her.

When they'd gone deep into the bush, he dropped the tub on the ground and grabbed her arm. She shrieked and struggled to get free, but he grabbed her other arm. Something heavy hit his head. He screamed and fell to the ground, holding his head. Several blows from heavy clubs hit his face, stomach and in between his legs. He fought back with blows and kicks. He broke free and took to his heels. He ran homewards.

He saw his neighbour, Sergeant Dauda, sitting on a bench in front of his own house, wearing a singlet and trousers.

"Good evening, Babawo," Sergeant Dauda greeted him.

Babawo darted into his house. It was a one-room apartment. A mattress lay to his left and a table to his right. The room was filled with the odour of dirty clothes and Indian hemp. Dark cobwebs created ugly designs against the white walls. The room had only one window, so it was stuffy. The bulb gave little light.

Babawo bent over and panted. Blood dripped from his head onto the floor. His shirt was soaked with blood. He took off his shirt and went outside to wash the blood from his head and torso at a tap.

"What happened to you?" Sergeant Dauda asked as Babawo washed himself.

"I fell," Babawo said. He closed the tap and returned to his room.

"You fell? Where?" Sergeant Dauda followed him into his room. He examined his wound closely. "Kai! This is not a fall! See the cut and the swelling on your head and face? What happened?"

"It was robbers," Babawo said, tying a piece of cloth around his head.

"Robbers? Where did they attack you?"

"It was in the bush close to the brewery."

"I have never heard of robbers around that place. None of my colleagues has reported any such case from there before. Are you sure it's not the vigilantes that look out for rapists? I know they hide in the bushes."

"No, no, no! They can't be the ones." Babawo waved his palms.

Sergeant Dauda looked at him suspiciously through the corner of his eye. "Babawo," he said, "are you sure you've not been troubling those girls again?"

Babawo took a deep breath. He looked down. "Do you blame me, Dauda?" he cried. "Governor Coulibaly killed my wife and my son. Now he is telling me not to get married – he and the leader. What kind of life do you want me to live?"

"Stop raping girls, Babawo! I advise you."

"I won't!" Babawo swore. "I will continue to satisfy my desires. And when the Kwaskwarima invade Tarayya city, I will kill Governor Coulibaly for killing my wife. I will kill Leader Gambo too, when we invade Birni."

PART III

THE HUSBAND

18

Professor Garba was eating jollof rice, turkcy and salad in the VIP section of a hotel restaurant. Eating with him was Mr Salman, a diplomat from the Middle East whom he had befriended some years ago during an international conference in New York. They had run into each other that night on the hotel grounds.

The hotel was in the finest section of Dakar. Professor Garba had been on official tours of several West African cities for the past two weeks.

A few other people sat eating at some of the tables around Professor Garba and his friend. The neatly dressed waitresses attended to them cheerfully.

After Professor Garba and Mr Salman had finished their food, they sipped orange juice, chatting and laughing.

"My king just recently deployed me to this country as his ambassador," Mr Salman began, switching from a lively discussion they had been having about Hasoumiya's maize wealth. "This is my first posting to Africa. I can see that your continent is blessed with a lot of good things."

"Really? What have you seen that makes you so excited?"

"Oh, there are so many things: the rivers, the wildlife, the zoos – many things. My eldest son saw something he loved most of all just last month. It has excited everyone in the family. He talks about it constantly."

"I see. And what is that?"

"He saw a girl – a nice girl!" Mr Salman announced. They both burst out laughing. "He's been working for some years now with an oil company in my country," he continued. "He had just travelled down here to pay me a visit when he stumbled upon this girl at a bank. The good news now is that they'll be getting married next week."

"That's great!"

"Yes, indeed! I hope you will stay behind to attend the wedding. It's just seven days away."

Professor Garba took a sip from his glass, set it down on the table and shook his head. "I'm sorry, but I won't be able to make it," he said. "I would love to attend, but I have to go back to Hasoumiya before—"

"Oh, that's not a problem. I understand."

"My leader wants me back in Birni in three days' time," Professor Garba persisted. "I wish the people in my country could get married just like your son. But Leader Gambo has banned them from marriage for five years."

"Ah! That's true. I have been following the news. But you have such an insane dictator! What good would a ban on marriage do for your country?"

"Nothing!" Professor Garba said, picking a serviette from the table and cleaning his mouth with it. "Absolutely nothing, but rebellion. I'm sure you've heard of the Kwaskwarima rebels. They've taken over most of the Hausa-Sahara region, where I come from."

"I learned they want to unseat Leader Gambo. Can they really do that?"

"Who knows? We are in a big mess!"

"You are part of the government. Why can't you advise your president to lift the ban?"

"I love my life, Mr Salman. I wouldn't do that!"

"Too bad!" Mr Salman drank up the juice in his glass. He glanced at his wristwatch. "I would love to ask more questions, but I've got an appointment to keep right now."

"Oh! We've had a nice visit together already," Professor Garba said.

Professor Garba followed Mr Salman to his car in the parking lot and bade him goodnight. He retired to his hotel room and changed into his pyjamas. He made some tea, and sat at the reading table to study the next year's budget of the Hausa-Sahara region. Governor Coulibaly had submitted it to him before he had left Hasoumiya. He sipped his tea as he studied.

He grabbed the phone receiver and dialled Governor Coulibaly's number. They exchanged pleasantries and began to discuss the budget.

"Coulibaly," Professor Garba said, "I asked you to include the drainage system for Masara town in the budget but you didn't do that. Why not?"

"Sir, you know the leader has not been willing to do anything for the town since its invasion," Governor Coulibaly replied.

"Should we allow that to continue? Your mother is from that town. I am from that town. We shouldn't neglect our people."

"Okay, sir. We'll update the budget."

"Thank you. How about Zaidou? Why haven't you released him yet?" Professor Garba asked. He had been thinking of how to get Zaidou released. He'd talked to the prison and police bosses. They'd both said that they couldn't release him. The previous month, he'd spoken to Governor Coulibaly.

"Sir, I told you that Zaidou is under investigation," Governor Coulibaly said. "He tried to kill me when I went to a rally in Masara. You saw everything."

"How long will it take you to finish your investigation? This man has been in jail for over two years now!"

"It's not my job to do the investigation, sir. That's for the police to do."

"Listen, Coulibaly: Zaidou is innocent. I have done my own investigation and I know this. Get him released immediately. If you don't do that, I won't recommend the leader to approve your budget."

"You are blackmailing me to do something illegal, Professor. And I won't do it. I must see that the investigation is concluded before I do anything. This man tried to kill me, so I won't let him go free." Governor Coulibaly hung up the phone.

Professor Garba paced round his room. He sat down again and sipped his tea. He dialled Zakiyyah's number.

"Hello!" Zakiyyah greeted him.

"Hello, Zakiyyah. This is Baba."

"Masaa'ul khair, Baba."

"Masaa'un noor, Zakiyyah," Professor Garba replied in a dull voice. "How is Lagos?"

"Fine, Baba. I just got home from work."

"Good."

"Are you still in Dakar?"

"Yes. But I will be back in Masara soon. I just spoke with Governor Coulibaly about Zaidou. He said he is still investigating him for attempted murder."

"When will this investigation end, Baba? Zaidou has been in jail for two years now!" Zakiyyah cried.

Professor Garba told her that he'd said the same thing to the governor. He pleaded with her to be patient.

"Haven't you gotten another suitor in Lagos?" he asked her.

"Baba, I won't betray Zaidou," Zakiyyah said. "I love him. I promised to marry him. So I will wait for his release."

Professor Garba ended the call. He dialled Kauthar's number and they talked about life in Dakar, his work, Zakiyyah and his return in two days' time.

◄○►

In the morning, Professor Garba set out to attend his last engagement in Dakar. It was a conference of West African countries with the theme of "Poverty Reduction and Economic Empowerment in West Africa: The Role of Agriculture and Education." Ministers and even heads of state were in attendance. He gave a speech about the elaborate and revolutionary agricultural policies Leader Gambo had been implementing in Hasoumiya since he'd come to power. He talked about how the country had developed through those policies. The applause he received was thunderous.

The conference ended at 2 p.m., and he went to his chauffeur-driven Peugeot in the parking lot. As he sank into the back seat, a Ghanaian minister approached him. Professor Garba came out of the car and exchanged pleasantries with him.

"Your speech made a lot of sense. It was very educative!" The minister smiled broadly.

"Thank you very much, sir," Professor Garba said.

"If I might ask: is Hasoumiya really experiencing the kind of development you talked about? I'm asking because the things we are hearing about your country are not nice at all! I've been hearing in the news that you people are not allowed to even get married!"

Professor Garba winced and scratched his neck. "Well, you know many of those journalists tell a lot of lies. They mix fact with fiction and feed it to the world. Part of the things you heard might be true, and others might be false."

"I see. So all those stories about marriage we've been hearing are actually—"

"I'm so sorry, sir, but I have to rush somewhere. We'll get to talk at another conference." Professor Garba returned into the car and the chauffer drove off.

◄○►

Professor Garba's convoy of four cars arrived at his house in Masara town and parked at the parking lot, one beside the other. They were all black Mercedes in mint condition.

An officer from his security detail opened the door for him. He climbed out, holding a briefcase. He was dressed in a white babban riga, a blue cap and black shoes. He walked through the paved parking lot and entered the house.

No one was in the sitting room downstairs. It was there that he usually received visitors. Adam and Moukhtar often sat there to watch television when he had no visitors. He had thought they would have run out to receive him upon his arrival as they usually did, but he remembered that it was only half past one in the afternoon and they were still at school. The maids were chatting and washing the dishes in the kitchen. He climbed up the stairway.

Kauthar was sitting alone on one of the couches in the sitting room. She was sipping some orange juice from a glass cup as she watched a cookery program. The woman on TV was pouring some chopped vegetables into a pot.

"Kauthar!" he called.

Kauthar shook with fright. Some of the juice spilled and poured on her black dress. "Oh, habibi!" she cried. "I didn't hear your footsteps." She got up and gave him a hug. She took his briefcase from him and placed it on the couch where she had been sitting. "Welcome back. How was your journey?"

"It was fine," Professor Garba replied, sitting down on the couch beside her. He didn't return her smiles.

"Let me get you some juice, habibi," she said, pecking him on the cheek.

Professor Garba continued to frown.

Kauthar came back with the juice on a tray and set it on the stool by his side. "I've brought you *fura da nono* as well. You're looking tired and sad. You'll feel better when you drink it," she said. She sat down by his side again.

He could feel her staring at him as he listlessly drank his fura da nono.

"You look worried, habibi. What's the problem?" she asked him.

He took three more sips from his drink and set down the cup on the tray. "Shouldn't I be worried, honey?" he asked. "I'm sure you're worried too. Just look at what Leader Gambo has turned the country into – a mess. People have asked me very embarrassing questions everywhere I've gone. I'm ashamed that even my daughter is suffering from this man's madness!"

"That's sad, indeed." Kauthar said.

"I wish Zakiyyah would listen to me and marry someone else. I don't think I can get Governor Coulibaly to release Zaidou. He is determined to destroy him, for reasons best known to him."

"Why don't you talk to his uncle, Chief Ousmane? He's back in town. I'm sure the governor will listen to him."

"Great idea, sweetie!" He pecked her on the forehead. "I had wanted to see him tomorrow to welcome him back. But I'll see him right away!" He rose to his feet.

"You've not had lunch yet, habibi!" Kauthar cried.

He ignored her and ran down the stairs, continuing outside to his car.

◄○►

When he arrived at Chief Ousmane's house, Professor Garba found its zaure full of people. He could tell that they were town and city chiefs from their elaborately embroidered babban rigas and white turbans. The chiefs stood up to receive him.

"Assalaamu 'alaykum, Professor! Good to see you!" Chief Ousmane cried.

"Good to see you too, Chief Ousmane! We thank Allah for your release." Professor Garba and his host fell into a warm embrace. The professor shook hands with all the chiefs.

"There's roasted mutton and tuwo for you. Help yourself, please," Chief Ousmane invited, pointing at the food as soon as they'd all been seated.

"Thank you, Chief,' Professor Garba said.

Chief Ousmane started in to tell him about his horrible experiences in detention. He thanked Allah that he'd survived. "It's not new to me," he remarked. "I survived a worse punishment when I was detained for five years after the invasion of this town. I am not surprised I survived this one."

The chiefs nodded and hummed in agreement.

Professor Garba was amazed that Chief Ousmane was looking strong and healthy.

When the chief began to speak about the condition in which he found Masara after his return, his voice became shaky. "I came back and saw that my daughter had been raped. Professor Garba, your government has harmed us all! Yet they have released me on the condition that I would stop challenging it. They want me to tell the people to be patient with the marriage ban. I can't keep quiet while people are being treated badly!"

Professor Garba consoled Chief Ousmane. He advised him to abide by the conditions of his release to avoid being arrested again. "I would like to see you privately, Chief Ousmane," he requested.

Chief Ousmane followed him outside. They stood under the mango tree. Professor Garba told the chief about Zaidou's arrest and about Governor Coulibaly's refusal to release him. He told him that Zaidou was Zakiyyah's fiancé, and that they planned to get married in Lagos.

"I thought you said your daughter wouldn't get married because of the ban," Chief Ousmane said.

"To tell you the truth, Chief Ousmane, I don't support the ban," Professor Garba confessed.

"Subhanallah! What made you change your mind?"

"That has always been my opinion."

"Alhamdulillah! The important thing is that you know the truth, my friend." Chief Ousmane patted Professor Garba on his shoulder.

"I want a favour from you, Chief Ousmane," Professor Garba said. "I want you to ask your nephew, Coulibaly, to release Zaidou. I believe he will listen to you. I'm sorry I'm making this request at this time when you deserve some rest. We have to act fast, because I suspect the governor wants to hang him."

"I know Zaidou is innocent. He deserves to be free. I will talk to Coulibaly. But remember: I told you that he is stubborn. That was why I didn't want him to be governor. I will still do my best. I will go to Tarayya tomorrow to see him."

"Thank you, Chief Ousmane." Professor Garba shook the chief's hand. "I will be going to Tarayya tomorrow also. We'll go together."

19

Chief Ousmane picked up his radio from the table and sat cross-legged at the centre of his zaure. The sun had just risen. There was enough light for him to monitor the pointer as he tuned the radio. He turned the knob carefully, passing one station after another. Many of the stations didn't have clear audio and they spoke in foreign tongues, especially French from the neighbouring Niger Republic. At last, he caught the station he wanted. It was clear and audible. A man was reciting a poem in Hausa:

> Our hearts thirst for love –
> The men and women amongst us.
> From the time of Adam, we've had this thirst.
> We've slaked it at the banks of our spouses.
> We've slaked it since the time of Adam,
> Until the time of Gambo, the time of the tyrant!
> Iron gates have been placed at the doors of our hearts
> And love cannot enter anymore, though it knocks
> so hard!

The recitation was interrupted by the theme music of the 7 a.m. news. The chief increased the volume. The newscaster was a man, and he read out the headlines, pausing after each one. All the headlines had one theme – the rebellion.

"And now the news in full," the newscaster said. "The Commander of the Kwaskwarima, Colonel Kaita, has announced that his men have taken control of the towns of Baladi and Gona in the Hausa-Sahara region. He announced this at a news conference yesterday in Baladi. He said that, although the government have released the Kwaskwarima's godfather, Chief Ousmane, his troops would continue to fight until the government reverses the ban on marriage and—"

"Assalaamu 'alaykum, Chief," a voice interjected.

Chief Ousmane looked up and saw his houseboy stepping in. "Wa'alaykumus salaam!" Chief Ousmane replied. "It's good you are early today, as always. Come in and listen to what these men are saying."

The boy came in, squatted before the chief and listened. He wore neither a smile nor a frown.

"Do their words make any sense to you? Have you seen any of those rebels visiting me?" Chief Ousmane asked.

"No, Chief. I don't believe them."

"Yet they call me their godfather!" Chief Ousmane switched off the radio. "How is your father?"

"He has joined the Kwaskwarima."

"Oh, that's true. You told me yesterday," Chief Ousmane said. He also remembered that the houseboy had said that his younger siblings had stopped attending school since their father's disappearance. Chief Ousmane had decided to increase the houseboy's wage.

"I want you to take me to Professor Garba's house on my motorcycle. I will be travelling to Tarayya city with him today." Chief Ousmane gave the houseboy the key to the small room beside the entrance to the zaure, where he kept his motorcycle.

"Okay, Chief." The houseboy collected the key and went out.

Chief Ousmane switched on the radio again. He produced a pink cola nut from his breast pocket, took a small bite and chewed.

He thought of how he could distance himself from the Kwaskwarima. Should he talk to the police? Or should he hold a press conference? Perhaps he should consult with the chiefs of the region. They were wise men.

Four cars ground to a halt in front of his zaure. A policeman stepped out of a chase car. He opened the door of one of the Mercedes, and Professor Garba climbed out.

Chief Ousmane stood up to receive him. "Assalaamu 'alaykum, Professor," he greeted him. "I was about to come to your house."

"Wa'alaykumus salaam, Chief! We have to hurry up. I have a meeting in Tarayya with General Oumar."

Chief Ousmane grabbed his leather bag, which had been by his side, and walked outside with Professor Garba. He asked the houseboy to return the motorcycle, climbed into the car with the professor and they took off.

"I heard that the Kwaskwarima have captured Baladi and Gona," Chief Ousmane said.

"Yes. Very sad."

"Do you think the government can defeat the rebels? They seem to be too strong to be destroyed!"

Professor Garba took off his spectacles. "We underestimated them, Chief Ousmane. Their leaders are military defectors, and they have support from foreign governments."

"Subhanallah!"

"The good thing is that they're only strong in this region. Birni and the Savannah-Fula regions are still in our control."

"Good! Ma'sha'Allah!"

"General Oumar is working hard to defeat them. He's determined to crush them all! The meeting I'm attending with him is all about how to stop them. Do you know that he was the one who advised the leader to release you?"

"Is that so?"

"He did. Unfortunately, the Kwaskwarima have not stopped fighting."

"I think General Oumar is a good man," Chief Ousmane remarked. "I wish he were our leader and not General Gambo."

"Everybody speaks of his kindness. I think I know him better than anyone else. I work with him closely. If not for him, Leader Gambo would have made this country worse than it is. He's blocked many evil things the leader would have done – assassinations and wicked policies!"

"Really?" Chief Ousmane asked.

Professor Garba told him about how General Oumar had been lobbying the leader to forgive the people and end the marriage ban. He had always argued that that was the only solution to the rebellion, but the leader had refused.

They came to a village about a hundred kilometres away from Masara. Some herdsmen drove their cattle across the road. They stopped to allow them to pass. The cattle crossed the road slowly and with poise, unaware that they were delaying travellers.

Apart from the herdsmen and their flock, no one seemed to be around the tiny village. Its mud huts were empty and deserted. Some of them were burnt – their thatched roofs had been reduced to ashes and their walls had all turned black.

"There was a battle in this village some weeks ago," Professor Garba revealed. "The rebels took over the village and conducted forced marriages. They raped and killed many of the villagers who refused to marry them. Soldiers came and drove them away."

"Where are the villagers now?" Chief Ousmane asked.

"They've all gone. This is a sacked town. Who would want to return to this kind of place?"

They continued with their journey as soon as the road was clear.

"You mean you risk your life by traveling this road every week, just to see your family?" Chief Ousmane asked.

Professor Garba put on his glasses. "I brought my family to Masara so that they can know their culture. They've lived all their lives abroad. But I can't continue to leave them in Masara now. It's dangerous, as you've said. I'm moving them to Birni."

"Better, Professor. As a government official, you are a big target for the rebels."

"Yes, indeed."

"I tell you, Professor, I won't allow those rebels to continue to do their wickedness in my name! They shouldn't do that simply because I was the one who began the struggle for freedom."

"Don't worry, my friend. This will pass, just like all your past troubles have come and gone! Trust me. I will help you out of it."

Their five-hour journey ended at noon. Tarayya city had developed dramatically since the time Chief Ousmane had attended the Teacher Training College there, four decades ago. With its beautiful network of roads, roundabouts and parks, it was now just as beautiful as Birni. Birni had more skyscrapers, though.

"I'll get you a hotel close to Governor Coulibaly's office. That will make your movements easy tomorrow," Professor Garba said.

"Ma'sha'Allah! That's nice of you, Professor." Chief Ousmane unwound his turban and wound it up again, so that it looked nicer. They reached Mountain Top Hotel. It was a lofty structure with four wings.

"Mamman is in this city too," Professor Garba said. "He'll be attending the meeting I am having with General Oumar today. He will be in touch with you after the meeting. You'll have a nice discussion. Trust me."

"Thank you, Professor." Chief Ousmane was happy at the thought of meeting Mamman again.

"I'll make arrangements for you to see the governor tomorrow. But please, be polite to him. I know he is your nephew, but you need to be polite if you are to get him to release Zaidou."

"Have no fears, Professor. I know how to handle him," Chief Ousmane said. As the chief climbed out of the car, Professor Garba told him that he'd be flying to Birni after his meeting with General Oumar.

"My driver will take you back to Masara tomorrow," Professor Garba said.

"Thank you, Professor." Chief Ousmane entered the hotel lobby.

◄○►

Chief Ousmane had just ended his 'Isha prayer when he heard knocks on the door of his room. Looking up at the clock, he saw that it was already 8:15 p.m.

The knocks sounded again. He put on his turban in front of the dressing mirror and sprayed perfume on his babban riga. He opened the door. "Ah! Assalamu 'alaykum, Mamman," he cried, embracing his friend.

"Wa'alaykumus salaam, Chief Ousmane. Good to see you again!"

Mamman was dressed in battledress. As they shook hands and exchanged pleasantries, Chief Ousmane thought he looked smarter and younger than the last time he'd seen him. They sat on the three-seater couch opposite the big well-laid bed.

"I have wanted to ask you, Mamman: how come you are heading our military as a Nigerian?"

Mamman laughed. "You see, what happened is that I left the Nigerian army to head your military. Leader Gambo invited me. I am a citizen of this country, too. My mother is from here." He crossed his legs.

He told Chief Ousmane about what he'd done to develop the country's military since he'd assumed office ten years ago. He had established its naval force and instilled discipline amongst its officers. The military now had the most modern weapons.

"The military is different today from what I met," he said. "When I came, many of the soldiers had potbellies and they couldn't march better than the secondary school students in my country. If I had not done the things I have done, the Kwaskwarima rebels would have defeated us by now."

Mamman spoke with courage. It made Chief Ousmane's blood run in his veins and made him feel like carrying a gun.

"I wish my son were alive," the chief said. "I would have made him join the army." Chief Ousmane looked down at the carpet and shook his head.

"That would have been a good idea, Chief," Mamman said. "We need more hands to fight the rebels."

"You never told me about the rebels while I was with you in Birni. Why?"

"I didn't want to discourage you from going back to your town, while that was what the rebels demanded. I wanted you back home, so that we could have peace."

"But we still don't have peace!"

"We don't, sadly." Mamman stood up and peeped out the window. He walked up and down the room and then returned to his seat. He licked his lower lip. "We are doing our best to teach the rebels some sense. But the leader doesn't want to understand that it's the marriage ban that is instigating them. It's a crazy ban to impose!"

"It is, Mamman." Chief Ousmane opened the refrigerator, brought out a bottle of water and gave it to his guest. "If you had come to Masara, I would have thrown a feast for you." He smiled.

Mamman took three quick sips and set the bottle on top of the refrigerator. He actually slammed it. He went to the window and peeped out again.

"Sit down, Mamman, please," Chief Ousmane invited.

"More than half of this region is now under the Kwaskwarima." Mamman continued to pace the room. "They say they are fighting rape, but they rape and kill wherever they go. They marry women by force."

"I heard that too. I am worried that they call me their leader, when I have no hand in their affairs."

"Yes, you don't. I know that." Mamman returned to his seat and looked Chief Ousmane in the eyes. "I know that you are not part of the Kwaskwarima because I have a lot of intelligence about you. I can tell you your story right from your childhood days."

"Hmmm!"

"Believe me. I'm the military chief. I have been trained in intelligence. There are people like Governor Coulibaly who don't have the information I have. And yet, they don't want to listen to me."

Mamman told Chief Ousmane about how stubborn Governor Coulibaly was: he supported Leader Gambo's stance to keep the marriage ban until its expiry. He had advised General Oumar to arrest Chief Ousmane again. He believed the Kwaskwarima had grown more audacious because the chief had been released.

"I am not surprised that he said all that," Chief Ousmane responded. "He respects me. But he has always been a problem child." Chief Ousmane's stomach rumbled.

"Should we go for dinner?" Mamman offered.

"Why not? I am quite hungry." Chief Ousmane laughed.

Two armed soldiers stood at the door of the room. They followed them to Mamman's car.

The barracks where Mamman lodged were not far from the hotel. His family hadn't come with him. A male cook served them dinner – fried rice, chicken, and sliced pineapple and pawpaw in crystal bowls.

"The government won't be fair to me if it arrests me again," Chief Ousmane said, pouring mango juice into his cup. "I have not broken any of the conditions of my release."

"Yes, Chief, you haven't. It's too early to say. General Oumar has never believed that you have a hand in the rebellion." Mamman was chewing excitedly, cutting a piece from the chicken on his china plate. He paused. "General Oumar is a good man. He likes you."

"Is that so?"

"He does. He's a lucky young man – a general at 32 years!"

"That's quite young." Chief Ousmane sipped his juice.

"Indeed," Mamman agreed.

Leader Gambo had upgraded General Oumar's rank from Colonel upon his appointment as the Deputy Leader seven years ago.

"Now, Chief Ousmane," Mamman began, "I think you should be the leader of this country."

Chief Ousmane chuckled.

"I mean it, Chief." Mamman hit the table with his fist. The cutlery clinked in the empty china plates.

Chief Ousmane stared at him. "Well, I am not a politician," he said. "And you know that Leader Gambo has had a firm grip on the country for more than thirty years now. No one else has a chance."

Mamman stood from his chair and paced round the dining table, his hands crossed behind his back. His boots knocked on the floor. He stopped before Chief Ousmane, looking down at him.

"You have a chance to be the leader of your country," he said.

Chief Ousmane didn't know how to reply.

Mamman sat on the chair closest to the chief and drew closer. His face looked like that of a man who was about to cry: his facial veins bulged and his eyes were red. He spoke in whispers. "I want to tell you something very serious," he began. "I trust that you will keep it secret. I have studied you closely and from far. I want to make you the leader of this country. Do you understand?"

Chief Ousmane shook his head, his heart pounding in his chest. "No. I don't understand," he said.

"I've completed plans with trusted friends – soldiers and politicians – to remove Leader Gambo from power. The country has had enough! We've decided that you should be the one we'll install to replace him. Do you now understand, Chief?"

Chief Ousmane's heart beat even harder. He looked unblinkingly into the eyes of his host.

"You are doubtful!" Mamman observed. "But I know you trust Professor Garba. He is part of this plan. You can discuss it with him."

"Okay, Mamman, in'sha'Allah," Chief Ousmane said.

Mamman shook his hand firmly, as if a deal had been struck. Bidding him goodnight, he got a driver to take Chief Ousmane back to his hotel.

◄○►

At the government house, Chief Ousmane was taken to a room to wait for his turn to see Governor Coulibaly. Ten other VIPs sat on the spotlessly white upholstered couches. Some were reading newspapers, others were chatting, while others were buried in thoughts. All but one were natives of the region – Kanuris, Hausas and Fulanis. The odd man out was a fat white man wearing a suit and expensive black shoes that shone under the light of the ornamental fittings. His wristwatch and rings glittered too. He was holding a newspaper up to his face, as if afraid of being recognised. He suddenly sighed and put the paper down on his lap.

"I give up!" he cried in Arabic, looking at Chief Ousmane. His words had a strong English accent. "My company has been growing maize in this country for ten years, but I give up now. I can't continue!"

"Why?" Chief Ousmane asked.

The man pointed at pictures of burnt cars and charred human limbs in his paper. On top of the pictures was the headline, "Kwaskwarima Bomb Police Station". Below the pictures was the news story.

"My farms in Baladi were attacked by the rebels this week. They killed fifty of my staff," the man said, his face flushed. "And now, just look at these pictures. We don't know where their next target is."

Chief Ousmane looked away from the pictures, telling the man he was sorry for his loss. "Peace will return to our country," he assured him. "No problem in life is permanent."

"For now, I have to look for safer countries I'll put my money in. When I'm sure peace—" The man went quiet. There was a sudden look of shock on his face. "Wait, aren't you Chief Ousmane?" he cried.

"Yes, I am."

"You are the rebels' grand patron, aren't you?"

Chief Ousmane felt like he'd been struck with a sword. "I have nothing to do with them, man!" he retorted. "If I did, I wouldn't be here."

Before he or the white man could say any more, someone appeared at the door and invited Chief Ousmane to follow him. The chief was led into Governor Coulibaly's office.

20

Zakiyyah stepped into the living room of her flat. She shut the door and dropped her handbag onto the centre table, beside a white ceramic flower vase. She'd just returned home from work. She filled a glass with water from the refrigerator and sat on one of the couches. Just as she was about to take a sip, her eyes fell on the telephone sitting on the stool beside her. She set the cup on the stool, picked up the receiver and dialled home.

"Hello!" It was her mother's voice. Zakiyyah could hear the noise from the television at the background. Her mother's favourite show, *Cook and Eat*, was on.

"Hello, Mum!" Zakiyyah responded. They spoke every day, so their voices didn't have the excitement of those who'd not spoken in months. "How's everyone?"

"Fine. Are you back from work?"

"Yes. Just now."

"Ah, you're late again today."

"Yes, but not like yesterday. I came home at 9 p.m. yesterday. It's just 7 p.m."

"You're right. Make sure you get enough rest."

"Mum, is Chief Ousmane back from Governor Coulibaly's office?"

"Not yet. He should be back tomorrow."

"Tomorrow? Good. I'll come home in two days, Mum. I'll come home to receive my husband into my arms," Zakiyyah promised.

Professor Garba had told her that it would be hard for Governor Coulibaly to say no to Chief Ousmane. Since then, she had felt like a princess about to be crowned queen.

Kauthar told her that the family would be moving to Birni from Masara the following day. The rebellion was coming closer to Masara, so she should fly to Birni when coming home.

"What?" Zakiyyah cried, putting her hand to her chest and rising to her feet. "They are not fighting in Masara, are they?"

"Not yet. Have no fears. We'll be safe. Good night." Kauthar hung up the phone.

With her mother's voice gone, the flat felt full of rebels hiding in remote corners. Zakiyyah looked about the living room. How secure she would have felt if Zaidou were with her! She went to her room, brought out his framed picture from her wardrobe and looked into his eyes. It was a candid photo of himself, smiling in his shop with his sewing machine in the background. He looked handsome all the same. The sight of his smile gave her some comfort. When he'd given her the picture, it wasn't framed. She had framed it upon her arrival in Lagos. She pecked it and thought of metaphors she could use to express her feelings. Making the picture stand on her reading table, she picked up a pen and scribbled in English:

> Your twinkle I see up in the sky of the darkest night.
> I seek to fly to reach your lofty position, and to bask
> in your light.
> But the roaring tyrant and the ravenous rebels
> Chain up my feet to the earth,
> And threaten me with war and death!
> But freedom, I know, is galloping along,
> Coming to cut my chains and soothe my pains
> So that I could fly high and be with you!

She looked at the lines and wondered whether she'd expressed her feelings sufficiently. She crossed out some words and wrote synonyms she felt would rhyme better. Then she turned a new page and began to write a new poem, this time in Arabic. She stopped halfway, looked at her lover's picture again and sighed.

Leaving the picture on the table, she went to the kitchen and soaked some garri in water. She added four cubes of sugar and a handful of roasted groundnuts. The groundnuts refused to sink, as if they were protesting about being forced to cohabit with garri.

She returned to her room and began to eat her dinner. It was a quick meal she'd learnt to make from her Nigerian colleagues. Whenever she felt too tired to cook a proper meal, she'd go for it. She finished up her meal and went to bed.

The following morning, she entered her boss's office as soon as he arrived. He was the head of the Legal Department. The name on his door read "Dr A.Y. Bagobiri, Esq." On the first day she'd reported to work two years ago, he'd looked at her and asked whether she was married. She'd said yes.

"Good morning, sir," she greeted him, as she stepped into his office.

"Good morning, Zakiyyah. How are you?" He pointed at the visitor's chair.

"I'm fine, sir." Zakiyyah sat down on the chair. No sooner had she sat down than he began to tell her about a conference they would be attending in the United States in four days' time. He wanted her to write a speech for him for the event. He wanted the draft for his perusal that very day.

Zakiyyah hit her fist on his desk.

Silence filled the air. Her boss looked at her with perplexed eyes.

She waved a timid apology.

"Why did you do that?" he asked her.

"I'm sorry, sir."

"I mean, why did you do that? Is there any problem?" he asked.

Zakiyyah looked at him.

"Tell me," he demanded, "What's the problem?"

"I'll write the speech, sir. It's just that I wanted to request two weeks off. I have to travel to Hasoumiya tomorrow. It's urgent."

"You want to go on leave?" Dr Bagobiri rested his elbows on his desk, straining his eyes.

"Yes, boss. It's urgent. Please."

"What's so urgent about it?" Dr Bagobiri leaned back in his seat.

Zakiyyah told him that her fiancé was about to be released from prison. She wanted to go and meet him.

"Your fiancé? Which fiancé? I thought you told me you were married." Dr Bagobiri leaned forward again, interlocking his fingers on his desk.

Zakiyyah maintained a guilty silence.

"Okay," he said, "I'll let you go, but on the condition that you finish the speech today."

"I'll definitely finish today, sir. I promise." Zakiyyah felt like jumping around the office.

Dr Bagobiri scribbled down some points and guidelines for her. He moved to the bookshelf to his right, selected three big books and gave them to her. He topped those with some documents he picked up from his table.

Zakiyyah looked at the resources. The task before her was worse than mountain climbing! She took a deep breath, zoomed off to her table and got to work.

It was a hard speech to write, on the topic "Oil, Economic Development and the Environment: The Way Forward for Nigeria." She needed to check many things in the encyclopaedia. She tried to work as fast as possible, ignoring the temptations to contribute to the conversations of her colleagues. Their conversations were distracting. They spoke about honeymoons, local politics and office intrigues. Their loud voices were punctuated with laughter. She struggled on with her work like a labourer carrying huge sacks in the rain.

Despite her efforts, she wasn't able to finish by the time Dr Bagobiri came out of his office at 7:30 p.m. to go home. Everyone had gone.

"Are you done?" he asked her.

"No, sir. I'll be done in twenty minutes," she said.

Dr Bagobiri looked at his wristwatch and then back at her. He didn't look angry at all. He caressed his clean-shaven chin.

"If you are to start your leave tomorrow, you'll have to finish this night and give it to me," he said.

"I'll do that, sir – in twenty minutes, as I said!"

"Good. I'll wait for you." Dr Bagobiri returned to his office.

Zakiyyah wrote fast. She was used to writing fast. Professor Garba used to give her his speeches to write for him under short deadlines. He loved her write-ups. Dr Bagobiri came out, strolled around and came over to look at what she was writing. He bent down, getting closer than was comfortable. Could it be because he didn't have his glasses on? She stopped writing and frowned at him. "Could you move back, sir?" she requested.

"Sorry," he said, standing up tall. "You've always made me think you were married."

"No, I'm not, sir," Zakiyyah said, continuing to write.

"Don't you think you've been spoiling your chances of getting a suitor to replace the persecuted one you have?"

"No, I don't."

"Why was your suitor arrested?"

Zakiyyah looked up. She told him the whole story.

He hummed and nodded as he listened. "Sad story," he said. His lips formed an arc like a rainbow.

Zakiyyah read the time from the tiny face of her wristwatch. It was 8 p.m. already. She continued to write. She had about two paragraphs more. Dr Bagobiri went back into his office.

She picked up her dictionary to see whether she should use the word "risk" instead of "uncertainty" in the sentence she was forming. The dictionary was snatched from her from behind. A bottle of Moontop orange juice replaced it. It was cold. Drops of water trickled down the bottle. She looked back and saw her boss smiling at her.

"You need to relax a bit, don't you?" he said. "All work and no play makes Zakiyyah a dull girl!"

Relax? She looked about the office.

"Yeah! It's a perfect situation – only the two of us!" Dr Bagobiri gulped from his bottle of Moontop orange juice and set it down on top of the paper she'd been writing on. It created a circular patch of wetness on it. He pulled up a chair and drew uncomfortably close to her.

She drew her chair back.

"Have no fears, Zakiyyah! It's just me and you." He smiled.

She could remember vividly how, one day, she'd taken a teacup to her lips and found out that she'd poured salt into her coffee. She'd never had such shock again until now. She screamed, gave her boss a slap in the face and ran out of the office. She raced down the stairs. She ran to the parking lot, swiftly got into her car and drove to her house on Victoria Island.

◄o►

Zakiyyah collected her boarding pass and entered the plane. Few passengers were inside. Her seat was by the window, beside a white man. He was reading a newspaper.

As the plane took off, she wondered whether she would be returning to Lagos. The slap she'd given Dr Bagobiri the night before might now have cost her her job. But wasn't he the criminal? He should be the one to be sacked, not her. She had only defended herself.

As the roads, bridges and buildings of Lagos grew smaller, she wished the city goodbye. Apart from her boss's misbehaviour, she'd had a nice time in the city.

"Excuse me, ma'am," the white man beside her said. "Are you a citizen of Hasoumiya?"

"I am," Zakiyyah replied.

"Why are there so few people going to your country? The plane is so empty. Could it be because of the rebels?"

"Perhaps."

"There aren't rebels in Birni, are there?"

"I don't think so." Zakiyyah looked away. She continued to look out of the window.

The man sighed and resumed reading his newspaper.

Zakiyyah got up and searched for another seat. She saw a row of seats where no one else was sitting. She sat there and continued to look out at the white clouds.

So she was leaving Dr Bagobiri to go to the Kwaskwarima rebels? From the frying pan to the fire? She knew there was no fighting in Birni. What if the rebels struck the moment their plane landed? What if they shot their plane down?

—◄o►—

Zakiyyah's room in Birni was bigger, cosier and more beautiful than the one she had in Masara. She stood at one of its windows, looking out into the morning and noting how it coloured the atmosphere at the Alqal'ah Villa.

The villa was in the most secured part of the country because that was where Leader Gambo's palace stood. She could see the white marble palace glittering under the sun. It had domes and lofty minarets. It looked as if the architect had designed it to humiliate the Taj Mahal. And he had succeeded! The mansion from which she was looking out was Professor Garba's official residence. It was one of the several mansions on either side of the palace.

Professor Garba's office stood opposite the palace. It was a tall building made of red marble. In the green area between it and the palace was a statue of Leader Gambo wearing a battle dress. Its arms were folded across its chest. It was looking into the future with the greatest optimism.

"Stupid man!" Zakiyyah hissed. She took her eyes off the statue and looked at the great walls far ahead, which surrounded the vast grounds of the villa.

"Zakiyyah!" Moukhtar called from outside her room. "Mum says breakfast is ready."

Zakiyyah had a quick shower and went downstairs. Her parents and her four brothers were eating at the table. The air was filled with appetising aromas. Bread, bean cakes, boiled eggs, omelettes and coolers of unknown contents were arranged neatly on the table.

"Good morning, everybody," Zakiyyah greeted them grumpily. She sat beside her mother.

"Still tired from your journey, eh? We are all up before you!" Kauthar said.

"Yes, Mum." Zakiyyah stretched.

"Next time, say *ina kwana* when greeting in the morning, Zakiyyah!" Professor Garba said, pouring coffee from a flask into a mug. "You've spent three years in Masara, but none of you can speak Hausa. It's your native tongue, mind you – and not Arabic."

Even though it was a Sunday, he was dressed in a babban riga, as if he were going out to work.

"Ina kwana," Zakiyyah repeated, reaching for a plate and cutlery.

"*Lafiya lau!*" Professor Garba smiled, stirring his coffee with a teaspoon.

"But Baba, we can all speak Hausa, can't we?" Zakiyyah said.

"Yes, we can!" her brothers echoed.

"Yes, you all can. But after spending three years in Masara, you should be professors. Now let me ask you: who knows what *manjagara* means?" Professor Garba asked.

Everyone stopped eating and looked thoughtful.

Professor Garba sipped his coffee. He produced a wad of crisp new notes from his pocket and waved it in the air. "The winner gets this!" he declared.

The boys began to consult amongst themselves.

"Well, Baba, for me, I just need to be close to the answer before I win the prize," Zakiyyah said. "I spent only one year in Masara while the boys spent three!"

Professor Garba set his cup on the saucer. "Okay, go ahead."

Zakiyyah had no idea what the word meant. She tried guessing by observing the way it sounded. Did it sound more like a utensil? Or was it a type of fruit? It sounded like *mangwaro*, the mango fruit.

"It's pawpaw!" she cried.

Professor Garba almost choked over his coffee as he tried not to laugh. "Boys, any answer?" he asked, browsing their faces.

The boys spurted their answers almost simultaneously.

"Lion!"

"Beans!"

"Mountain!"

"Aeroplane!"

"Kauthar, what about you?" Professor Garba waved the wad of notes in front of his wife.

"I'm an Arab!" Kauthar smiled, pushing a morsel of fried yam into her mouth.

"The answer is 'rake'!" Professor Garba declared. "So my money goes to the winner." He pushed the money back into his pocket and sipped his coffee.

The boys protested and said that he shouldn't be the questioner and the winner at the same time; they should all get something for their guesses.

Professor Garba smiled and tossed the money at Zakiyyah, asking her to share it with her brothers.

The boys clapped and cheered.

"I'll be travelling to Tarayya this morning," Professor Garba announced with a serious look. "General Oumar has gone there again to see how the fight against the rebels is going. We'll be meeting with him over there."

"Okay, Baba," everyone replied.

"And I'll be going to Masara too because—"

"Habibi!" Kauthar cried, dropping her cutlery in her plate. "Last night you only told me you'd be going to Tarayya. Masara is too dangerous now."

"I know. I'll have to go and meet Chief Ousmane about Zaidou, remember? I'll be safe, sweetie. No one get worried, please." Professor Garba looked into the faces of his children in turn.

Zakiyyah was pleased that he had not succumbed to her mother's advice not to go to Masara. If not for the rebels, she'd have requested to follow him.

"Will you come home with Zaidou, Baba?" she asked.

"If he is released, yes." Professor Garba got up.

They all went to him to receive a peck on the forehead.

"Lest I forget, I've told your mother that you all will be going to greet Leader Gambo today. Your appointment with him is at noon. Please behave yourselves, okay? Do you hear me, Moukhtar?"

Moukhtar nodded.

Professor Garba made for the exit. They all followed him to the parking lot, waving at him as his convoy drove past the fountain and out of the huge, grey ornamental gate.

"Mum," Zakiyyah said, meeting her mother in her room, "do we really have to meet Leader Gambo?"

Kauthar was sitting on her big bed, folding some garments and arranging them into a small pile. "You're not afraid of him, are you?" Kauthar asked, continuing with her activity. "I've always told you to work on your cowardliness, Zakiyyah."

"Not that I'm afraid, Mum. It's just that we shouldn't be visiting such a bad man."

Kauthar arranged the garments into a box. "Listen, my daughter," she began. "We are now the leader's neighbours. Do you want us to be bad neighbours? Go and get ready, please. Wear your best clothes. It's 11 a.m., already."

By 11:45 a.m., everyone was ready. Zakiyyah had never seen her brothers dressed up so gorgeously. Like their father, they wore babban rigas. Kauthar was dressed in an expensive black abaya, just like Zakiyyah herself. Even though the palace was a walking distance away, they drove out in two cars.

The interior of the palace was more beautiful than its exterior. It was the most beautiful sight Zakiyyah had ever seen. Everywhere was white. It glittered from the light of the ornamental light fittings. They were made to sit in a parlour where they were served cold drinks. Zakiyyah trembled the whole time. The air conditioning made her nervousness worse. Her brothers chatted in whispers and took their drinks calmly. Their mother took a few sips too. She kept an eye on Moukhtar.

At exactly 1 p.m., a plump man dressed in a white suit came and led them into a big living room. Everything there looked, felt and smelled heavenly. The colours were white and golden – the curtains, couches and tables. Something that didn't quite look heavenly sat on a throne-like chair at the extreme left of the room. He was dark, old and had a mass of white moustache.

―◄○►―

"So tell me, Zakiyyah, what has happened now? Has Leader Gambo beaten you up?" Kauthar asked, sprinkling some spices into a pot on the gas cooker. Zakiyyah was chopping vegetables on the table while the maid washed tomatoes in the sink. The afternoon sun came in through the door that opened out to the backyard. The maid was teaching Kauthar how to prepare a porridge called *fate*. Zakiyyah had decided to join the class.

"Tell me, Zakiyyah: did Leader Gambo hurt you when we saw him yesterday?" Kauthar asked again.

Zakiyyah wished her mother would stop talking about her cowardliness in front of the maid.

"No," she muttered, chopping faster and noisily.

"You had no reason to be afraid of him," her mother said. "He is a human like you and me."

Leader Gambo had treated Zakiyyah better than he had the others. He was nice, kind and sweet. After the pleasantries, he'd ignored all the others and pestered her with questions about her work, education, likes and dislikes.

The phone in Professor Garba's living room rang. Zakiyyah rushed to get it. It was Houssein – her brother who'd just finished university in England. He'd had an accident about two months ago, leaving him with a broken leg.

"How's your leg, Houssein?" she asked.

"It's much better," he replied. "I can walk without crutches now."

"Ah! That's good news."

"My flight is tonight. I'll be arriving Birni around 9 p.m. London time."

"Great! That should be eleven p.m. Birni time. Or is it—"

The doorbell rang. Zakiyyah continued talking about the time of Houssein's arrival. The doorbell rang again, yet no one went to get it. She ended the call and got the door.

It was the plump man who had ushered them into Leader Gambo's living room the day before.

"Good afternoon, Madam," he greeted her, handing her a parcel. "This is from Leader Gambo. You're Zakiyyah, I suppose?"

"Yes."

"Good. It's for you. The leader says you should come for lunch and dinner today."

"With my family?"

"No. Only you." The man left.

Zakiyyah returned to the living room and opened the parcel with trembling hands. Jewellery? Gold and diamonds? She stared at them for some time. She unwrapped the parcel further and saw a letter. She unfolded it and read:

APPOINTMENT AS FOREIGN AFFAIRS MINISTER

Dear Zakiyyah,

Greetings!

I am, with this letter, informing you about your appointment as my minister of Foreign Affairs. This is effective a week from the date of this letter.

Accept the assurances of my best regards.

Yours sincerely,
Leader Gen. Gambo Sarajo (retired).

"Mum! Mum!" Zakiyyah screamed, unable to get off her seat.

"What is it?" Kauthar came running into the living room. The maid ran behind her.

Zakiyyah showed her mother the items.

"Where did you get these?" her mother asked.

"They are from the leader," Zakiyyah gasped.

Kauthar took the letter and read. She flushed as she read. It took her about ten minutes to read it. "I'll take them to my room," she said, wrapping everything back into the parcel. "Your father should see them when he comes back."

"The leader says I should come for lunch and dinner today."

"You are not going anywhere!" Kauthar cried.

They returned to the kitchen and worked silently. Nothing was said about anything. They continued chopping, blending, cooking and tasting.

At 2 p.m., the boys came in for lunch. Moukhtar took the *fate* eagerly. It was hot and well peppered. It caused him and the others to sweat. "What do you call this, Mum?" he asked.

"*Fate*," Kauthar replied. "Zakiyyah, you've eaten very little. Eat well, please."

Zakiyyah ate slowly. "Houssein called earlier," she announced. "He said his plane will land by 11 p.m. tonight."

"Yeeeeee!" Moukhtar and his brothers cried.

"Ah! That's good news," Kauthar said, setting her cup of water on the table. "How's his leg?"

"He says it's better."

"Good. So, everyone, we'll all be going out to the airport at 9 p.m. tonight. Do you hear me?"

"Yes, Mum," came the chorused reply.

Zakiyyah left her food and went up to her room. Standing at the window, she looked out at the palace. She looked at it for a long time. Then she lay on her bed to get some sleep.

At 9 p.m., her mother came in.

"You're not crying, are you? You should stop crying over small things, Zakiyyah. Let's go to the airport."

Was her situation a small thing? Zakiyyah wiped her tears and joined the rest of the family in the parking lot. Like their outing to the palace, they went out in two vehicles. A chase car full of bodyguards escorted them.

The parking lot at the airport was full of cars. They found somewhere to park after some hard effort. They walked towards the terminal in a single group, the bodyguards following close behind them.

It was a busy airport. People were moving up and down, attending to one flight concern or another. Two planes flew in from different countries, polluting the air with the noise of their engines. A female voice announced the arrivals over the speakers. Travel-worn passengers of all races trooped in with luggage of various sizes.

Houssein's plane landed after they'd waited for two hours. They kept an anxious lookout for him as the passengers streamed in. The number of passengers was not large, but they were of all sorts: white businessmen in suits, a couple of Rastafarians with their dreadlocks and Rasta caps, aged couples supported by their walking sticks in their feeble gaits, and young families bubbling with the excitement of adventurous tourists. None of them had a broken leg. There was no Houssein.

"He's not here!" Kauthar cried, looking about. Moukhtar began to sob. Adam asked Kauthar silly questions about plane crashes.

Zakiyyah ran out of the terminal and made for a phone booth at a remote corner. There was no queue of people waiting to use it. She grabbed the receiver and dialled Houssein's number. It rang, but there was no response. She dialled a second time, and then tried once more, getting apprehensive. Houssein didn't pick up. She slammed down the receiver and ran back towards the terminal.

Just when she was a little way from the entrance, she sighted her mother hugging Houssein. Why had it taken him so long to deplane? She smiled and ran. A plump man blocked her at the entrance – the same plump idiot from the leader's palace. His perfume smelled horribly like garlic.

"Good evening, madam!" he greeted her.

She gasped.

The man smiled. "I'm sorry," he said. "I did not intend to scare you." He pulled out an identification card from his breast pocket and flashed it before her eyes. "Remember me?" he asked. "The leader complained that you didn't come for lunch. He wants me to fetch you for dinner. You will be safe in my hands, I promise."

Zakiyyah pushed the man away so that he fell. She ran to the parking lot.

The driver was dozing inside the car. His legs were crossed on the steering wheel. She opened one of the rear doors and dived inside, slamming the door shut.

The driver awoke with a start.

"Take me home!" she screamed at him.

He looked around in a confused manner.

"Take me home, I say!" she yelled.

"But the others are not here, madam," the puzzled driver said.

"Do as I say, man!" she shrieked. "A demon is after me!"

The driver looked out the car window and saw the plump man approaching. He made a dangerous reverse and drove off.

As they sped through the streets, Zakiyyah kept telling him to drive faster. When they got home, she dashed upstairs to her room and locked the door. She let down the curtains of her window, switched off the light and buried herself in the duvet. She listened for movements.

A car purred into the compound. It was followed by footfalls on the stairway.

"Zakiyyah!" Kauthar called angrily, storming into the room. "What's wrong with you tonight?"

Zakiyyah remained as still as a statue. The duvet was pulled away from her. She quickly covered her face with her hands.

"Zakiyyah!" Kauthar called sternly. "Why did you run away with the car?"

"It's the man from the palace, Mum. He stopped me at the airport, and I had to—"

Chaotic noises sounded outside. Kauthar rushed to the window, drew the curtains apart and looked out.

Zakiyyah followed her and looked out too.

A group of soldiers were engaged in a scuffle with the domestic bodyguards at the gate. The soldiers were trying to force their way into the house. The bodyguards were pushing them back. A gunfight broke out.

Zakiyyah shrieked. She dived to a corner of the room.

Kauthar ducked, crawled to the telephone and began to dial. "Hello! Hello!" she gasped.

A bullet smashed the window. She let go of the receiver so that it dangled from the nightstand. She joined Zakiyyah at her corner and put an arm around her. The gunfight raged on.

Silence.

Footfalls sounded on the stairs. The plump man and seven soldiers entered the room.

"There she is," the plump man cried. "Get her!"

Two soldiers grabbed Zakiyyah's arms.

She fainted.

21

Professor Garba's convoy reached a village a few kilometres from Masara town. It had a strong military presence. A tanker blocked the middle of the highway. On the kerb, a pickup van was in flames. The soldiers were scattered between the huts, looking on all sides. Thick black smoke billowed from different parts of the village. Corpses were sprawled on the highway, by the roadside and on the pathways. The villagers and soldiers carried wounded people and corpses into two waiting ambulances. Women followed the casualties, wailing. The wounded were unconscious, drenched in blood or had some limbs amputated. They yelled in pain.

"We are lucky, sir!" said the bodyguard sitting in front of Professor Garba.

"We really are!" Professor Garba replied.

An army officer standing atop the tanker beckoned to them to pass. He saluted them as they manoeuvred past the tanker. They continued with their journey.

Masara was peaceful. It had an increased presence of soldiers and policemen. They looked battle-ready.

Professor Garba reached Chief Ousmane's house.

Chief Ousmane rushed out of his zaure, smiling from ear to ear.

They exchanged pleasantries. Professor Garba craned his neck to see if Zaidou was among the visitors in the zaure. He couldn't recognise any of the faces.

"Come in, please." Chief Ousmane held Professor Garba's hand as though he were a child and led him into the zaure.

Professor Garba greeted the men inside. Zaidou was not among them.

Chief Ousmane pulled him to a far corner of the zaure. They talked in hushed tones. "How was your journey?" Chief Ousmane asked him.

"It was terrible, Chief. Terrible!"

"Subhanallah! What happened?"

"We passed through a village that had just been attacked by the Kwaskwarima. It's not far from this town." Professor Garba brought out a handkerchief and wiped the sweat from his forehead.

"Allahu Akbar! This is serious!" Chief Ousmane exclaimed.

"Let's talk about Zaidou, Chief. Has Governor—"

Before Professor Garba could finish his question, Chief Ousmane grabbed his hand and shook it. "He has agreed. Alhamdulillah!" the chief said, smiling. "He said that the investigations have shown that Zaidou is innocent."

"So where is he?" Professor Garba's excited voice rang in the zaure.

The other visitors looked back at him.

"I didn't come with him," Chief Ousmane said. "Coulibaly says we should expect him in Masara today or tomorrow."

Professor Garba hugged him, patting him on the back and whispering *thank you* a dozen times. If Zaidou returned to Masara that day or early the next day, the professor would be able to travel with him back to Birni the following day. "Let me allow you to attend to your visitors," he said, rising to his feet. "I'll come back tomorrow morning for Zaidou."

Chief Ousmane followed him outside. "Can we talk privately in your car?" Chief Ousmane requested.

"Why not?" Professor Garba opened the car and they entered. He told his driver to excuse them.

Chief Ousmane scanned the neighbourhood and then whispered, "Mamman spoke to me about something. Are you aware of it?"

"Coup?"

"Yes."

"Have no fears, Chief. It's a good arrangement for you and for the country. You are the best for this country. Have no fears." Professor Garba gave Chief Ousmane more details about the coup. "I don't know all the plans," he explained. "Mamman is the coup leader."

"You think he can do it?"

"I trust him," Professor Garba said. "Let's trust him. He has a lot of experience."

Chief Ousmane thanked him for his advice, bid him farewell and climbed out of the car. The door banged as he slammed it shut. It was followed by another bang – a much louder bang. More bangs followed, so loud that they seemed to shake the town.

Professor Garba came out and looked about. Two green army vehicles sped into the neighbourhood, dust rising behind them. They stopped with a screech in front of Chief Ousmane. Six soldiers jumped out. Three of the soldiers bundled the chief into one of the jeeps, while the others went into the house. The visitors in the zaure ran out and went in different directions. The soldiers that had entered the house came out with Chief Ousmane's wife and children and led them into the jeeps.

"Where are you taking them to?" Professor Garba asked the soldiers.

The soldiers ignored him. They climbed into the jeeps and drove away.

Professor Garba stood watching, unable to move. The sounds of gunfire and explosions kept sounding from different directions. His security detail fired their weapons into the air. "Get into the car, sir!"

One of the policemen opened the car for him.

He climbed in and they darted out of the town.

22

Zaidou opened his eyes, stretched and looked out the train window. The light of the dawn was bluish. He could only make out the trees of the forest they were passing through. The only sound he could hear was the noise of the train moving along the tracks.

Most of the passengers had odd sleeping postures. Some had their heads resting on their neighbour's shoulder; others had their heads on their knees, while still others slept on the floor. They reminded Zaidou of the way he had slept in prison for the past two years, though the conditions in the prison had been worse. He and other inmates had been packed like sacks of maize in a tiny cell that had only one small window. Despite the congestion, he'd had to battle with mosquitos, rats and cockroaches. Many of his cellmates had died of disease. He was lucky not to have fallen sick even once.

He stretched again and looked at the man by his side. He was an old man dressed in a kaftan with many patches. He was looking blankly ahead of him, apparently with nothing on his mind but the much-anticipated arrival at Masara.

"Will we be there soon?" Zaidou asked him.

"Yes," the man croaked. "Our journey is twelve hours, so we should be there later in the morning. Is this your first time travelling this route?"

"Yes, sir. I had never left Masara until I was arrested and taken to prison two years ago."

"Oh! Are you just out of prison?"

"Yes. I was taken to a prison in Birni. They moved me to another in Tarayya. They said I was innocent, so they let me go."

"I was in prison, too. The one at Baladi," the man said. "I was set free by the Kwaskwarima. They captured the town, you know."

The man told Zaidou about how he'd gotten arrested after the ban because he'd gotten his daughter married. He had been set free a day before his execution.

Zaidou asked him whether the Kwaskwarima were a group of armed robbers.

The man said that they were rebels trying to take over the country.

"Rebels?" Zaidou cried.

"Yes, my son," the man said. "They have been fighting the soldiers. Many people have died."

Zaidou thought about Larai and her children. How were they? Where on earth was Zakiyyah? Thoughts of her had been his best companion in prison. He'd often heard love songs from the prison officials' radio, and they'd always reminded him of her.

The day got brighter as the sun rose. Many of the passengers woke up and began to chat. Some children in the villages they passed through waved at them. Zaidou smiled and waved back. In other villages, some huts were on fire. The people seemed to be running away from something.

"What's happening in that village?" he asked his neighbour.

The old man frowned. "The Kwaskwarima and the soldiers are fighting," he said.

The train's horn sounded several times. It slowed down and came to a halt.

The old man stretched. "You are back home, my friend," he said to Zaidou.

"Is that so?" Zaidou cried. He looked out the window to see if he could recognise the surroundings. He saw men in strange brown camouflage carrying guns around the train station. He disembarked from the train with the other passengers.

"Put your hands in the air, everyone!" one of the men in camouflage barked. "Put your hands in the air!"

Zaidou put up his hands.

The armed men shot their guns into the air and made the women scream. Zaidou screamed too. He heard the passengers in front of him whispering that the armed men were Kwaskwarima fighters.

The rebels asked everyone to go into the town peacefully and without any mischief, otherwise they would be shot.

Outside the terminal, Zaidou saw the corpse of a soldier by the roadside. Blood had pooled around his head. Flies hovered over him. He saw many more corpses as he got deeper into the town, some belonging to soldiers and others to civilians and policemen.

A truck had stopped in front of five dead soldiers lying at a checkpoint. The men in the truck tossed the corpses onto the back of their vehicle and proceeded.

Zaidou wondered whether it was safe to enter the town. Where else could he go?

A jeep approached, carrying some Kwaskwarima fighters. Zaidou fell on his buttocks and awaited the worst to happen. The jeep pulled up in front of him.

"Are you hurt?" the jeep's driver asked him.

Zaidou said no.

"Then what are you doing here?"

"I am afraid!"

"Afraid of what?"

"Bullets!"

"Do you hear any gunshots in the air?"

"No, sir!"

"Then get up and go into the town. The soldiers are all gone. We are in control. Go to the field and choose a wife. Go!" The driver took out a gun and fired it into the air.

Zaidou jumped up and took to his heels.

At the Peoples' Drinking Place, people were drinking and laughing. The brewery was open for business, hawkers were hawking, boys were playing in the streets, herdsmen were moving about with their flocks and the market folk were buying and selling. Rebels, armed to the teeth, were scattered all over the town. Burnt houses were here and there. Large, dried bloodstains stained the roads.

The big field was crowded. It looked like a market. Five trucks full of women arrived. Kwaskwarima rebels jumped out from the trucks and led the women in the trucks into the field. Armed men manned the borders of the field, shouting, "Go inside and choose! Go inside!"

Men were trooping to the field, smiling and laughing.

"You!" a rebel barked, pointing his gun at Zaidou. "Have you chosen?"

"Chosen what, sir?"

"Are you mad? Go in and see! Enter the field!" He kicked Zaidou's thigh with his boot.

Zaidou ran into the field.

There, he saw women sitting in hundreds of rows. Men walked between the rows, picking the women of their choice. Rebels monitored the choosing exercise. Some of the women jumped and clapped when they were taken; others were in tears, weeping bitterly, like bereaved women. At every end of the field, an elderly man pronounced couples husband and wife. After the pronouncements, the couples were allowed to leave the field.

Some women were flogged. They rolled in the dust as they cried and pleaded for mercy. The whips cut the skin on their faces and necks. Blood ran from their cuts and stained their clothes.

"Why are they flogging those women?" Zaidou asked a man browsing the rows of women.

"They are stubborn. They don't like the men who chose them!" the man said and continued to browse.

"What are you waiting for?" A rebel nudged Zaidou. "Haven't you gotten a wife yet?"

Zaidou browsed the women's faces. Several eyes looked into his. Other women waved at him, women of all sorts and ages.

"Haven't you decided?" the rebel barked at Zaidou.

"No, sir. I'm looking for my fiancée."

"Call out her name!"

"Zakiyyah! Zakiyyaaaah! Zakiyaaaaah!"

"Yes!" Five women in their fifties and sixties stood up.

"Is she among them?" the rebel asked.

"No!" Zaidou said.

"If you don't see her, pick someone else! Maybe somebody has taken her," the rebel said.

Zaidou's eyes met those of his neighbour's daughter. He beckoned to her.

She got up and followed him to one of the men at the end of the field. He was busy marrying off the crowd of couples around him.

"I pronounce you husband and wife. Go home!" he said to Zaidou and the girl.

"If your wife refuses to stay with you, come and report to us!" one of the rebels told Zaidou. He allowed them to leave the field.

"Thank you, sir!" the girl said to Zaidou as they walked homeward.

Zaidou pretended not to hear her. He walked very fast and she trotted after him.

"Where is your father?" he asked her.

"He has joined the Kwaskwarima. He is guarding the motor park," the girl said, panting.

"What of your mother?"

"She is at home," the girl said.

They reached their neighbourhood. Zaidou asked her to go to her father's house and wait for him. He turned the doorknob of his own house and found it locked. He knocked hard. There was no response. He knocked even harder. Still, no one responded.

"Larai!" he barked through the window. His voice returned to him in an echo: *Laaaaaraiii!*

"There is no one inside," a woman hawking cooked groundnuts informed him.

"Where did they go to?"

"Larai got married to a trader in the Marmari market two years ago. They fled to Nigeria with her children," the woman revealed.

Zaidou guessed she was referring to Ya'u. He scratched his head. His hair had grown bushy, like that of a woman who had not plaited her hair for ages. He made his way to Chief Ousmane's house. There were lizards playing in the zaure and cobwebs on the doorway.

"Assalaamu 'alaykum, Chief!" he cried. "Assalaamu 'alaykuuuum!"

He stood akimbo and looked thoughtfully at the ground. He sat under the mango tree to rest. Ants played on his dusty feet. He hadn't worn shoes throughout his stay in prison, so his feet were cracked. His toenails had grown long because he couldn't bite them off the way he'd done to his fingernails.

His stomach rumbled. He plucked one of the ripe mangos hanging low from the tree and took a huge bite. He ate it up hurriedly, threw the seed away and plucked another mango. He ate it up and belched.

A truck entered the neighbourhood with some women in it. Five Kwaskwarima fighters jumped out of the truck and searched the houses in the neighbourhood. They brought out every unmarried woman and put her in the truck. They came to Chief Ousmane's house.

"Whose house is this?" one of the fighters asked Zaidou.

"It's Chief Ousmane's house," Zaidou replied.

"Ah! So this is his house? Is there any woman inside?"

"I don't know."

"We love Chief Ousmane. We won't let any woman in his house stay unmarried," the rebel said. He entered the house and came out alone.

"You! Have you married?" he asked Zaidou.

"Yes, sir. I took a wife from the big field today," Zaidou said.

The man and the other rebels returned to the truck and it drove away.

Zaidou got up and made for Professor Garba's house. Several trucks of women drove past him on the streets, going towards the big field.

"Zaidou!" a man stopped him. It was Audou. "Zaidou, you are back!" Audou hugged him.

"Yes. I am back," Zaidou said. He didn't return his friend's smile.

"When did you come back?"

"Today."

"Oh! Good to see you, my friend." Audou hugged him again. "Where are you going?"

"I'm going to Professor Garba's house."

"What? Don't you know that the Kwaskwarima have taken over the house?" Audou's last sentence was said in a whisper.

"What of Zakiyyah? Where is she?" Zaidou grabbed his friend by the shirt.

"Calm down, Zaidou. Calm down. Come, let's talk." Audou took Zaidou to the roadside and made him sit on a rock.

"Zakiyyah is now a minister in the government," he said. "She is in Birni with Leader Gambo. It was announced on the news."

"Shut up!"

"I'm telling you the truth, Zaidou! Come. Let's go to my house." Audou held Zaidou by the hand and led him home.

Audou's wife served Zaidou with masa and taushe soup.

"Eat very well, Zaidou," Audou urged him. "You are looking pale and sick."

Zaidou took a few morsels. Audou spoke to him, but he neither listened nor responded. At night, Audou took him to the Dandali and bought him suya and mint tea. The men spoke of their new wives, Leader Gambo and the battle that had happened in the town.

"I advise you to stop worrying," Audou said to Zaidou. "Zakiyyah is gone. She is not the only woman in the world. Marry a different girl."

"I love Zakiyyah, and I promised to marry her," Zaidou said.

"I didn't say you don't love her. I am only telling you the right thing to do," Audou said.

That night, Zaidou couldn't sleep much. At the break of dawn, he sneaked out of Audou's house. He went to the motor park to take a bus to Birni.

◄○►

At the motor park, Zaidou learnt that he would have to take a bus to Tarayya first. From there, he would take another to Birni. He didn't have money, so the conductor allowed him to stay at the back of the bus with the passengers' luggage.

It wasn't as uncomfortable as he'd feared. He had enough space to sit and stretch his legs. The only discomfort was that whenever they rode into a pothole, some bags would fall on him. He would put them back in place. He enjoyed the view as he looked out the back windshield. It made him feel that they were moving farther away from Masara and closer to his heartthrob.

Two of the passengers talked about the Kwaskwarima.

"Those people are evil!" one man said.

"Don't say that!" the other retorted. "We couldn't get married for two years. These people have come and given us wives."

"They are evil! Is it right to force women to marry?"

"Whether by force or not, we can now get married. Life is better that way."

The other passengers joined the conversation. A hot debate ensued.

They came to a checkpoint and the bus stopped. The passengers kept quiet.

A soldier, with leaves hanging from his uniform and headgear, peeped into the bus. "Driver!" he barked. "Why are you carrying this man in your boot?"

"We usually do that, sir! That is how we help our people who don't have money," the driver explained.

"Are you sure he is not a Kwaskwarima man?"

"No, sir!" the driver said.

The soldier knocked on the bus. The driver drove off.

Zaidou heaved a sigh. He didn't know how many hours they had spent on the road by now. He'd heard the passengers saying that they'd be in Tarayya by noon. By the time the sun was in the middle of the sky, he started seeing tall buildings and fine wide roads. Though Tarayya was beautiful, it reminded him of prison.

The driver slowed down as they inched closer to the motor park. Several sighs were heard in the bus.

"Ah!" one passenger yelled. "I see corpses!"

"Where?" the others cried, craning their necks.

"There!"

Bang!

"Yeeee! Get down! Get down!"

Bang! Bang! Bang!

"Help! Yeeeee!"

The rear windshield of the bus smashed. The bullet flew over Zaidou's head and pierced the rear seat. Blood splashed him. He ducked even lower. His heart beat very fast and he feared he would faint. The bus swerved right and left, hit a wall and came to a stop.

The explosions and gunfire did not stop. Something exploded not too far from the bus, shattering its windows. Flames and smoke erupted around the bus.

Zaidou prayed hard. He pissed his pants and whimpered. The passengers were quiet, and he imagined that they were all dead. Then someone groaned. Zaidou wished he could move close to the groaner, closer to the living.

The battle did not end until dark. The bus was lit from the yellow flames around it. The air smelled of burning tyres.

Some of the passengers whispered, "Should we go out?"

"Let's wait and listen more."

"What do we need to listen to again? Can you hear any gunshots?"

"Let's wait, please! Let's not play with our lives."

Zaidou pulled a bag over his body and stayed still. He hoped that none of the rebels or soldiers had heard the soft noise he'd created in doing it.

He heard voices around the bus. A torch shone through the window. The light cast round the interior, then went off.

Silence.

The torch flashed again.

Zaidou heard the rattle of the door as someone meddled with it, and then the dragging sound of it opening.

"Get out! All of you!" came the order.

Zaidou heard a few passengers complying.

"If you're alive and still in the bus, I swear I will kill you if you don't come out – *now!*" the voice said again.

Zaidou pushed the boot open, climbed out and fell on his buttocks. His knees were knocking on each other. Something sharp and painful hit his neck. "Yeeee!" he yelped. He looked up and saw a whip aiming for his neck again. He ducked, but he couldn't avoid it. He yelped again.

The man lashed him thoroughly. "Next time, you don't delay in obeying orders!" the man said. "Get up!"

Zaidou got up. He was made to stand with the other passengers in two rows of three people each. Fifteen of them had boarded the bus, so nine were dead.

Many other rows of passengers were spread across the motor park. In some rows, the passengers had their hands in the air. Many of the buses were burning or riddled with bullet holes or had smashed windscreens. Many corpses lay on the ground: soldiers and civilians alike.

The minder of Zaidou and his co-passengers pointed his gun at them. "If you move, I will shoot you, so remain still!" he warned.

A hefty man accompanied by his bodyguards came and inspected the rows.

Zaidou gasped. It was Babawo.

Babawo began to address them. He told them that the Kwaskwarima had taken over the motor park and all the suburbs around it. He told them that they would be used as ransom for the release of Chief Ousmane and other rebels in government custody.

"Is that clear?" he thundered.

"Yes, sir!"

"Is that clear? Say 'yes, Commander'!"

"Yes, Commander!"

"Whip them all!" Babawo waved his hand in their direction. "Let them learn how to speak out." Their minder lashed their necks.

Zaidou yelped.

"Did you hear what I said?" Babawo asked.

"Yes, Commander!" they shouted.

"You! Zaidou!" Babawo barked. "Come here!"

Zaidou went to him, and Babawo held his hand. Babawo warned the minder not to allow the passengers misbehave and he walked away with Zaidou.

Babawo took Zaidou to one of the kiosks in the motor park. Its door was padlocked. He asked one of his bodyguards to shoot it open, which the man did. It was a provision shop, full of biscuits, soft drinks and snacks. Babawo picked up a loaf of bread and ate. He asked Zaidou to take whatever he wanted. Zaidou took a pack of biscuits and a bottle of yoghurt.

"What are you doing here?" Babawo asked him, sitting on the freezer. He opened a soft drink with his molars. He threw away the cap and took a long gulp.

Chewing his biscuit, Zaidou narrated his story to his old customer. He told him how he'd suffered hard labour in prison. Upon his release, he'd learned that Leader Gambo had stolen Zakiyyah from him.

"Do you want revenge?" Babawo asked him.

"Yes. But it's my fiancée that I want back the most!"

"You can get revenge and your fiancée, if you work with us. You can't do it alone." Babawo drank from his bottle. "We are about to take over this city from Governor Coulibaly. We won't surrender until we kill Leader Gambo and take his head to our boss, Colonel Kaita. Once we do that, you can take your Zakiyyah back."

"Can't we travel to Birni straight away and kill Leader Gambo?"

"No! We do everything in stages. We take one town after another. Our task now is to take this city and move to the next, until we get to Birni."

Zaidou threw his biscuit on the floor. "How long will it take for us to do that, Commander?"

Babawo didn't say anything. He continued his meal with enviable calm. He threw his bottle to the floor so that it broke. He belched and dusted his hands. He rolled some hemp in a piece of paper and began to smoke it. "With the pace we are going," he said, exhaling smoke, "we should capture Birni in two weeks. So you should be back in Masara with your wife in two weeks!"

—◦—

By morning, all the flames in the motor park had extinguished. What remained were charred remains of vehicles. The corpses were taken out for burial. Some trucks came in with weapons. Some of the guns were very big – types that Zaidou had never seen before.

Babawo spent the whole morning telling Zaidou how important the Kwaskwarima's mission was to the country and to him personally. He told him that the Kwaskwarima were stronger than the government, so he should have no doubts that they would succeed. After lunch, he asked one of the rebels to teach Zaidou how to use a gun. Zaidou was taken to an isolated part of the park.

"Hold the gun like this," the rebel said, holding the gun with both hands, one in front of the other. He gave it to Zaidou. "Now put your finger here. No, this finger! Yes. Now lie down like this."

"Like this?"

"No! Is that what you see me doing? Look at me very well, idiot!"

"Like this?"

"Good. Now you are going to pull the trigger. It is going to fire. Press it like this." The man moved his index finger and Zaidou copied him. Bullets shot out, hitting the wall.

"Yeeee!" Zaidou threw the gun away and ran to a safe distance.

"Come back here!" his teacher barked.

When Zaidou came back, his teacher gave him several blows to the face. Blood oozed from Zaidou's nose. "The next time you run, I will kill you," the teacher warned. "We are not cowards here!"

The training continued till evening. Once Zaidou grew accustomed to the noise and the kick of the gun, he felt shooting was easier than he'd imagined.

Babawo gathered Zaidou and some other rebels together. They stood at attention as he told them about the plans ahead. He told them some dos and don'ts. He told them that he'd received instructions from his superiors to assassinate Governor Coulibaly. Zaidou would be one of the assassins. They'd go when the time was ripe.

Zaidou continued to train the following day. His teacher taught him many things about a gun: its parts, how to load it and the various positions from which he could shoot. Firing a gun was even easier than sewing a babban riga! The ease with which he fired reduced his anxiety over his impending mission. Raising up his gun, he began to dance, singing a love song. His teacher laughed and clapped.

Babawo called him and his teacher into the kiosk. He was standing with Sergeant Yunusa, a policeman who spied for the Kwaskwarima.

"How good is he with the gun now?" Babawo asked the teacher.

"He is very good. His only problem is that he needs to be more confident. But he can strike anything!"

"Good!" Babawo said. He turned to Zaidou, pointing at Sergeant Yunusa. "Zaidou, we will be going out with Sergeant Yunusa tonight. Is that okay?"

"Yes, Commander!" Zaidou said.

"Are you ready?"

Zaidou's heart pounded. "I am," he said.

"Good! Governor Coulibaly will be flying to Birni this night. We will attack him at the airport," Babawo explained. He gave Zaidou a police uniform to wear and asked him to ensure that his gun was fully loaded.

Zaidou wore the uniform, praying silently. The clothes were a little bit oversized. The beret fit perfectly, but there were no boots. Babawo gave him new slippers from the kiosk to wear.

"We will have to get some fuel, Commander," Sergeant Yunusa announced.

"Are you mad?" Babawo pointed at his own head. "Why didn't you get that before coming?"

"Sorry, Commander!"

"Now go, you and Zaidou, and get the fuel. Come back on time to pick me up. I'll give you thirty minutes!"

Zaidou set out with Sergeant Yunusa in a police saloon car. Many of the streetlights had been damaged. Burnt vehicles littered the roads, but traffic flowed smoothly.

"We are going to infiltrate the governor's security detail and strike," Sergeant Yunusa told Zaidou. "We need a lot of fuel, because we'll have to make a getaway. We don't know how far we have to drive to do that. We have fighters all over the city. They will give us backup."

They got to the filling station. The fuel attendant began to fill their tank. The station was in a government-controlled street. Soldiers and armoured personnel carriers were positioned in and around the station.

"Behave as confidently as you can, or else they will suspect you," Sergeant Yunusa whispered into Zaidou's ears.

Zaidou nodded, frowned and swallowed hard.

It was now 7:30 p.m. They needed to be at the airport before 8 p.m., when the governor's jet would be taking off. Sergeant Yunusa sped towards the motor park. He manoeuvred between motorcycles, cars and pedestrians, blowing his horn. When they neared the park, a jet flew low over them. Its noise was loud. It flew towards the motor park like an arrow. Two loud explosions suddenly shook the ground.

Sergeant Yunusa applied the brake so that the tyres screeched. "Ahhhhh!" he screamed.

The plane continued its flight. Fire and clouds of smoke rose from the motor park. Sergeant Yunusa sat watching, his hands on his head.

"What is it?" Zaidou asked. His teeth knocked on each other as if he'd had a cold bath on a cold night.

Sergeant Yunusa drove to the motor park. It was filled with smoke, dismembered bodies and flaming cars. Zaidou and Sergeant Yunusa climbed out of their car and moved round. Many of the passengers Zaidou had travelled with were dead. The injured were yelling on the ground. The rebels were moving helter-skelter, trying to help them. The kiosk that Babawo had used as office was in flames. His dismembered, bloody body lay in front of the kiosk.

Zaidou fell to his knees.

"We don't have time to waste, man!" Sergeant Yunusa pulled him up. "We have a mission to finish." He warned Zaidou to remain strong, because they would be killed by the Kwaskwarima leaders if they failed.

They returned to the car and sped out. They drove so fast that Zaidou feared they'd hit something.

"I don't have a gun with me," Sergeant Yunusa said. "So you will be the one to shoot. You must be brave, or else we will fail!"

They reached the government house just after Governor Coulibaly's convoy had set out. They followed it. Sergeant Yunusa switched on the siren.

The convoy passed through the gates of the airport. Sergeant Yunusa increased his speed to reach the gates before they were closed. They made it!

"Get your gun ready!" Sergeant Yunusa barked.

Zaidou held his gun tighter.

"Are you ready?" Sergeant Yunusa barked again. "Don't fail us, man!"

"I won't fail," Zaidou said.

The gates of the runway were guarded by soldiers. An army officer flagged them down. They stopped, their tyres screeching.

"Where are you going?" the officer asked them, peeping into the car. The light from the streetlights lit their faces well.

"We are part of the convoy!" Sergeant Yunusa punched the steering.

The soldier looked at their faces intently in turn. "Are you sure?" he asked them.

"Yes!"

"I don't think so. Turn off the car! Fake policemen! You're all fakes! Get out of the car, all of you!"

Zaidou's hands trembled.

"Put your hands in the air!" The officer began to search them, groping their pockets. He brought out Sergeant Yunusa's identification card, perused it and returned it.

"Where's yours?" he asked Zaidou. "And why are you in slippers?"

"I . . . I . . . was just wearing this uniform to disguise—"

Zaidou was silenced by gunshots and explosions at the gate.

The security operatives around began to move towards the scene. The officer left Zaidou and the sergeant, barking orders at his boys. The armoured personnel carrier standing at the gates of the runway moved, leaving the runway entrance bare.

"Get in the car! Let's go!" Sergeant Yunusa dived into the car and Zaidou followed suit. They drove through the gates and onto the tarmac. The convoy had stopped in front of the jet.

"There he is!" Sergeant Yunusa cried. "I will drive by and you shoot. Take out your gun, quick!"

Governor Coulibaly had just come out of his Peugeot. They darted towards him. When they were close enough, Zaidou aimed and pressed the trigger. He let it down and refused to let it go. The gun vibrated as the bullets flew out of it.

The governor fell. Zaidou shot other men around. Sergeant Yunusa made a quick U-turn and made for the exit.

They came under fire. Zaidou ducked into the car and fired back. At the gate, their tyre burst. The car hit the gate at its hinges. Blood splashed Zaidou. Sergeant Yunusa slumped. Zaidou ran out of the car, shooting back at the governor's security forces as he ran out of the gate.

He felt an excruciating pain on his shoulder and back. He screamed, threw his gun away and grabbed his shoulder. He fell to the ground, crying for help.

23

Professor Garba looked at the front page of the *Daily Truth Newspaper*. A big headline read:

"INVESTIGATE THE WHEREABOUTS OF CHIEF OUSMANE," EMIR OF TARAYYA APPEALS TO GOVERNMENT.

The emir's picture stood at the centre of the news report. He was wearing a big white turban that left only his eyes visible. The writer wrote of how soldiers had taken Chief Ousmane from his house, but the government had denied being behind his abduction. In his appeal, the emir warned that Chief Ousmane's disappearance could worsen the rebellion.

Professor Garba put down the paper and looked at Mamman. The latter was sitting on the settee beside him, dialling some numbers.

"You've not told me where you've hidden Chief Ousmane and his family. Is he really fit for office? Injured?"

Mamman held the receiver to his ear and listened. He dropped it. "Chief Ousmane and his family are fine," he whispered. "Chief Ousmane is going to read the takeover speech on TV this night. Believe me."

Mamman dialled again and waited for response. He dropped the receiver and took a deep breath.

"What time are we going out?" Professor Garba asked him.

Mamman looked at the clock. "It's not time yet." He sat down and looked at some notes he'd scribbled down on a jotter. He flipped through the pages, mumbling as he read.

Professor Garba brought out a handwritten document from his pocket. He turned its pages with shaky, sweaty hands. He looked at the portrait of Mamman on the wall, side-by-side with that of Leader Gambo. In the picture, Mamman was dressed in ceremonial military regalia. He looked brave and intelligent.

"Will the takeover speech be read tonight or in the morning?" Professor Garba asked Mamman.

"Tonight," Mamman replied, still looking at his notes.

"Have the soldiers taken positions at the palace yet?" Professor Garba asked.

Mamman slammed his jotter on the stool where the phone sat. His eyes grew wide and the veins on his face showed. "Calm down, Professor! Everything will be fine. Trust me," he cried.

"It's okay, Mamman. I was just—"

Professor Garba took off his spectacles and stared at the TV. The newscaster was announcing that Governor Coulibaly had been left in a coma after a rebel attack. Professor Garba dropped his spectacles onto the armrest and moved to the edge of his seat. "Governor Coulibaly? Attacked?" he exclaimed.

Mamman marched to the TV and increased the volume.

"This is shocking! Kai! Isn't that Zaidou?" Professor Garba jumped to his feet and moved closer to the TV. Zaidou was being carried on a stretcher with blood on his police uniform.

The reporter explained that the person on the stretcher was a member of the Kwaskwarima who had carried out the attack. The police chief spoke to reporters, saying that the arrested rebel would help in intelligence gathering.

"But he was just released from prison! How can he be one of the rebels? This is a lie!" Professor Garba punched his right fist into his left palm.

"It's not surprising," Mamman said. "He could have come into contact with them and they used him. He's just a victim, perhaps."

"He was supposed to marry my daughter! That was why she came home – to run back to Lagos with him and get married."

"I see," Mamman said.

Professor Garba wondered whether the image of Zaidou was a mix-up. But could the cameras commit such an error? He sat down and heaved a sigh. He covered his face with his hands, shaking his head. "I wonder if he'll survive his wounds," he moaned.

"Hmmm," Mamman hummed, making coffee at the dining area. He returned to his seat, sipped some coffee and set the cup on the stool. "So, who would you recommend to the leader to replace Governor Coulibaly if he doesn't survive? His deputy?"

"Maybe. I'm sad for my daughter. Leader Gambo has taken her. Now her fiancé is wounded!"

"It's okay, Professor. Don't let that destroy your courage. We have serious business at hand tonight."

"The coup?" Professor Garba lifted his head.

"What else? Once the coup is done, your daughter is free." Mamman looked at his wristwatch. "The soldiers will take over the TV and radio stations by 11 p.m. Leader Gambo is attending the banquet for your daughter's inauguration now. We'll arrest him as soon as he returns to his palace."

"Are we the ones to arrest him?"

"I have assigned some officers to do that." Mamman stood up and paced the parlour, his hands crossed behind his back.

The news ended at 9:45 p.m. A live broadcast began of the banquet the leader was hosting for Zakiyyah's inauguration as minister. About one hundred and thirty dignitaries were present. They sat at the beautifully arranged round tables, eating and drinking. Each table held expensive alcoholic wines, which the guests drank from crystal goblets. The smartly dressed waiters moved from table to table to keep every mouth happy. General Oumar sat at a table next to that of the leader. He had seven other people with him: two emirs, two foreign magnates, two ministers and a white diplomat. Zakiyyah, dressed in shiny silver-coloured garments that glittered like stars under the light, sat next to Leader Gambo.

Professor Garba winced. Zakiyyah's face was dull and unsmiling, like one who'd not slept for days. He read the time from his watch. It was 10 p.m.

The master of ceremonies called on General Oumar to make some remarks. General Oumar was dressed in a white babban riga.

"Have you noticed any resemblance between General Oumar and Chief Ousmane?" Professor Garba asked Mamman.

"Yes," Mamman replied. "Let me tell you something I've found out: did you know that Chief Ousmane once had a son called Oumar?"

"I know. He died during the attack on Masara over thirty years ago – he and his mother, Falmata."

"His mother died, yes. But Oumar didn't die. He is this same Oumar you are watching on the screen!"

"Are you serious?" Professor Garba jumped to his feet.

"Yes, I am, Professor."

"How do you know this?"

"I had to conduct a lot of investigations on Chief Ousmane before I decided that he should be president," Mamman said. He told Professor Garba about how a woman called Kande had taken care of Oumar after his mother had been killed. She had been able to raise him with the support of the non-governmental organisations that had offered to care for the babies orphaned by the attack on Masara. He'd been under her care until he'd gone to the military academy in Tarayya city.

At the academy, General Oumar had met his wife, Ayesha. She was Leader Gambo's only child. Ayesha had died shortly after given birth to their son, Fahad. The leader had wanted power to be passed on to Fahad so that it would be retained in his progeny. That was why he had made General Oumar the heir to the throne.

"This is interesting!" Professor Garba cried.

"It is, indeed," Mamman replied.

"But why didn't Kande return Oumar to Chief Ousmane?"

"She had no other child, so she decided to keep him. She was selfish. I told her that to her face." Mamman got up from his seat, walked to the window and peeped out into the night. He walked round the parlour and then returned to his couch.

"Have you told Chief Ousmane this story?" Professor Garba asked him.

"No. I've not told General Oumar either, but I will tell them both. The good thing is that Kande is still alive to confirm the story. It's 10:30!" Mamman jumped up from his seat. "Where is the takeover speech?"

Professor Garba waved the handwritten script he'd been holding. His legs felt like jelly as he rose from his seat. He followed Mamman out of the house.

Mamman brought out his pistol from its holster, examined it and returned it.

Professor Garba wondered whether he shouldn't be holding a gun, too.

Mamman drove. Many soldiers were in his house, but none escorted them. They zoomed through the streets and reached the Crown Castle, where foreign guests of Leader Gambo used to lodge. That was where the leader was hosting Zakiyyah's inauguration dinner.

Professor Garba heaved.

The castle was well lit and guarded. It was smaller than the leader's own palace. It also had gold-plated domes and marble minarets. On the lawn opposite its entrance, the drivers and orderlies of the dignitaries were having a good time. They gulped from their beer bottles, laughing and chatting. Lamps lined the lawn. One man stood urinating at one of the lamps.

"Are we going in? Are we making the arrest now?" Professor Garba asked.

"No." Mamman climbed out of the car. An army officer walked up to him. They spoke in hushed tones.

A lady, escorted by five policemen, emerged from the castle's huge ornamental double door.

"Zakiyyah!" Professor Garba gasped. He rushed out of the car. Before he could even begin to approach them, a black jeep cruised along the road and stopped in front of Zakiyyah. She and three of the policemen climbed in and the jeep drove away.

The jeep was driving too fast for the empty, quiet road. The man who had been urinating on the lawn walked unsteadily onto the road.

"Stop! Stop!" Professor Garba shouted at him.

The jeep tried to avoid the man. The edge of its bumper brushed his thigh and sent him falling, his bottle of beer smashing on the road. The jeep continued its journey out the gate.

Mamman and the officer talking with him rushed to the scene. Professor Garba joined them. They pulled the man to his feet. He wobbled as soon as they had let go of his arms.

"Are you hurt?" Professor Garba asked him.

"I'm fine," he said and walked away. His steps weren't steady. He went straight to Leader Gambo's limousine and sat at the wheel.

"He's the leader's driver," Professor Garba revealed.

"I know him," Mamman said, going back into the car. "The leader will be coming out any moment now."

They drove out of the castle grounds. Professor Garba kept craning his neck to see if he could sight the jeep that had driven Zakiyyah away, but it had disappeared.

They reached the headquarters of the Hasoumiyan Broadcasting Network. Soldiers and APCs were there already. Two officers met them at the gate and led them into the studio. Professor Garba sat at the table, feeling like a newscaster. Two other chairs were to his right, where Mamman and Chief Ousmane would be sitting. The cameramen were standing behind the cameras, awaiting orders.

"You still have the takeover speech with you, don't you?" Mamman whispered into his ear.

"Yes," Professor Garba replied.

"I'll be back," Mamman said. He dashed out of the studio.

Professor Garba remained there for over three hours. He paced up and down the studio, ignoring the cameramen as if they were statues. Returning to his seat, he brought out the takeover speech from his pocket. It was ten pages long. He browsed through the pages. The sentence he loved most in the speech was "The marriage ban is hereby lifted." He read it a dozen times.

The door of the studio was thrown open. The script fell out of his hands. Mamman and Chief Ousmane appeared at the doorway. The ferocious look on Mamman's face had disappeared. Chief Ousmane was looking calm and healthy.

"Let's go home, Prof!" Mamman cried.

"Home? Isn't Chief Ousmane going to read the speech?" Professor Garba asked.

"That is no longer necessary, Professor." Mamman smiled.

◄○►

Zakiyyah was awakened by the phone ringing on the nightstand. She remained motionless on the bed. The phone continued to ring, until it finally stopped. Her stomach growled. Her limbs felt weak and she could hardly move them. She hadn't eaten anything during her inauguration party the night before, so she had requested some food upon her return to the palace. She looked at the coolers of food arranged on the well-varnished dining table at one end of the big room. They were inviting, but she wouldn't touch them. She'd overheard one of the ladies who had brought them asking the other, "Did you put the love potion in the food?"

The other lady had hushed her up, and they had gone out in a hurry.

Even before that, Zakiyyah had not been eating well since she'd been brought to the palace.

The phone rang again. Zakiyyah picked it up.

"Good morning, Your Excellency," a lady's voice greeted her.

"Mhmm," Zakiyyah hummed.

"What would you like for breakfast?"

"Anything you like."

"We have fried plantain, toasted bread, fried potatoes, baked beans, boiled eggs, masa, sandwiches, chicken wings, custard, coffee—"

"I have read everything on the menu you gave me. Bring whatever you like. Put as much poison or love potion in it as you wish." Zakiyyah said all this in a calm voice, but her rising temper got the better of her. She shouted into the phone, "If you like, don't even bring the food!"

"I brought you sandwiches and coffee yesterday morning. Should I bring you fried potatoes and egg sauce with tea today? I will get you some apples and—"

Zakiyyah slammed the phone on the cradle. She rose from her bed. Her feet sank into the soft blue carpet as she walked to the window. She lifted the white silk curtain and looked outside. The window was sealed with bulletproof glass. A garden stretched out in front of her room, and many soldiers were there. They chatted on the benches, smoking and loitering. Each of them had a gun. The window gave a good view of the palace grounds. She couldn't see her father's house, though. She saw statues of warriors on horses. They looked as if they were erected there to scare her.

The door of her room was opened with a key and unbolted from the other side. Two young ladies wearing spotless white aprons and toques came in with silver-plated dishes.

"Good morning, Your Excellency." They greeted her with smiles.

"Don't greet me!" Zakiyyah spat. "Witches! I will never love Leader Gambo, no matter how much love potion you put in that food. I won't be his mistress! I won't be his minister!"

The girls stood and stared at her. They set the food on the dining table and collected the coolers of dinner.

"We didn't put any bad thing in your food, Your Excellency," one of the girls said, standing at the exit.

"You did! Get out of my room!" Zakiyyah yelled. The girls went out. The room was locked again.

Zakiyyah's stomach growled. She went to the dining table and opened one of the containers. Steam rose from the egg sauce. It smelled of curry and it made her stomach rumble again. She brought her nose closer. It didn't smell of anything strange. As she opened another dish, she heard shouts outside her room. She moved to the door and put her ear to it.

The shouts went on, accompanied by jumps. The voices were those of the soldiers who guarded her room. They sounded just the way her brothers celebrated when their football team scored a goal. They were speaking in Fulani, so she couldn't understand all that they were saying, but she knew they were talking of Leader Gambo.

She ran to the window and saw the soldiers in the garden jumping and hugging each other. They danced on the lawn and on the benches. She couldn't hear anything they were saying.

Her door flew open. General Oumar stepped in, with about ten other officers. They were all smiling. General Oumar wore a blue beret and green military outfit. His black shoes shone. He had sideburns, thick eyebrows and a straight nose. He was just about her age. As he walked up to her, she could smell his cool perfume.

He smiled. "Good morning, Zakiyyah."

"Good morning, sir," Zakiyyah replied.

"How are you?" he asked her. Tears welled in Zakiyyah's eyes. They ran down her cheeks. She shook her head, looking into his eyes.

"It's okay," he said. "Come. Let's get you out of this place. Have no fears. I am the president." He beckoned to her, and she followed him out of the room.

—◄○►—

When Zakiyyah returned home, her mother rushed out to the car park. As soon as Zakiyyah stepped out of the car, her mother screamed so loud she could be heard by the neighbours. She hugged Zakiyyah tight and lifted her.

Zakiyyah buried her face on her mother's shoulder and cried. They stood there and cried together. Her mother caressed her back and her hair. They went into Professor Garba's living room downstairs. Her mother took off her scarf and cleaned Zakiyyah's face with it. She inspected her daughter's face, arms and feet for any injury.

"Did they beat you?" she asked.

"No, Mum. I'm fine." Zakiyyah sniffled.

"Did Leader Gambo touch you?"

"No!" Zakiyyah said. "But he wanted me to be his mistress. He tried to cast a love spell on me!"

"We thank Allah that he is no more!" Kauthar raised her eyes and hands to heaven. She prostrated herself on the carpet and then sat back on the upholstered couch.

She asked Zakiyyah so many questions, and Zakiyyah wished she would stop. Her mother invited her to the dining table to have breakfast. Zakiyyah's hands shook from hunger. Her mother poured steaming water into a cup and made tea for her. She buttered her bread and put fries by its side on the china plate. The smell of the food made Zakiyyah hungrier. She ate quickly.

"Has Zaidou been released?" she asked her mother, stirring her tea.

Kauthar sighed. "Your father knows all that!" she said. "He will tell you when he comes."

"Didn't he tell you?"

"He did. He said he's been released. But I . . . I don't know where he is. Your father knows it all!" Kauthar looked thoughtful as she spoke.

Zakiyyah's brothers came in. They yelled and jumped to her. She hugged them in turn. They sat in the living room upstairs and chatted till afternoon. It was as if they'd not seen each other in many years.

At night, Zakiyyah could not sleep well. She kept having dreams about Zaidou and Leader Gambo. She'd wake up with a start each time. She switched on the light and looked at the wall clock. It was 12:30 a.m. She sat up in bed and allowed different thoughts to run through her mind.

She went downstairs to the dining table and made some tea. The whole house was quiet. The teaspoon clinked against the china cup as she stirred her tea. The clinking seemed to fill the whole house. She took three quick sips, put down the cup in the saucer and stirred the tea again. She buried her chin in her two palms.

The sound of the gate being opened hit her ears. Some cars purred into the compound. The doors of the cars were slammed shut. The door of the living room opened, and she heard shoes knocking on the marble floor.

"Zakiyyah!" her father cried, appearing in the living room.

She raced to him and they fell into a warm embrace. They sat on the couch and talked. He asked her similar questions to her mother's. He spoke to her about Leader Gambo's death. He told her that his driver had crashed the leader's limousine. The driver had survived, but Leader Gambo and his bodyguard had died on the spot.

"I knew you were back home," he said. "President Oumar told me he released you himself."

"Yes, he did," Zakiyyah said.

"I have been in a meeting with him since morning. He has appointed me as the chief mediator to end the war."

"Okay, Baba. I wish you success."

"Thank you. It's not going to be easy. I will be meeting the rebel leaders tomorrow morning."

"Okay. Where is Zaidou?" Zakiyyah asked.

Her father cleared his throat and faced her squarely. "You are now a minister, Zakiyyah. Do you still want Zaidou?" he asked.

"I don't want to be the leader's minister, Baba!" Zakiyyah cried.

"The leader is no more, remember. President Oumar is a good man. You will enjoy working with him."

"Does he still want me as a minister?"

"Yes. We discussed that this night. He wants to be your husband, too. I think you will like him more than Zaidou."

"I like Zaidou better, Baba. Where is he? Please, Baba, tell me!" Zakiyyah clasped her hands together.

Her father looked down at the carpet and thought for some time. "Zaidou has been released," he said at last. "But he is a rebel. He killed Governor Coulibaly and he has been arrested."

Zakiyyah recoiled in horror. A rebel? How could such a jovial, lovable tailor metamorphose into a killer-rebel? "It can't be true!" she said.

"It is true, Zakiyyah," her father insisted. "I'm sure you wouldn't like to marry such a man."

"He can't be a rebel. Where is he now?"

"He is in the military hospital here in Birni. Maybe you would like to see him. That will make you believe me."

"Yes, Baba. I will see him," Zakiyyah said.

When Zakiyyah went back to her room, she couldn't sleep again. She stayed awake till the sun was up. She had a shower and went downstairs.

Her father was in the living room, all dressed up for work. He was making a phone call to someone, stating that his daughter would be coming to see the rebel in Ward 156 of the military hospital.

"So, you can go and see Zaidou," her father said to her, hanging up the phone. "One of my aides is waiting for you outside. He will take you whenever you are ready. I hope you will have made a wise decision by the time you come back."

"I won't change my mind, Baba," Zakiyyah said, standing at the door. "I've always known Zaidou to be a rebel. And that is what he should be. We all were rebels. None of us liked Leader Gambo. We are all happy now that he is gone."

She went out, and she was driven to the military hospital. It was a lofty steel and glass building. Professor Garba's aide led her to Room 156, accompanied by an army officer. The door was opened.

She entered and stood still, looking at the man on the bed. Was that Zaidou?

He was lying on his belly, facing the door. His hair was dishevelled. He was pale and his eyes were sunken. His right arm was bandaged up to his shoulder, and a dressing covered his back, close to the spine. He was on an intravenous drip. His healthy arm was handcuffed to the metal bed. The grimace on his face spoke of pain, worry, fear and misery, and she could hear him moaning quietly.

He stopped moaning and looked at her. He stared at her steadily without moving. Was he dead?

She walked up to him and touched his bandage. "Zaidou!" she whispered. "They shot you!"

The grimace on Zaidou's face evaporated. He smiled. It was a weak, gentle smile. It was natural.

The army officer brought her a plastic chair and kept it by the bedside. "Sit down, Your Excellency," he said.

She sat on the chair. She and her suitor stared at each other without saying a word.

"They shot you, sir?" Zakiyyah asked.

"Zakiyyah," Zaidou said in a weak voice. "Is that you? I'm happy to see you."

"Yes, it's me, sir. What happened?" Zakiyyah asked again. Tears rolled down her cheeks.

Zaidou began to tell her his story – from prison to rebellion. He could barely utter a sentence without moaning. His voice grew more and more inaudible as he spoke.

24

Zakiyyah opened the wardrobe and brought out five sets of new babban rigas and five new caps. The babban rigas were nicely packaged in transparent nylon bags. The bags crackled as she brought them out. The caps were well starched. She dropped them all on the bed, walked to the window and drew the creamy curtains apart. The lukewarm rays of the morning sun flooded in, falling on the furniture in the room.

It was a big room. Its carpet, curtains, bedcover and wallpaper had designs of white and cream flowers. The dressing mirror adjacent to the windows reflected the light that flooded in very nicely. On the wall were portraits of General Oumar, Chief Ousmane and Zakiyyah herself.

Zakiyyah looked at the caps. They looked thicker and finer than the ones her father used to wear. They were all woven in different colours. The babban rigas were white, blue, brown, grey and cream. She lined up the caps in one row and the babban rigas in another row beneath the caps. She was trying to see which babban rigas matched best with which caps. She held her chin in her hand as she regarded them.

Getting the right match wasn't as easy as she'd thought. She could easily spot which tie and shirt colours matched best, but matching caps with babban rigas was a different sport all together.

It looked like the brown cap would match best with the white babban riga that had brown embroidery. She put those colours apart and returned the others into the wardrobe. She squatted and glanced at the shoes at the bottom of the wardrobe. They were all brand new shoes of different colours. She chose the black pair that had no design. She removed the price tag and kept the shoes by the bedside.

General Oumar entered. He was wearing a blue dressing gown and blue bedroom slippers. He was the most handsome man she'd ever seen, more handsome than Zaidou.

Zaidou had remained still, shortly after he'd told her his prison-to-rebellion story. He had not moved again since then. Never.

Oumar was smiling radiantly. It was a smile from his heart. She could tell from his glittering eyes.

"Have you had breakfast, habibi?" she asked him, returning his smile.

"Yes. The cooks did a nice job!" he replied.

Zakiyyah frowned. "The cooks?" she asked. "Well, I was the cook!"

General Oumar laughed, sitting with a soft thud on the settee at the centre of the room. "Okay!" he said. "The First Lady did a nice, beautiful, splendid job!"

Zakiyyah smiled. "I've brought out a nice match for you." She pointed at the clothes on the bed.

"Ah! Good match, sweetie!" he said, pulling the babban riga out of the nylon bag. He dressed and admired himself in the mirror. She helped him gather the big sleeves of the babban riga onto his shoulders. She patted his cheeks.

"Now tell me, sweetie," he began, "with these white clothes, which of my citizens will ever think I'm a tyrant?"

"Well, they don't have to look at your clothes to see that. Your smile alone says a lot!" she laughed. She regarded him to see if any other adjustment was needed. He looked perfect.

He browsed the perfumes on the dressing table. He picked one and sprayed it all over his clothes. Its scent filled the room. He had worn the same perfume on the day he'd saved her from the room where Leader Gambo had locked her up. Its cool scent reminded her of the freshness of the sea.

"Did you get that when you went to England last week?" she asked him.

"I got it here in Hasoumiya," he said. "Don't you know we have companies that export perfumes?"

She picked up the perfume bottle, reading its label. Its name was in Hausa and was written in cursive print.

"*Turaren Sarki*," she read. "My Hausa is not too good. What does that mean?"

"It means the King's Perfume." General Oumar sat on the bed to tie the laces of his shoes.

"Oh really? It's just the right one for you!" Zakiyyah laughed.

President Oumar turned serious. "I have a meeting with your father and the Governor of the Hausa-Sahara region today," he said. "It's at 10 a.m. this morning. They are submitting a budget for rebuilding the region."

"Those rebels did so much damage!" Zakiyyah frowned.

"Yes, indeed. Good riddance to them!" President Oumar picked up his briefcase and walked to the door.

"You told me you'd be receiving the report of the inquiry into Leader Gambo's death yesterday. Have you received it?" Zakiyyah followed him.

"Ah! I did," President Oumar said. "His driver didn't crash the limousine on purpose, as we had thought. He was drunk!"

"Wow! Interesting! But why did it take six months to get the report?"

"They had to do a thorough job. Where is Fahad?"

"He left for school at 7 a.m."

"Excellent. Chief Ousmane – I mean Baba – and his wife will be coming from Masara today. He will be attending the swearing-in of Mamman as my vice president. That will be tomorrow."

"Will he wait to attend the send-off dinner you'll be hosting for my father? He'll be retiring next week, remember?"

"Ah! That's true. I'm sure he'll wait. They're friends, after all."

"No. In-laws!" Zakiyyah wore a playful frown.

"That's correct, sweetie!" President Oumar pecked her on the cheek. "Your father has served the country for more than forty years. I'll be honouring him with the Presidential Medal of Peace at the send-off."

"Oh! That's beautiful, habibi!" Zakiyyah hugged her husband.

She thought her father deserved the medal. He was the one that had signed the peace agreement with the rebels on behalf of the government. With that agreement, President Oumar had lifted the marriage ban, and the rebels had dropped their arms. But shouldn't Zaidou get a medal too? He'd defied the ban in his quest for marriage. He'd fought Leader Gambo's forces because of love. And that had cost him his life. When President Oumar returned from work, she would tell him about her plans to launch an award to honour the first couple in Hasoumiya to get married every year. She'd call it the Zaidou Prize for Love.

President Oumar patted her on the back. He broke the hug and she followed him to the living room downstairs. He pecked her on the forehead and gave her that radiant smile of his.

"Goodbye," he said.

"Goodbye, habibi!" Zakiyyah replied.

He marched outside to his convoy.

Printed in the United States
By Bookmasters